# A FAERIE'S TOUCH

*Memory Guild Book 7*

# WARD PARKER

Mad Mangrove Media

# CONTENTS

## CHAPTER 1

# OBLIGATIONS

Life was about as normal as it could be—I mean, normal after you've discovered you're the human incarnation of an ancient goddess. I didn't believe this revelation changed me much. Maybe, I was wrong.

"You were absolutely divine last night," Cory said as we snuggled in bed one morning.

"Ha-ha, very funny."

"I'm not joking. You were truly a goddess, as in beyond human in your skills. It felt like I was being sacrificed on your altar."

"Knock it off." I couldn't help but giggle.

"You're the daughter of the mother-earth goddess. You make me want to have kids with you."

"I think it's too late for that."

"I'm not so sure," he said, kissing me. "Danu is a fertility goddess, right? Isn't that why seedlings keep appearing in all these places they're not supposed to? Who knows what could happen?"

He was getting frisky, but I had breakfast to prepare for our guests.

"We'll continue this topic later," I said as I jumped out of bed and headed for the shower.

Yeah, life was normal if I ignored my new role as Daughter of Danu. And if I forget the impending war between the Fae and every other creature on the planet.

If only I could push those matters from my mind, I could take comfort in the mundane details of daily life. In my case, it was running our historic bed-and-breakfast in the nation's oldest city. And it was trying to avoid, for my sanity, the constant manifestations of the paranormal and supernatural from the ghosts, witches, vampire, and gargoyle who call our inn their home.

So eager was I to live a mundane life after my recent adventures, I started wearing thick rubber gloves to neutralize my psychometry. The gloves made handling things awkward, but at least I didn't pick up the memories other people left upon objects and surfaces around me.

The only thing paranormal I couldn't completely avoid was my telepathy. It was pretty spotty, though, so I didn't worry about picking up unwanted thoughts as I went about my daily routine, serving the breakfast buffet to my guests.

That is, until my daughter's thoughts intruded into my head, ultimately setting off my next crime-investigation adventure.

And I truly didn't want or need any adventures, thank you.

I had just pulled from the oven a fresh batch of scones and was arranging them on a tray. Sophie was in the kitchen, her back to me, washing something in the sink.

*How in the world can I raise bail money for him?* Her question appeared in my mind unbidden. *I don't own anything for collateral, other than my car, which isn't even paid off yet.*

My gut clenched. Who needed to be bailed out of jail, and why were they arrested?

But I couldn't just ask Sophie that. Being a telepath makes you unintentionally rude, an invader of privacy. I refused to say anything unless she brought it up herself. Being her mother made the situation even more delicate.

Sophie was anxious and distracted throughout the rest of the breakfast service and continued to be as I was bringing the chafing dishes back into the kitchen. This part, the cleaning, was her responsibility. By this time, I usually headed to the utility room to meet Bella, the housekeeper, and give her the list of rooms that needed to be cleaned or turned over.

Sophie opened her lips, about to say something, but changed her mind. It was my cue to swoop in.

"Anything on your mind?" I asked her.

"Why do you ask? Have you been reading it?"

"You seem like you have a weight on your shoulders."

She sighed as she gave in to the urge to share.

"Dad's been arrested," she said, her face twisting slightly as she fought tears.

Oh no, I thought. Buddy's been busted again.

"What did he do now? DUI? Indecent exposure? Public urination?"

"Mom! You have such a horrible opinion of him."

My first husband was the iconic Florida Man, the guy you read about in the news who gets in trouble for doing idiotic things. Usually, while drunk and naked.

"I'm sorry. That wasn't fair of me. I need to be more charitable. What is he accused of?"

"Murder."

"Oh, that's all? Something perfectly minor. How terrible of me to think it was something serious, like driving his car into a miniature golf course." Which he actually did years ago, by the way.

"Your sarcasm isn't helping," she said. Tears were flowing now. "Dad's business partner was found shot to death, and Dad's been accused, with no justification. It's a perversion of justice."

"Is that what he says?"

"Yes. I need to help him."

"You are not giving him any money for bail, and neither am I. Partly because we have none to give. But mostly because he can use a bail bondsman just like everyone else. They have numbers for those guys posted at the county jail. I don't see why he needed to bother you."

"Maybe because he's scared."

I could believe that. Buddy's previous arrests for Florida-Man stunts never threatened to put him away for good. I admit I felt sympathy for him. The man had squandered my youth, drained our bank accounts, and cheated on me. But he was my partner in bringing Sophie into the world. We did have some fun together. Well, before we got married, that is. And I was the one who filed for divorce, not him. I really couldn't bring myself to hate the guy.

"I'll ask around for recommendations for a good defense attorney," I said. "Although, he probably will have to go with a public defender for financial reasons."

"Thanks, Mom."

I think simply the appearance of trying to help made Sophie feel a little better.

Later in the morning, I called my old friend, Jen, and asked her if she knew of any attorneys. She wanted to know why, of course.

"Poor Buddy," she said. "Why has he always been such a disaster?"

"Born that way, I guess. He always bounced to his feet whenever he messed up in the past which, I guess, was part of his charm. He's been this way since high school."

"I work with real-estate attorneys. The only defense attorney I know is Ron Dutton. I recently ran into him at a fundraiser. Remember him?"

"Yeah. I saw him in the news representing that guy whose pet tiger ate a landscaper. I can't believe he won the case."

"Maybe since Ron knew us all from high school, he'll take on Buddy at a reduced rate."

"It would have to be *very* reduced," I said. "Like, pro bono."

Jen snickered. "Good luck with that. Ron drives a Maserati."

"Let's hope he has warmth for Buddy in his heart. And a lot of generosity, too."

Jen promised she'd give Ron a call, and I thanked her profusely.

I felt I had performed my good deed for the day. Well, actually I outsourced it, but hopefully, it would be helpful to Buddy.

And I wouldn't need to be involved any further.

I found Sophie laundering sheets in the utility room. She looked miserable.

"I told you that working at a bed-and-breakfast was not a glamorous job," I said as I entered the room.

She wiped a tear from her cheek. "I'm upset about Dad."

"My friend, Jen, knows an excellent defense attorney. She'll call him about Buddy. If he agrees to take the case, Buddy will be in good hands."

"Thank you." She didn't appear any happier.

"It's the best we can do."

"I said, thank you."

"Who was his business partner?" I asked. "I didn't know he

had a business. Isn't he still working for the pest-control company?"

"He still works there. I don't know what this business is. He called it his 'side hustle.'"

I wouldn't be surprised if it involved a gray area of the law. I didn't say that out loud, of course.

"I'm sure it wasn't illegal," Sophie said resentfully.

I guess she didn't need to be a telepath to read my mind.

Cory popped his head in the kitchen.

"Morning, Sophie. See you guys soon. I have to go to the hardware store so I can replace some door hinges."

Yeah, not much glamor in the bed-and-breakfast business, especially when your inn is nearly 300 years old and in a constant state of falling apart.

But I wouldn't trade it for a job in some cubicle farm, not in a million years. My closest approximation to a desk job is managing reservations and keeping up with the accounting. Oh, yeah, and marketing. That task, I haven't quite mastered yet, evidenced by the constant vacancies. I headed for the desk in the foyer to pay invoices, serene in the mundane nature of my world.

Until the supernatural intruded into my life once again.

"Hey!" The exclamation came from behind me as I walked down the hall past the first-floor suite.

The voice had the vaguely European accent I'd become too familiar with of late. My scalp tingled from the realization.

I stopped and retraced my steps. The door to the suite was ajar. The freakish doll-sized face of a faerie peaked around the edge of the door. I say freakish, because, with the faerie in his natural two-foot-tall form, his face had hominid features proportionately a little too large.

"Divine Mother, how are you doing?" the faerie asked with a hint of sarcasm.

"You must not be seen by my guests," I said, pushing past him into the room and closing the door.

He looked familiar. Now I remembered: he was Jaekeree, the faerie who had given me the pearl and told me the Fae had high expectations for me.

"Um, how are you doing?" I asked. "What brings you here today?"

Jaekeree smiled devilishly.

"I am here only to say hello, and to congratulate you on your ascension to goddess status. Our prophesies about you turned out to be true."

"I guess. At the moment, I'm living a normal life. The goddess thing seems bizarre to me. My life hasn't really changed, except for the plants and seedlings that keep appearing in the inn."

"How boring, my dear. We need to talk."

Jaekeree was no longer standing by the door. I turned to find him in human form, sitting on a chair in the suite's living room. The slight, dark-haired man was handsome and not at all freakish, like he was in his natural state. But there was something menacing about him, despite his gleaming smile.

"If you recall from our last conversation," he said, "I shared our belief that you would either be a great friend or foe of the Fae."

I nodded, dreading where this was going.

"You have not been very friendly."

"Dorn sentenced me to death. How was I supposed to act?"

"He did so because of your prior behavior."

"Because I knew he had his wife murdered."

"And because you had a certain key that Dorn stupidly mishandled."

"I don't know what you're talking about."

He smiled ruefully. "Humans are not skilled at lying, are you?"

"Why do you care about the key? Pandora's Box was opened by the Faerie Queene, and everything remaining in it has escaped."

I kept my thoughts away from the second box I had seen in the memory of the ancient artisan who had installed the lock on Pandora's box. I had to be careful, in case Jaekeree could read minds.

"I'm not here for the key," he said.

"Good. Um, then why *are* you here?"

"The pearl."

My heart seized up. Jaekeree had given the pearl to me as a gift, or so I had thought. I didn't steal it. But I truly did not want to return it to him. It had been extremely valuable for the purposes of magic, mostly used by my witches-in-training, Cory and Sophie.

"It's a very pretty pearl," I said, lamely.

"It is, indeed." He stared at me with no expression.

"Um, are you here to take it back?"

"What kind of gift-giver do you think I am? I'm insulted that you would think I'm so petty."

"I don't think you're petty. You said you're here for the pearl."

"No, not *for* the pearl. *Because* of the pearl." He folded his arms and slid downward in the chair into a more relaxed position. "You must have learned quite a bit about faeries since I last saw you, no?"

"I've learned a little."

"Surely, you must have heard the old stereotype of the Fae: that we expect a great debt in return for each gift we give."

Uh-oh. I didn't like where this was going.

"No, I haven't," I lied.

"Well, unfortunately, the stereotype is true. As you must have learned by now, the pearl is extremely powerful and useful in so many ways. When the Faerie Queene ordered me to give it to you, she expected much in return."

"Um, like what? I'm just a non-magical human."

"You were non-magical when I gave the pearl to you, though our priests had prophesied a pivotal role in your relations with the Fae. Well, now we've learned you're the daughter of Danu, a goddess we, too, worship. What role you will play for us is clearer."

"Well, I don't quite have my goddess act together yet."

"Oh, but you will, my dear, you will. And we shall expect much generosity from you."

I didn't know what he meant, but I knew for a fact that Danu wanted me to stop the Fae's mad campaign to enslave humans and other creatures as they attempted to reclaim their ancient dominance. I had no clue how I would stop them, only that I had to do so.

"How about if you just take the pearl back?" I asked, hating to part with it, but dreading more what the Fae would ask of me.

"Oh, but you've made such good use of the pearl. How could I take it from you? Please don't insult me. All I ask is that you prepare to repay your debt, or else there will be severe consequences. The Fae never allow debts to go unpaid."

"But how do I pay?" I asked.

"I will tell you when the time is right. The matter is extremely sensitive."

And just like that, the chair was empty. Jaekeree had disappeared.

Thanks for nothing.

# CHAPTER 2

## LIQUID GOLD

"Well, well, look what the cat dragged in," I said as Buddy appeared in the inn's foyer. In my case, it wasn't a cliche. I felt as pleased to see him as I would a dead mouse.

"Darla, good to see you." He gave me a quick, chaste hug. He smelled of unwashed clothes and desperation. "Thanks for hooking me up with your attorney."

"He's not my attorney. Just a friend of a friend."

"You look good. There's a, well, glow about you. You aren't pregnant, are you?"

I laughed. "No, that ship has sailed long ago." I couldn't mention that what he saw in me was probably the goddess effect. Who would believe his ex-wife was the daughter of a goddess?

Buddy had aged drastically since I'd last seen him only about a year ago. He wore his typical outfit of a tropical-patterned shirt, shorts, and boat shoes. The goatee and obvious comb-over were the same. But he had lost several pounds, and his eyes were ringed by more worry lines than before.

He had a desperate air about him, but I suppose that was to be expected when you were charged with murder.

"Ron got me bonded out, but I don't think he's going to represent me," Buddy said. "He's too expensive and he'll only handle my case if it would get him good publicity. He kind of hinted that I'm a lowlife who's guilty."

Which was probably true.

"But I'm not guilty. Honest."

I nodded, trying to look sympathetic, but not going so far as to agree with him. Why was Buddy telling me this? I tried to read his thoughts but heard only jumbled fragments of worry and fear.

"I don't mean to sound callous," I said, "but why are you here? I don't believe there's any way I can help you."

"A small loan—that's all I ask. I need to hire a private investigator to prove I didn't kill Damon. And I have a bail bondsman hovering over me. My freaking bond is half a million! The bail bondsman's fee is fifty grand. He took all my cash and the title for my car. I had to use my house as collateral."

"Buddy, I'm sorry. We're mortgaged to the eyeballs with the inn. Business hasn't been great, and the expenses have been slamming us. I'm truly sorry, but we can't spare anything."

I put extra emphasis on "we," reminding him that Cory was back in my life. Buddy had a manipulative side, and I didn't want him to take advantage of me.

"Doesn't your attorney have investigators?" I asked.

"Like I told you, it doesn't look like he's going to take on my case. He thinks I'm a bad bet."

"What about Esmerelda's attorney?"

She was his ex-fiancée, currently serving time for assault,

arson, kidnapping, and attempted murder. Against me, my inn, and my cousin, Missy. She was a black-magic sorceress who had been running around behind Buddy's back with an evil rich guy. Long story.

Buddy visibly shuddered. "I don't want to get anywhere near that witch. Besides, her lawyer didn't do such a great job, did he?"

When he said "witch," he didn't mean it literally. Buddy never knew about Esmerelda's magic. He didn't even believe in magic at all. He thought my mother's reputation as a witch was just an old wives' tale.

Needless to say, I never told him that his own daughter inherited Mom's magic genes and was now a witch of growing powers.

"I've heard rumors that you're kind of an amateur sleuth," he said.

"How would you have heard that?"

"Aw, you know San Marcos is a small town at heart. Word gets around that you're buddies with a detective and helped him solve some cases."

More like Sansom helped *me* solve them.

"How could I do that?" I hoped he'd reveal if he knew I was psychic.

"I honestly don't know. Maybe that old joke that you could read minds is true. Is it? I heard you helped find Jen Howell when she was kidnapped."

"All I do is a little research and a little snooping."

"Maybe you could do it for me. I need all the help I can get."

He sure did.

"Who was the detective on your case?" I asked.

"Some jerk by the name of Siwicki. Why? You know him?"

"I wanted to make sure it wasn't the detective I work with.

He would have told me, anyway. It would have been a conflict of interest for him to investigate my ex-husband."

"Well, the guy who arrested me was a total sleaze."

I should have shut the entire conversation down, but my curiosity was getting the best of me. And that usually led me into trouble.

"So, what was this little business you and your partner had?" I asked.

"Liquid gold," he said, smiling with pride. "Pee."

"What in the world are you talking about?"

"We have a special arrangement with a lab that does medical testing. I found out about them when I worked for the city. We provide drug testing for addiction recovery companies. There are tons of them here in Florida. They find patients with great private insurance that covers rehab—housing, counseling, testing, the whole shebang. We give them kickbacks to get samples from their patients as often as every day, ordering tests for, like, every drug in the book. The insurance companies pay for it, and we rack up the dollars."

"So, it's a scam?"

"No! How could you say such a thing? We provide a critical tool for helping patients stay sober. Maybe they don't need to be tested so often and for so many drugs. Okay, maybe it's totally unnecessary. But it doesn't hurt anyone, right? And the insurance pays for it, so we're all good."

My blood pressure built up from anger until my head was throbbing. You see, I'd clashed with a criminal drug recovery company once to save Sophie's life. After she fell into a dangerous crowd and was using, I got her into an expensive, well-regarded rehabilitation center in South Florida. She left it and ended up at a sleazy company. Which gave many of its patients to a gang of vampires who were co-owners.

Sophie had been nothing but livestock to these fiends. With luck, and the help of Missy, we rescued her before it was too late.

Hearing again about the dark side of the recovery business got me all riled up.

"Was your partner killed because of your business?" I asked.

Buddy flinched. A haunted look filled his eyes.

"Yeah. It had to be that."

"Was he using drugs? Did he have any large debts, or any other reason someone would want to take him out?"

"I don't think Damon was using drugs. But some of the recovery companies we work with are pretty bad."

"What do you mean?"

"I mean giving drugs to their patients to keep them addicted and in recovery."

"That's disgusting."

"Yeah. You see, Damon worked with the companies directly, selling them our tests. I worked with the testing lab, delivering the samples, and forwarding the results. I don't know what kind of stuff Damon got into on a day-to-day basis."

"How was he killed?"

Buddy rubbed his face nervously. "He was found shot to death in his car. That's what the cops told me."

I didn't know how I could help Buddy in a hardcore criminal case like this. The previous cases I'd been involved with usually involved the supernatural to some degree. I'm just an innkeeper with paranormal abilities. I wasn't a hard-nosed private investigator.

My anger at the illegitimate recovery companies that took advantage of vulnerable people prodded me to do something, though. Sophie had almost been drained to death by vampires because of one of these evil companies. Or she could have been turned. Being a mother is hard enough without your daughter becoming a vampire.

"So, do you think you can help me, Darla?"

"I told you I can't lend you any money for a lawyer or an investigator."

"I know, I know. I guess I'll need a public defender. What I'm hoping is that you can be my investigator. I mean, however you can."

"I'm not sure how much help I could be."

"Any little thing you uncover could help. We need to point Detective Siwicki in another direction. Maybe, if I'm looking innocent, the high-powered attorney, Mr. Dutton, will take an interest in me. Maybe he'll take me on for free if he can get a lot of publicity."

There were missing pieces in the story, though.

"Why were you accused of Damon's murder, anyway?"

Buddy's eyes darted back and forth. "You know, they always suspect the business partner. And the spouse. He didn't have a spouse."

"No, tell me. Do they have any evidence tying you to the murder?"

"My gun. It was my gun that shot him."

"Wonderful."

"It's easy to explain. I lent it to Damon for protection. Someone used it on him, that's all."

"What motive do the police think you had to shoot him?"

"They think Damon was hiding a bunch of profits from me."

"Is that true?"

"If he was, it's news to me. I, uh, wasn't on top of all the paperwork and stuff."

Maybe I'm a sucker, but I believed Buddy. You can question my judgement for marrying the guy. But I was very young when I fell in love with him. He was always a walking disaster who challenged the blurry line between right and wrong, but he was a likable one. His self-effacing humor always provided a way for him to laugh off whatever trouble he'd gotten himself into.

Until the trouble included blowing all our savings and cheating on me with a bartender. He couldn't laugh his way out of all that.

And now, he faced life in prison, or worse. Nothing here to laugh off. Buddy is the father of my daughter. How could I turn my back on him?

There was one other thing making me inclined to help: no supernatural forces were involved. I didn't have to deal with the Fae, nor would I discover new creatures I never knew existed. Sordid humans were the only characters in this story.

"I'll see what I can do, but no promises," I said.

"Thanks, babe!"

I hated when he called me that.

"You don't deserve to go down for a murder you didn't commit. But you're going to be on your own if you're charged for the testing scam."

His face fell. "Hopefully, I won't be."

"And I need access to Damon's possessions."

"Why?"

"To look for clues," I said, hoping he would let it drop. I didn't want to tell him about my psychometry. "You said he's not married?"

"He's long divorced."

"Can you get me into his home?"

"I think so. His landlord knows me. I'm sure the police have already searched there."

"Yeah. But not the way I can."

He looked at me with a raised eyebrow.

"I can't explain," I said. "If you want me to help, don't look a gift horse in the mouth."

"Right. Okay. I'll do whatever you ask."

"First, you need to go through the list of all your clients and let me know which ones were up to no good."

"I guess most of them."

"Great. Just wonderful. Are there any clients you suspect would have killed him?"

"I don't know. Most of his day-to-day dealings with them were unknown to me."

"Well, you need to go through all of Damon's paperwork and records to look for the most suspicious stuff."

"Really? Oh, okay." He sounded depressed, like I just gave him a homework assignment. Buddy had a habit of blowing off homework in high school.

"It's much better to study your office paperwork than law books in the prison library."

He went pale and nodded. "I hear ya. Um, by the way, we didn't really have an office."

"You didn't?"

"Nope. We worked out of our homes and our cars."

"Okay, then talk to Damon's landlord and get access to his apartment. Let me know when I can stop by."

"I will. And thank you so much, Darla. It means a lot to me that you're helping. Even if you don't find anything, just being there for me, and not turning your back on me like everyone else, is a blessing."

He smiled in the cute, goofy way that used to tickle my heart. It didn't work on me anymore, but it did score him a few points.

I'm such a softie.

"Why would you get involved in this?" Samson asked when I called him.

"I'm helping my daughter's father. Wouldn't you?"

"Look, Darla, this is politically very awkward. You're known at the department as my kooky little psychic consultant. No one realizes how amazingly effective you are, but at least they think you're harmless. Detective Siwicki's case has nothing to do with me. Nothing to do with the paranormal. It will look bad for me to intrude on his investigation."

"The San Marcos Police Department is tiny. Why can't you simply offer your help?"

"Siwicki wouldn't want my help."

"Why? Don't you get along?"

"Not exactly. He hasn't been here very long and hasn't gone out of his way to make friends."

"But I need access to the victim's car. His memories could tell me right away who actually killed him."

"And possibly tell Siwicki he made a mistake and charged the wrong guy. He wouldn't want to hear that. Besides, you expect him to believe you read the victim's memories?"

"Don't you guys care about catching the right guy?"

Samson paused. "*I* do."

He left hanging the implication that Siwicki didn't.

"Siwicki would be angry if I intruded on his case without being invited. And I can't get you into the car without letting him know."

I thought of a possible workaround.

"Mike, the way we've worked together is I learn stuff with my psychometry, and it can't be used in court. But the information does help you find other information using conventional means that confirms what I discovered. You sort of reverse-engineer the investigation based on what I found paranormally."

"Yeah, right. So what?"

"If you get me inside the victim's car, and I find out who killed him, you can tell Siwicki you heard from an informant that this guy is the killer. Siwicki can then follow up on it in his own way."

"It's still not proper protocol."

I sighed. "Then introduce me to Siwicki. I'll convince him he needs a psychic on his case."

"Yeah, good luck."

I hung up and walked into the kitchen. Sophie looked up and rushed to me, hugging me tightly.

"Dad called and told me you're helping him," she said, her face buried on my shoulder. "Thank you so much, Mom."

"Of course, Sweetie."

There was no backing out now.

# CHAPTER 3

## LAST CORN DOG

S iwicki was much younger than Samson. He was probably in his late twenties, and his swagger immediately turned me off, because experience and time on the job were critical for detectives. This guy was simply too young to be as awesome as he thought he was.

He had dark hair with a week's salary worth of gel in it. His cheeks and chin were peppered with deliberately cultivated stubble. And he had a large, bushy mustache. Since when were mustaches back in fashion?

Before I'd even exchanged words with Siwicki, I became enemies with his mustache. It stood between us like a growling guard dog.

"Laz Siwicki, I'd like you to meet Darla Chesswick," Samson said, ushering me into the cramped office of the detective bureau. "She's the psychic consultant I occasionally use."

Siwicki raised his eyebrows. They were almost as bushy as his mustache.

"Detectives actually use psychics?" he asked snidely. "I thought that was only in TV movies."

"She's been of great assistance to the department," Samson said. "She found a kidnapping victim whom we had no means of locating. And that's just one example."

The eyebrows arched even further. If the two eyebrows joined together, they could probably beat up the mustache.

"Interesting," he said with obvious disbelief.

*Why is he introducing me to this kook?* was his thought that came into my head.

"He's introducing you to this kook because he's polite," I said. "I stopped by to see him, and he wanted me to meet the new detective."

I couldn't help putting emphasis on "new."

Siwicki was taken aback that I repeated his thought, but it didn't throw him off balance.

"It was a pleasure to meet you," he said. He turned his attention back to his computer screen.

"I'm happy to provide my services if you'd like," I said. "I don't charge anything."

"Then your help must be worth a lot," he said sarcastically. "Thanks, but I don't need a psychic to solve crimes for me."

"Don't think of me as solving crimes. I can help you confirm hunches and find new avenues for you if you hit a dead end. Sometimes, I can find mistakes."

"I rarely make mistakes."

I had to bite my tongue to avoid telling him he was making a mistake with Buddy.

"She can read thoughts left behind at crime scenes, from victims as well as perps," Samson said. "It's really handy for backing up your work."

"You can't use a psychic in court."

"I know. Like I said, she can confirm if you've got the right guy and flag it if you don't."

"Oh, come on. Is this a practical joke? You're trying to get me to take the bait so you can laugh at me."

"Not at all," I said. "I want to take a look inside the car belonging to Damon Borgia. "

I hadn't meant to blurt out my true intention, but it was too late now.

"The victim is a friend of a friend," I said. "I want to learn more about his death."

"Forensics has been all over that car several times," Siwicki said. "There's nothing more the car can tell us."

"There might be something it can tell me."

He laughed. "What do you want from me? Go ahead and let her look in the car, Samson. But keep her out of my freaking case."

Samson nodded and quickly led me out of the room.

"I didn't think he'd say yes," I said.

"Neither did I. But he was making me so mad I would have finagled a way to get you in that car, no matter what he said. I have to do the paperwork to authorize this. Meet me at the impoundment lot in an hour."

I knew exactly where the lot was, in the outskirts of the city, since I'd been there before. I parked on the street outside of the large parking lot surrounded by a tall chain-link fence with barbed wire at its top. This wasn't where your car went if it was towed by the city. All the cars here were involved in crimes.

Some, like the one I was about to visit, were spattered with blood.

Damon Borgia's car was a Mercedes coupe that would give bad vibes to the least paranormal observer. It wasn't simply that the car was old, dirty, and ill-kept. I had the feeling that it had been in bad neighborhoods and witnessed bad things, both inside and outside of the vehicle.

It didn't help that the drivers-side window had two bullet holes in it.

Samson unlocked the door with the key fob branded with a red plastic tag. The reek of stale cigarette smoke radiated from the interior. And the coppery, sour smell of old blood.

"Great," I muttered.

Samson's nose wrinkled at the smell, too.

It also didn't help that the passenger seat was covered with dried blood.

"Looks like the shooter came up to the car and shot him through the window," Samson said. "The victim fell sideways onto the passenger seat."

"Do you mind opening the glove compartment and the center console?" I asked. "I want to see what's inside without touching them."

The container between the seats held an open pack of cigarettes, empty pill bottles, and a tire-pressure gauge. Samson stepped around to the passenger door, opened it, then unlatched the glove compartment.

A pack of condoms fell out. Other lovely accessories included tiny plastic bags, the kind used by drug dealers, a box of bullets, sunglasses, and a small rubber ducky. Don't ask me why he had a rubber ducky in his glove compartment.

"Funny, but Damon doesn't seem like my kind of guy," I said.

"Yeah, I wouldn't think that you hung out with him."

I looked at the grimy interior with dismay, already feeling the energy of years of memories, most of them not the sort I wanted to experience.

"This is going to take a while," I said.

"You know, you don't have to get involved in this."

"I promised Buddy I would help." I took a deep breath to fortify myself. "There's no need to discover this guy's life story. I just want to see if there's a memory of who shot him. Or who he thought *would* shoot him."

"Okay. Don't push yourself. I'll go wait in my car."

"Wait," I said. "Where exactly was the car found? I take it the murderer didn't shoot him in front of the murderer's own house."

Samson snickered. "I heard they found it parked at a Mega-Mart. The victim was eating a corn dog when he was popped."

I eased myself into the driver's seat, as if I was taking a dip in a cesspool. The psychic energy Damon left in the car was of corruption, perversion, decadence, greed. Pick your vice—you can tack them onto the list. He also left the essence of self-hatred, as if he were aware of what he had sunk to but couldn't change.

There must be some happy, innocent memories in this car, but they would take some digging to find them. I only wanted to get out of here quickly.

As I settled into the seat, feelings of anxiety came to me through my legs and back. Recent anxiety. Maybe he knew he was in a risky situation before he was shot.

First, I held my hands close to the steering wheel, but not quite touching it. This is where cars held most of the drivers' memories, obviously. The problem is, for all the hours you spend driving, you do a lot of thinking, though most of it is random subconscious thoughts while you're focused on the road. It's a lot of stuff for a psychometrist to sort through.

As I've honed my craft, I've learned how to test the memories for freshness and pluck out the most recent ones. With Damon, his most recent thoughts left upon the wheel probably weren't his last if he was parked and eating at the time.

The freshest ones were near the top of the wheel—in two places at the same time. Which meant both hands on the wheel and no corn dog eating. I steeled myself, then placed my own hands—

—*Right in front of me like she's not in a parking lot. I could have hit the idiot. And what the heck is she wearing? There's too much butt crack showing, even for Mega-Mart . . . Okay, here's a good spot. Only have a half hour to eat before I have to get to Grady's joint. Man, I dread going there nowadays. He used to have hot chicks there that he'd string along for months with free drugs. Like Rita, man was she sweet. She was the best, since she took care of herself, unlike the others.*

*(Turn off ignition.) Why does Grady move patients in and out so fast now? I never heard of clients getting better in only a few days or a week at the most. They don't even look like they're on drugs. No wonder he's ordering fewer urine tests.*

*It really bugs me, because I wonder if they're undocumented, and he's helping smuggle them into the States.*

*Still, it bothers me. Got to hurry and—*

—The memory ended when he let go of the wheel, the sensation of his hunger for lunch affecting me, even though the thought of eating was the furthest thing from my own mind in this disgusting car.

I used my hands to scan the interior for another recent memory. There was a brief one on the inside handle of the driver's door as he pulled it closed, thinking about the corn dog on a stick he held in his other hand.

On the center console, he placed his right hand here very recently. Let me see if—

*—Willie thinks he has us over a barrel. Thinks he can raise the dang price for the testing. That freaking guy. Forgets that he wouldn't be anywhere if it wasn't for Buddy and me. He'd be testing old people's pee for their annual physicals and would be driven out of business by the big testing chains. Good luck, Willie. Mess with us, and we'll stomp on you. We know about all the other shady stuff you're up to, trying to rip off Medicare. You squeeze us, and we'll squeeze you right back.*

*I never fully trusted Willie. Buddy said he met him when he worked for the city. Buddy worked for the Public Works Department. How would he be in contact with a chemist? And why is a chemist working for the city? I dunno. Maybe Willie worked in a waste-water-treatment plant. Ha! That would teach him about pee all right! Hm, maybe he worked for the medical examiner's office, testing dead people for chemicals in their blood. Yeah, if I had to do that, I'd sure want to quit and start my own business.*

*Hey! That moron almost rear-ended me. I've got a trunk full of urine samples. Could you imagine the mess if he crushed my trunk? It would be—*

—a waste of time to keep reading this memory. It was turning into brain-dead ramblings of trivial nonsense.

I continued scanning the car's interior. There had to be something else useful here. It wasn't easy searching. Damon obviously spent a lot of time in here, and not only driving. Buddy had said the two of them worked out of their cars instead of offices. So, there were plenty of thoughts created in here and not a lot of useful introspection.

And wait—there on the armrest, something strong and recent. His elbow rested here while he ate. I touched the spot and fell into his memory of—

*—the first bite. Aw, man, the danged thing was sitting under the heat lamps too long. I should have expected that, since it's kind of late for lunch now. Still, nothing beats a good corn dog when you're—hey! Watch*

*it, buddy! (Honk the horn.) Freaking Lexus drivers! He pulled in way too close to my car. What if I needed to get out? The old dude wearing shades in the passenger seat better not ding my door . . . say, is that the Emerald Man? Haven't seen him in ages! He's lowering his window to say hello. Well, I'll—a gun? I know that gun. It's—*

The memory abruptly ended with a bright flash of white.

It's hard to explain experiencing someone else's death. Damon's was unexpected and quick. I didn't read in his memory any awareness that he was being killed. Most people say they'd prefer to go like that—so quickly they don't even know what happened to them.

The thing is, his animal instincts knew. His lizard brain sensed death was coming before his logical brain did. I felt the first surge of adrenaline course through his veins as his lizard brain told his body to evade destruction.

I heard the soft pop of the gunshot fired through the silencer, the crack as the slug broke through the window, and the impact of it against his skull. I sensed the electrical chaos run through his neurons.

But it was mercifully quick, and Damon never knew what hit him. Only his body, and I, did.

The second bullet was overkill. Pardon the pun.

NIGHT WAS FALLING BY THE TIME I LEFT THE MERCEDES AND breathed air free of the taint of cigarette smoke and dried blood. I walked to Samson's car, idling on the street, and rapped on his window. He lowered it.

"Anything?"

"Buddy definitely didn't do it. It was some guy he called the Emerald Man. Older Caucasian. Damon didn't have a great view of him, so I don't know if I could spot him in a lineup. That's all I know. A car pulled into an adjacent spot, too close to allow Damon to open his door, and the Emerald Man, the passenger, shot him through the window. Damon didn't have time to think about it. Are you familiar with anyone with that nickname?"

"Nope. I'll have to ask around."

Yeah, you do that, I thought. Meanwhile, I would check to see if Buddy got permission from Damon's landlord to enter his apartment. I bet I could find out the identity of the Emerald Man before Samson did.

"You know what I'm going to say next," Samson said.

"You bet. We can't use my psychic findings in court. We have to find traditional evidence tying this Emerald Man to the murder before the DA drops the charges against Buddy."

"I'm glad you understand. Do you mind if I ask you something?"

"Go ahead."

"You and your ex—I don't see you two being a couple. Was there something I'm missing?"

"We were high-school sweethearts, and I was young and dumb. People change."

Samson nodded. He had no idea how much I had changed. I hadn't simply become older and wiser. No, I became a psychometrist on top of my telepathic abilities. Then, I also became a goddess. Well, the daughter and human representative of one.

He didn't know about the goddess thing. I wasn't sure if I would tell him. It wasn't the kind of news you simply drop into a conversation: *Oh, by the way, I'm the daughter of Danu now.*

No, I'd keep that little change in Darla to myself for now.

# CHAPTER 4

# CRAZY SHIZZLE

I have a habit of being at the wrong place at the wrong time. It's not my fault. Really. I stumble upon crazy shizzle by accident. Completely by accident.

As darkness filled the city, brightened by strings of Christmas lights wherever I looked, I realized I was late for Wine Hour. However, while I drove back to my inn on my newly repaired motor scooter, my mind was focused on how I could find out who the Emerald Man was.

The shortest route from the impound lot included several blocks of Seville Street, one of which was blocked by construction barriers. So preoccupied was I that I didn't stop until I had passed through a gap in the big orange plastic cylinders, almost clipping the sign that said, "Detour" with an arrow pointing left.

Ahead of me, two utility hole covers had been removed in the middle of the cobblestone street. A city sewer department vehicle the size of a garbage truck was parked in the middle with a large hose snaking from its rear into the nearest utility hole. It looked like a vacuum of some sort.

No workers were present at this hour. And there was plenty of room for a motor scooter to navigate past the obstacles to the next block, which was open. I said the heck with it and continued ahead.

I passed the utility hole with the large hose stuffed into it, then dodged a smaller truck and a generator on wheels. I was halfway down the block when I braked suddenly.

There was movement in the second open utility hole twenty feet ahead of me.

A doll-sized head with pointy ears appeared in the opening. Tiny human-like arms reached out to press upon the cobblestones as the creature pulled itself from the hole. Insect wings came out of the hole with it.

It was a faerie in his natural form.

The creature stepped onto the street, a spear in his hand and a quiver of arrows strapped to his side. Then, another faerie followed it from the hole.

The two slipped into the shadows of a darkened storefront as more faeries emerged from the utility hole. Soon, there were more than a dozen. What were they doing here in the middle of Old Town, early enough in the evening that many humans were still out and about?

To avoid detection, I had cut the engine of my motor scooter and walked it to the shadows of another closed store across the street from where the faeries were gathering. I didn't know what to do. Was there someone I should call to report the faerie incursion? Certainly not 911.

I could call Samson, but what was he supposed to do? Technically, the faeries weren't breaking any laws. Technically, they didn't even exist as far as normal humans were concerned. The Executive Council, comprising the heads of the city's supernatural guilds, was supposed to be leading the response to the Fae's impending war. But I had no way of contacting them.

So, I group-texted the Memory Guild and described the situation.

"Be careful," several of them warned.

"Don't let the faeries see you. Go home immediately, Dr. Noordlun said.

"Okay," I replied.

And, of course, I ignored everything they said.

The last faerie had crawled out of the hole. I strained to see into the shadows across the street to determine how many of them there were and what they were up to.

They were gone. How could they have disappeared without my seeing them?

I should have slipped away and headed home. But, no, I had to stick my stupid nose into the faeries' business.

Leaving my motor scooter parked, I crossed the street to the storefront where they had been gathering. More than a dozen of them had been huddled here. Where could they have gone?

I tried the most obvious approach: I checked the doorknob of the store, an art gallery that had closed an hour ago.

The door was unlocked.

The faeries must have gone into the gallery. But why? What would they want in a high-end gallery of contemporary art?

Me being me, I couldn't leave this question unanswered. I carefully opened the door and went inside.

The gallery was completely dark, except for the light from streetlights that made their way into the large display windows fronting the street. Immediately facing me was a hyper-realistic statue of a naked man with a potbelly and a computer tablet covering his naughty bits. A video played on the tablet of bees gathering nectar from flowers. I didn't have time to reflect on the symbolism.

The space was enormous, broken up by various alcoves and partial walls. There was no movement of any faeries I could detect. And no sounds, either. I moved slowly across the floor.

Paintings ranging from abstract to Impressionistic to bonkers covered the main and partial walls. Statues, installations, and kinetic art were placed here and there.

Faeries were not among them.

Behind a counter at the end of the room was a corridor leading to stairs. Figuring the faeries must be doing something dastardly upstairs, I quietly ascended the staircase. It ended at a door that was locked. There was nothing I could do.

Returning downstairs, I headed for the exit, relieved that the locked door had stopped my dangerous and foolish search for the faeries. Until something caught my eye.

It was an installation of multiple shovels and spades protruding from a sphere in a way that mimicked a plant. Pretty eye-catching. But what had drawn me to it was its awkward placement on the floor. It wasn't positioned for optimal viewing, and it was tilted slightly, not sitting on its base properly.

Why can't I control my curiosity?

I walked up to the artwork. Below its base was a wide crack in the floor. That was odd. I nudged the base with my foot, and it moved easily, as if mounted on a turntable. The crack now was much wider, revealing darkness below the floor.

There was still time for me to quash my curiosity and get out of there.

But, really, wouldn't you be curious, too?

I pushed the installation with my foot and both hands. It rotated about forty-five degrees. And where the base used to be, was now a large opening in the floor. Cool, humid air wafted up from below. There was clearly a large expanse of space down there.

In Florida, we rarely have basements because of the high underground water table. In the strata of limestone beneath the soil are occasional pits and caverns through which water flows. They often lead to sinkholes, which Florida has in abundance, that seem to enjoy swallowing cars and sometimes even homes.

I knew for a fact that the Fae have been living in these spaces, since they recently brought me down there and tortured me near the estate owned by Dorn, AKA Dick Gilley.

You'd think that memory would send me running. But the underground tunnels near the estate were inaccessible without magic. There were no obvious openings, and a full-sized human —even a petite one like me—needed to be magically transported into a cavern, since we wouldn't fit through the narrow tunnels even if we could locate them.

So, why was this such a large, obvious opening to a subterranean world? It was a question that needed to be answered, right?

Yeah, I'm my own worst enemy.

As I chewed over this question, I glanced up at the ceiling of the gallery. Attached to it was a track of steel beams that followed the perimeter of the space and led to a large garage door at the rear.

Above me, not far from where I stood, was an electrical winch on wheels hooked to a beam with a hook dangling from it.

The casual observer would conclude the winch was used to move large, heavy statues and installations into the gallery and to their display locations. But, with this opening in the floor, the more astute observer could only guess that heavy objects were also lowered into the space below the floor.

For storage, you might say.

But we don't have basements in Florida, I would say. Plus, more than a dozen faeries came into this gallery and disappeared. They had to have gone into the space below me.

It was also likely that if any object was lowered into this hole, it had something to do with the Fae. What sort of item would they be moving around?

I feared it was a gigantic bomb. Since the invention of gunpowder, armies have dug tunnels to place mines beneath their enemies. It was a very effective tactic.

If the Fae were using it in San Marcos, that would be devastating. Think of all the people who would die. And all the historic buildings and objects that would be destroyed.

I needed to find out if this was the case, so I could warn the guilds and law enforcement.

At the edge of the opening was the top of a steel ladder descending straight down into the darkness. Before I could even think of a plan, my hands were planted on the floor at the edge of the hole, and my right foot was feeling for a ladder rung. My left foot did the same. Soon, my feet stepped downward, my body followed, and once my hands grasped the uppermost rung, I climbed downward into the darkness.

I couldn't see where I was going. But by now, it was too late to turn back.

# CHAPTER 5

## STUCK IN A HOLE

W hy, you ask, am I climbing by myself into a dark hole where I suspect several faeries recently went? Am I completely nuts?

Not completely.

I often act impulsively, without fully assessing the risks. That's a characteristic of an adolescent brain that hasn't fully developed into adulthood. Here I was in midlife, and my brain had apparently regressed to its adolescent state.

It must have something to do with not only my hormones, but all the paranormal changes happening to me.

However, let me be clear: I was only taking a quick look to see what was down here. If there appeared to be an extensive network of faerie tunnels, then we humans were in big trouble. It was one thing to have faeries burrowing underneath a forest in the middle of nowhere. But it was extremely dangerous beneath a city filled with humans and tourists. (Yes, I admit tourists are humans, too.)

Especially if the faeries were planting mines or bombs of some sort. If so, they would be set to go off in the future. Probably not within the next couple of minutes, while I took a quick look.

I descended only far enough for my head to clear the bottom of the floor. It was colder down here than outside and too dark to see.

Now, I hooked my right arm through the ladder and pulled my phone from my jeans pocket with my left. Holding the phone carefully with both hands, I activated the flashlight app to give me a look at what was down here.

Nothing. It was just a cavern—a sinkhole about the size of the average home's living room with a very high ceiling. The walls were jagged limestone, and the floor was dirt with a puddle in the corner. There was no sign of tunnels leading from the space.

See, no big deal. Obviously, the faeries didn't come down here. There was no gigantic mine set to explode. My curiosity satisfied, I pushed my phone back into my pocket so I could climb back up.

I'm not as nutty and irrational as you think I am.

Somehow, my phone slipped and landed on the dirt below.

Okay, maybe not nutty, but definitely clumsy.

My phone sounded like it landed right at the bottom of the ladder. I climbed down to get it. As soon as my feet touched the ground, I searched with both hands, patting the dirt around my feet until my hands seized the phone.

This time, I made absolutely sure it was deep in my rear pocket and stepped back onto the ladder.

That's when I heard the muffled cries.

Yep, the sound of people in distress.

Do you really expect me to scramble up the ladder and get out of here, without seeing who needed help?

I shined my phone's flashlight around the cavern once more. What I missed the first time were all the footprints in the dirt floor.

And the three openings in the cavern's walls. I swear, these were not there the first time I looked around.

More cries. It sounded as if their mouths were covered. The sounds came from my left, from one of the openings in the wall. I hurried over and pointed the light into the opening.

Three people huddled inside a much smaller sub-cavern: two women and one man who were bound and gagged. They grunted and whimpered for help, though they didn't seem sure if I was friend or foe.

"Hi, I'm Darla. I'll help you out of here."

First, I removed their gags, untying heavy strips of linen that were holding thick wads of cloth in their mouths. I started with the older of the three, a woman with a silver-haired bob and a short, expensive-looking Navy-blue dress stained with dirt. She must be cold down here.

"Thank you so much!" she said, tears streaming down her cheeks. "I can't believe this happened to us."

"What exactly happened?" I asked as I untied the other woman's gag.

"Men barged into my gallery, tied us up, and forced us down here. I had no idea this cave was down here or that there was a hole in the floor of my gallery."

"When did they abduct you?"

"What day and time is it?"

"Tuesday," I glanced at my watch. "Six p.m."

I had missed Wine Hour. I hoped Cory covered for me.

"They kidnapped us last night."

That meant she was already in captivity when I saw the faeries enter the gallery. The tunnel openings I hadn't noticed before meant the faeries had probably gone into one of them. And maybe they put bombs in them. So, we had to hurry.

"Thank you, this is such a nightmare," said the other woman, a blonde who appeared to be in her twenties.

I set to work removing the man's gag. He was in his thirties and wore the yellow reflective vest of a utility worker.

"The men who abducted you were in human form?" I asked.

The older woman looked at me like I was crazy. "Of course."

"Were they handsome?"

"They were dreamy."

"They're terrorists," said the man. "They grabbed me while I was working beneath the street on the water main, and said I was going to be killed as a sacrifice. Those dirty terrorist maniacs and their false religion."

I didn't mention that their religion was nothing like what this man thought it was. It existed before humans existed.

"As a sacrifice?" I asked. I wasn't aware the Fae did that kind of thing.

"That's what they said. I don't know what they meant. I guess they meant beheading me."

I was trying to remove the ropes that bound the three prisoners. The man was first, because he seemed the best-suited for fighting in case the faeries attacked us. The knots were intricate and too tight for my fingers to loosen. Good thing I carried a multi-tool on me. It came in handy with minor repairs and such that came up at the inn. I never imagined I'd be using the little penknife blade to cut rope bindings from someone's wrist.

Finally, his hands were freed.

"I'll let you untie the rope around your feet yourself," I said before I went to work on the older woman's bound wrists.

"The thugs said nothing about the two of us being sacrificed," she said. "They told me they'd already been using my gallery as a transfer point at night—they didn't say what they were transferring, probably drugs—and they needed it full time now. I can't believe the burglar alarm never went off on any night."

Once her hands were freed, I turned my attention to the younger woman. As soon as their legs were untied, we could all go up the ladder to freedom.

Wait, what were those noises coming from the main cavern?

Footsteps scraping across the dirt. *Heavy* footsteps.

"What's that?" the guy asked in a quavering voice.

I shushed him and turned off my phone's flashlight.

The footsteps came closer. Whoever or whatever it was snorted and huffed.

You could almost feel the immense size of the creature as the air was displaced by its presence moving toward us.

"I don't want to be sacrificed," the guy whimpered.

"Shhh!" I considered putting the gag back on him.

It was too late—the creature already knew we were here.

The footsteps shuffled right to the opening of our little cavern. The creature sniffed deeply.

It smells us, I thought.

My heart was thudding like a jackhammer. In fact, I think I heard the other three hearts beating, too.

It was pitch black in here, but my eyes had adjusted to it. And with the faintest of light that came down from the hole—illumination from streetlights coming through the windows of the gallery—I could make out the silhouette of the creature.

Looming before us was a giant so tall its head nearly scraped the ceiling of the cavern, so brawny it made King Kong look like a weakling.

It snorted again. Then, it reached into our sub-cave.

The maintenance worker screamed as a hand half as big as he wrapped around his body and yanked him from our hiding place.

I turned on my phone's flashlight.

"Holy Moly," I said under my breath.

The creature had a massive human body, clothed in what looked like boat sails stitched together.

And it had the head of a bull.

It was a minotaur. A freaking minotaur. An entity that was supposed to be only a myth.

Despite my panic, the thought crossed my mind: was this what the Fae lowered through the hole in the gallery floor? It figures that their idea of a major weapon was a mythical monster.

The minotaur carried the maintenance worker out of our view. The man shrieked, as did the two women with me.

We were trapped in this alcove. The minotaur blocked our escape route. If we tried to run, it would be right into his hands. And mouth.

We couldn't simply cower here, though. We would only be delaying our deaths. How could we fight back? I had no weapons on me—remember, I had just come from the police department. I doubted the art dealers had anything on them stronger than pepper spray. Even if we had guns, this beast didn't look like it would go down easy.

With trembling fingers, I dialed 911, wondering how the heck I was going to explain this.

Then I had an idea. A gateway had saved the day when the faeries attacked the Hall of Records. Maybe, just maybe, I could summon one to get us out of here.

*Please, I need a gateway to save us,* I pleaded telepathically. *Save us now!*

"Nine-one-one," said a woman's voice over my phone. "What is the nature of your emergency?"

"A minotaur is eating a city worker and is about to eat me and two other women."

"What is eating you?"

"A minotaur."

"Is that some sort of dinosaur?"

"No! Don't you know the Ancient Greek myth of the half-man, half-bull? In the labyrinths below the palace of King Minos of Crete?"

"Is this a joke? You realize it's a felony—"

The maintenance guy shrieked again.

"Was that the man the dinosaur is eating?"

I desperately hoped a gateway would arrive and take the minotaur away, like the one that had plucked the faeries out of the air. Finally, nausea swept over me, indicating a gateway was nearby.

I swung my light around and saw it behind us, against the rounded wall in the back of our sub-cavern. No, the gateway would take *us* away, not the minotaur. But because of the confined space, the gateway was only large enough to take one person at a time.

"Crawl this way, into the shimmering air," I shouted at the hysterical women.

"What is it?" the gallery owner asked.

"It will get us out of here and to a safe place. Just go."

She didn't hesitate and crawled right into the shimmering before disappearing.

The younger woman hesitated, though. Until I grabbed her and pushed her through.

"Is this a prank or not?" the 911 operator asked.

"No. The guy getting eaten is below the Pendergast Gallery on Seville Street. There's like a sinkhole beneath the floor. You need to tell them to look for the hole in the floor."

"Is the dinosaur still there?"

I hurried through the gateway.

# CHAPTER 6

## THE FAE MAFIA

"Where the heck am I?" the gallery owner asked, after we appeared standing on the roof of my inn in the moonlight.

The gateways and I were truly becoming simpatico, but there was still a lack of understanding on their part. In the future, I hoped they'd deposit me inside the inn, or at least on the ground beside it.

Blessedly, the gateway did not take us to the In Between. I would have hated trying to explain the alternate plane of existence to my art dealer friends. Even if they could get their heads around the concept, and not freak out being in a new world that was slightly off from reality, they had to deal with the trauma they'd just experienced.

I mean, I don't recall ever seeing anyone post photos or videos on social media of encounters with minotaurs. This was a brave new world, and my new friends had to come to terms with what they just went through.

I only wish I could have saved the maintenance worker. I

hoped he didn't suffer too much.

The gallery owner repeated her question.

"This is my bed-and-breakfast," I said. "The Esperanza Inn."

"You mean the Hidalgo Inn?"

"That was its previous name. I renamed it when I bought it."

"The previous owner of the Hidalgo Inn was a friend of my mine."

"Yeah. I'm sorry. We recently cleaned his remains from beneath a third-floor bathtub. It's my inn now."

"Thanks for saving us, but how do we get off the roof?" the assistant art broker asked.

"We climb down a ladder as soon as my husband puts one up." I pulled out my cellphone. It had already been about to die from all the flashlight use, then being transported by the gateway completely fried it, as tended to happen with gateways.

"Just one moment," I said.

I inched my way to the edge of the roof on the side that faced the courtyard and our cottage.

"Cory!" I shouted. "Cory, get the ladder!"

No answer. Where was he? I feared he was inside in a room where he couldn't hear me. Or, worse, he was in bed already. He'd better not be! He should be sitting around, worried about where I was. It occurred to me, much too late, that I should have contacted him when I first saw the faeries.

"Cory!"

"Who's Cory?" came a male voice from the courtyard.

Reluctantly, I got on my stomach and inched closer to the edge of the roof to see the courtyard better. Being at a downward angle made me nervous. I reminded myself that I just survived a near-fatal encounter with a minotaur. Falling three stories from the roof would be half as horrifying a death.

Our small, heated swimming pool came into view. Though it

was night, a large man wallowed in the shallow end, his big gut protruding from the water like a cartoon island. All it lacked was a palm tree growing on it. I vaguely recognized the man. He must be the husband of the couple staying in 202 with the ghost of the Elvis impersonator.

"Cory is my husband, the co-owner of this place. Can you please call the front desk and ask for someone to help us down?"

"Sure. Careful, that's a steep roof."

"Tell me about it."

I pushed myself away from the roof's edge and sat near the peak with the two women.

"We didn't have time for introductions," I said. "I'm Darla."

"I'm Francis Pendergast," said the older woman. "This is Bebe. I appreciate your helping us escape, though I don't understand any of it."

"Why was the bull eating that poor man?" Bebe asked in a robotic voice.

"It was a minotaur," I said.

"A what?"

"A man who had the head of a bull." She obviously didn't know the legend of the minotaur. Such was the state of our culture.

"I didn't see a man. Only a bull."

Interesting, I thought. Perhaps she was incapable of seeing the supernatural.

"I'm sorry for what you guys went through. Can you tell me more about the men who abducted you?" I asked Francis. "Did you know them?"

"I knew one of them. Gorgeous-looking man named John Balen."

Balen! He was Dorn's assistant and one of the faeries who had captured and almost executed me.

46

"Mr. Balen first came to my gallery posing as a customer. He was charming and appeared to have a lot of money to spend. He bought a piece from an up-and-coming Ecuadorian I represent for the high five figures. But then, he changed."

"How so?"

"He started hanging around all the time, bringing his assistants with him. Once, he asked me if I needed a loan, which I politely declined. Next, he claimed a ring of art thieves was in the area, and he offered to provide security. Again, I declined. I have an excellent security system. But thieves broke in the very next night."

"How convenient," I said.

"Yes." She smiled grimly, her eyes flashing with anger in the darkness.

"I lost a work that was priced at twice what Balen paid for his purchase. It was clear to me now that what they wanted was not security work, but protection money—a racket, just like the Mafia would do. I honestly thought they *were* the Mafia. Until I learned more."

"Like what?"

"My security company told me they couldn't figure out how the alarm was compromised. There were absolutely no signs that anyone had physically disabled it. It has a backup battery in case the building's power is cut. They said the circuits were fried, but there was no evidence of a power surge, and even if there had been, it wouldn't have fried the circuits like that. The technician joked that magic must have been used."

"I'm afraid it was," I said.

"I realize that now. For the next few weeks, the alarm was disabled every night. But it wasn't fried; it was simply turned off, as if the intruders had the code. And morning after morning, I'd come to work to find signs that someone had been inside the gallery overnight, occasionally stealing art, or moving things around, like the winch. I didn't know about the hole in the floor, though.

"Finally, when Bebe and I were abducted, I realized Balen and his gang *did* have magic. They paralyzed us and bound our limbs without even touching us. They didn't need the ropes they tied on us, except for when their magic wore off, which it did by the time you rescued us."

"I'm glad it had worn off, or I would have had to drag you into the gateway."

"And finally, there was the monster, the minotaur, that was going to eat us. What kind of organized crime are Balen and his gang involved in?"

She'd already seen too much. There was no reason to hold back information from her.

"There's a species of supernatural creatures called the Fae. They're like the faeries in your childhood storybooks. They have magical abilities and can appear in human form, generally as really good-looking humans."

"Criminal ones."

"Yeah. Their existence has been a secret for all of modern history, but they've been coming out of the woodwork lately. Basically, they want to reclaim what they believe is their rightful place as the dominant intelligent species. Only the supernatural creatures and paranormal humans have known about them. They haven't messed with normal humans until now."

"What do you mean by reclaiming their rightful place?"

"Ruling us all. I thought it would be in more subtle ways than acting like organized crime thugs, though."

"Why do they have a minotaur? And why is it in San Marcos?"

"I guess it's for fighting. Humans have tanks. Maybe this is the Fae version."

"What are Bebe and I supposed to do now? We can't go back to work in the gallery after what they did to us. Especially with that thing living right below us."

"I wish I had an answer for you. I'll let all the right people know about this and tell you what they say. And I'll help you in any way I can."

She frowned. My answer wasn't good enough.

All three of us jumped at the sound of the aluminum ladder hitting the edge of the roof. I guess our nerves were simply too frayed. They were smoothed by the sound of someone climbing the ladder and the sight of Cory's head popping up above the roof's edge.

"I put the ladder on the roof of the utility annex, so it's only a two-story climb," he said. "Um, can I ask where you've been and how you got up here?"

"I was rescuing them from a minotaur, and a gateway dropped us off a little inconveniently," I said.

He ignored the part about the minotaur. I didn't blame him.

"Couldn't you have taken a gateway from the roof to the ground?" he asked.

I must admit I hadn't thought of that. "To be honest, I'm not used to having them respond to my requests. And I still don't enjoy traveling with them."

Cory nodded. He didn't enjoy the Barf Bus, either.

I introduced Frances and Bebe to him. Since they appeared nervous about climbing down the tall ladder, he offered to descend right below them to make sure they didn't slip.

Once we all were down, we went inside the inn, and I served coffee laced with brandy so the two women could warm up and relax. I took my coffee, with extra brandy, into the front room where I called 9-1-1 again to make sure they had taken my first call seriously. It turns out they had, but they didn't report if they found the maintenance man.

I gave Cory a brief synopsis of what I'd been through. Needless to say, he was not happy with my foolhardiness. Then, I tried Samson despite the late hour.

"Yeah, I heard about a call regarding a city worker being attacked in a sinkhole beneath a gallery," he said.

"It's more of a cavern than a sinkhole, but that was easier to explain."

"They didn't find anything."

"What do you mean?"

"The first responders searched the gallery, went down into the hole, and didn't find a victim."

"Wow," I said. "Then, he was completely consumed."

"Will you please explain yourself?"

I told him the entire story, from seeing the faeries climb out of the sewer to the attack by the minotaur.

"First, you were warning me about faeries," he said wearily. "Now, a minotaur."

"Who says there's just one minotaur?"

"How can I do something about this without being accused of having delusions? Do we really want to get the police involved with the supernatural?"

"If this keeps up, they won't have a choice," I said. "If you don't want to do this officially, you need to help us by freelancing. The Executive Council of the Supernatural Guilds is still dithering, while the Fae is getting increasingly aggressive."

I explained what Francis told me about Balen's shakedown.

"There you go. That's a crime, and he and his crew are committing it while in human form. If she's willing to file a complaint, we can put pressure on that Balen character, even if he's magical."

"That doesn't work. At least not in the mafia movies I've watched. And the mafia don't have magic."

"Don't underestimate the power of a good racketeering charge. I'm not saying this will stop the Fae from invading, but it might stop them from harassing businesses. Ask the gallery owner to call me in the morning. Tell her we'll post an officer nearby for security."

Archibald, who was his typical stony slumbering gargoyle self when I entered the room, chose this moment to animate.

"Pardon me, but did you speak about a minotaur?"

"Yep. What about it?"

"There are no minotaurs in this part of Florida. I've heard of one spotted in Tarpon Springs, where they have a significant Greek population. And Montana has a few minotaurs, I'm told. More bulls there than men, they say. But never in San Marcos."

"Whatever," I said. "There's one here now."

"Don't you realize what this means?"

"It means the Fae shipped one here, probably in some sort of circus trailer, because this guy was huge."

"No. It means the Fae have torn open the veil."

"What's that?"

"You haven't heard of the veil? I realize you're human, but one would think someone would have briefed you on this, your being in a supernatural guild, and all. Not to mention all this goddess business."

"No, I haven't heard of the veil. It would have been nice if you had told me before now."

"The veil appeared when humankind first showed signs of modernity. If you ask me, you're all still a bunch of uncivilized barbarians, but I'll leave that aside for now. The veil shields the human world from the gods and monsters of ancient religions and folklore."

"Really? But it seems I come across crazy supernatural creatures all the time that I thought didn't exist."

"Yes, those that humans continued to believe in after your so-called modernity because they remained with you, like vampires and faeries. Not so creatures like the minotaur. No one believes in them anymore. No one frightens little children into behaving by telling them the minotaur is going to get them."

"True. Not in my house, at least."

"If the veil has been torn asunder, there's no telling what nightmarish creatures the Fae have unleashed. They could be the secret weapons for defeating us."

I couldn't imagine the creatures he was talking about. I didn't want to.

"The Fae can control them? What if they attack the Fae, too?"

"We shall see."

"I need to know more."

"I believe you have guests to attend to now. We'll discuss this matter at the next guild meeting."

In a blink of an eye, he returned to stone. Such a frustrating fellow, my gargoyle housemate.

When I returned to the living room, my guests were getting ready to leave.

I scribbled Samson's phone number on the back of the inn's business card.

"Call Detective Samson tomorrow, and he'll post an officer near your gallery for extra security."

"I wonder if I should move the gallery," Francis said. "To another city, perhaps."

"Please don't, I can't leave my family," Bebe said.

"How can we keep it open when there's that thing below it?"

"By the way, they didn't find the maintenance worker," I said.

"The beast probably dragged him into its lair. I can't go back to that building."

I understood how she felt. Even if I broke protocol and set her up with the Magic Guild to protect her from the Fae, Francis and Bebe would never feel safe there again. Plus, I doubted the Magic Guild could do much for them.

"I understand," I said, giving each of them a hug. "You both have been through too much. Please, call Detective Samson, though, and report the harassment by Mr. Balen."

We say our goodbyes, and once again, I promised myself I would focus on my family and business, letting the guilds battle the Fae.

How long do you think it will be before I break my promise?

# CHAPTER 7

# MEMORIES OF THE DEAD

It was a normal day at the inn. Breakfast was followed by cleaning. Cleaning was followed by washing sheets and supervising the housekeeper. This was followed by getting Cory to fix a broken bathroom fixture in 302, followed by calming a guest who didn't realize 303 was haunted, despite our brochure saying so. Dealing with the ghost was followed by a food delivery.

And then, Buddy called.

Man, I had almost forgotten about him. An encounter with a savage minotaur made Buddy's sordid little world easy to forget.

"Hey, babe, I got the key from Damon's landlord."

"Weren't you supposed to stop calling me babe when we divorced?"

"Force of habit. I call lots of women babe."

"Maybe that explains why you haven't remarried."

"Anyway, do you think you can go there and do your sleuthing thing?"

"I'm too busy today."

"Come on, please? That high-powered lawyer won't represent me unless I show him evidence someone else did it. I met with a court-appointed attorney, and the guy doesn't even have time to help me. He wants me to plea-bargain for a shorter sentence. I told him I'm innocent, and he doesn't care."

I sighed theatrically to make a point. "You can't rely on me for your defense. I'm just a psychic, and I'm too busy."

"Come on, Darla. All I'm asking is for you to visit the apartment like you suggested. Spend like an hour there, tops. Will ya do it?"

I sighed again. "I'll be there at noon. Before I get there, look the place over so you can tell me what possessions Damon handled the most. But don't touch them."

"Handled?"

"Yeah. I'll explain later."

"Okay. I'll see you there. And thanks, babe."

I stifled a curse and clicked off. Then, I got a text from Bella about a room that a guest had apparently used to host a mud-wrestling match.

This is my life.

DAMON'S APARTMENT WAS IN A SEEDY NEIGHBORHOOD ON THE outskirts of San Marcos. I passed a liquor store, a stripper club, and two pawnshops before I reached the cluster of two-story buildings. They were sad and rundown. All the units had porches or balconies, and the place might have been decent when it was first built. But that was probably forty or fifty years ago, and no improvements had occurred since.

Buddy had made it sound like their drug-testing scheme was highly profitable. Well, it looked like Damon hadn't spent much of his profits, at least not on his living arrangements. Maybe he had been blowing them instead on gambling, drugs, or other vices.

I went up an exterior staircase to find the door of his apartment open. I smelled the lingering cigarette reek before I even reached the door. Buddy was inside, inspecting the place.

"It's amazing how I worked with the guy for so long and didn't know jack about his personal life," Buddy said. He was examining a multi-photo frame on the wall of a boy and girl in their stages of childhood. Nudging a golf bag with his foot, he added, "I didn't even know he played. It's sad."

It was always sad visiting a dead person's home when all their stuff was still there. As a psychometrist, I had to build up a wall to protect myself, especially when, as in this case, he had lived here for a long time and accumulated tons of memories on his stuff.

Before I started searching, I needed some answers.

"Do you know someone nicknamed the Emerald Man?"

Surprise, then fear, crossed Buddy's face.

*Oh crap.* I picked up this thought.

"Nope."

"Don't lie to me," I said with a tone.

"What, did you read my mind?"

"You gave it away with your facial expressions."

Buddy kicked the golf bag lightly and wandered in front of the TV.

"I don't know The Emerald Man personally. Never met him. I know *of* him. He's sort of a fixer for a lot of bad guys."

Buddy was avoiding my eyes.

"Sounds like you might travel in the same circles as him," I said.

"I told you I don't know him."

"He might be the one who killed Damon."

"How do you know this? Do you have more psychic stuff I don't know about?"

"It doesn't matter. Why would the Emerald Man kill him? And would you be next on his list?"

Buddy swallowed hard. "He's got no reason to kill me. Damon must've gotten his nose into matters that didn't concern him."

"Like what?"

"I already explained to you our business model. It just so happens that some of our clients aren't exactly choirboys."

"Breaking news."

"I don't want to talk about it anymore. Just drop it, okay?"

"To clear your name, you're going to have to find probable cause that someone else killed Damon. We need to know more about the Emerald Man. You should have the police show you mugshots and try to identify him."

"I'm not going back there on my own free will."

"And we have to explain why your gun was used."

"I lent it to Damon for protection. The killer must have grabbed it and used it on him. I can't see the Emerald Man doing that. I was thinking Damon had some chick in the car with him, and he got a little too forward."

"No. Let me explain this." I had to speak slowly so he would understand. "I saw a vision of what went through Damon's mind. A car pulled up beside his with a man that Damon identified as the Emerald Man. Then, the man shot him through the window."

"You saw that in a vision? Man, you're more of a psychic than I thought."

"Yeah. I prefer not to talk about it, but I want you to believe what I'm telling you. I can read people's memories—what was going through their minds—when I touch something they touched."

"Wow, that's crazy! Have you always been able to do this?"

"No. I discovered the ability when I moved back to San Marcos."

"Hey, I wonder if it has anything to do with your age, like, you know, going through The Change."

"Shut up. Now, give me some time by myself to see what I can find here. Did you locate anything he was fond of?"

"Not really. Just that Jacksonville Jaguars cap on the table over there. He would wear that fairly often."

I thanked him and ushered him out the door, closing it behind him.

The cap was the typical adjustable ball cap with the Jaguars' logo on the front. Its bill was dirty from frequent handling. The inner liner band was soiled from hours of touching a sweaty, greasy forehead.

Anything your skin touches can transfer your psychic energy. However, skin in some locations is better than others. Despite being so close to your brain, the skin of your forehead isn't a great conductor of memories. You don't use this skin for sensory input; you just wear it. I wasn't eager to touch the disgusting sweatband, and a cursory scan of it told me there wasn't much in the way of memories on it.

The hat's bill was a different story. Damon's fingers touched it frequently, and your fingers are among your best conductors of memory. Most people only touch the bill when putting a hat on or taking it off.

Wait, Damon seemed to be the exception. I found images of him grabbing it frequently to adjust his hat in a nervous habit. He also spent a lot of time with both hands on the bill, repeatedly pushing its edges inward to curve them downward.

I brushed the bill lightly with my fingers and received a jumble of memory fragments. Killing time in the car, chatting with sober home workers, working out a deal with a prostitute who sat in the passenger seat, buying drugs from someone standing outside the driver's window, drinking in a bar at midday, counting the crates of urine samples in the trunk of the car.

Then, a strong memory, a poignant one: asking a security guard at a sober home what happened to Rita, an image of her face matching the woman who had sat in the car. Sadness filling him as he heard she had been transferred with other patients to another facility far away.

He vowed to find her. He actually loved her.

I dove deep into this memory because it seemed so important. He spoke to the guard outside a two-story apartment building with outdoor breezeways providing access to the units. A man and woman leaned against the upstairs railing, smoking cigarettes. I fell into a reverie so I could read the name—

—*Shady Palms Apartments. I'm telling Sam they can't just transfer patients somewhere else without their permission. "Yeah, we can. It's in the contract they sign." But something doesn't smell right. Rita told me that some of her friends had left one night, and they hadn't known they would be moved. Yeah, something is fishy. And I deserve to know what the deal is, because every time people leave, it means fewer tests for us. I'm going to stake out this place and try to find out where they're sending the residents. I have to find Rita 'cause I miss her. I put my—*

—hat back on, and the memory ends.

I scanned the hat more thoroughly, hoping to find memories

of his stakeouts, but, surprisingly, couldn't find anything recognizable.

Glancing around the small, cluttered apartment, I didn't know what to investigate next. There were old newspapers and magazines lying around. An ancient computer that I doubted worked. Empty beer cans scattered about. An end table with a half-full bottle of vodka.

Just inside the front door was a narrow table that looked like he would drop his keys here and other things he brought inside from his car. There were no keys, of course. Among an empty fast-food soda cup and a pile of mail, I spotted them.

A pair of binoculars. An essential tool for a stakeout.

THE BINOCULARS WERE LOADED WITH PSYCHIC ENERGY. THESE instruments are not casual tools. When you're using binoculars, you're intent on finding or studying something. You're just as focused as the lenses are.

I hovered my fingers above the hand grips and felt a mix of longing, desperation, boredom, and then, excitement. I cleared my mind, took a deep breath, and—

—*walk along the second-floor breezeway. The man bangs on each door, and when it opens, he yells at the people inside. He does this until he gets to the end of the building, then turns around and returns the way he has come. By now, people are drifting out of their studio apartments. He gestures to them to head for the stairs.*

*I pan the binoculars and see the second man standing by the stairs. A big, mean-looking white guy holding a rifle. This is serious. The residents drag their feet and complain, until they see the guy with the gun. They're heading downstairs now. I think there are eight of them, men and women, ranging from their twenties through their forties.*

*A passenger van pulls up to the bottom of the stairs. We call these vans "druggy buggies," because they transport patients to therapy sessions and drug tests. Everyone piles inside with the guards behind them.*

*The van leaves the parking lot. I start my car and—*

—put the binoculars down. There's a gap in the memory, but it picks up again. I allow myself to be sucked into—

*—a swirl of cigarette smoke as I light yet another one. It's risky for me to park outside the gate of this ranch. I'm too easy to spot. But that's the problem with being out here in farm country. Why are they all the way out here? I've never heard of sober homes being this far from town. Maybe this is one of those working ranches where they make the patients shovel horse dung, kind of like boot camp.*

*I'm tired of sitting out here where I can't see anything except for the main house and the barn. The house seems dead, but there are lights on in the barn. I take the binoculars, leave the car, and slip through the narrow space between the gate and the barbed-wire fence. There better not be any sensors or anything that I'll trigger.*

*Crouching in the bushes where it's nice and dark. Have a good angle on the barn. Focusing on the windows. There are people moving around in there. No clue what they're doing. Man, I need another cigarette, but can't light it out here.*

*Wait, no one is moving past the windows anymore. Maybe they're all sitting. The lights just went out. That's weird. Get down—a door opens on the side of the barn. The two guards walk out and go into the main house. They didn't lock the door behind them.*

*I need to check this out. Sneak across a wide dirt driveway and up to the barn, on the side where I can't be seen from the house. I'm looking through a window. I don't see anyone inside. Even though it's dark, I can tell it's empty. What did they do to the patients? I slip around the side of the barn and try the door the guards came out of. It's unlocked and I enter.*

*Yeah, there's no one in here. Where the heck did everyone go? There's no loft. Is there another room somewhere? I'm pretty sure this place isn't a sober home. No sign it's even a working ranch. I haven't even seen any animals.*

*What's that? A car coming up the driveway! Dang, they would have seen my car parked next to the road. Looking out the barn window at the car, a Lexus. It parks by the house. Two men get out and walk into the house.*

*Time to bail out of here. Jogging down the driveway, slipping out of the space next to the gate. Badly disappointed that I learned nothing to help me find Rita.*

*Jump in my car and drop—*

—the memory as he releases the binoculars.

Did I learn anything of value? Heck, yeah. I recognized one of the men who showed up and went into the house. I'd seen him in Damon's memory of the moments before his death. It was only a shadowy image of him, but I knew who it was. The Emerald Man.

What was he doing out there? Does he own the place?

I also learned this particular sober home is up to something crooked. What exactly happened to those patients?

Fortunately, the crooked business didn't seem to involve Buddy and Damon. However, Damon got himself involved as a witness, which would be dangerous if anyone knew he followed the van to the ranch.

Namely, the Emerald Man.

I left the apartment and went downstairs. Buddy was pacing back and forth in the parking lot, speaking on his phone.

"Yeah, I need the extra money bad, but if they do a background check, they'll find out I'm indicted. It's only Mega-Mart, but I have just as much of a chance of getting hired there as getting elected mayor."

He nodded while the other person talked.

"Hey, you've got a good point there," Buddy replied. "There are tons of politicians who get elected while they're under indictment. Maybe there's hope for me yet."

He noticed me standing there, listening.

"Gotta go. I'll call you later."

He stuffed his phone in his pocket. "Learn anything?"

"I didn't solve the mystery, but I picked up some interesting things."

"From this new psychic stuff? You've got to explain to me exactly how this works."

"Maybe someday, Buddy. I think it's a bit too complicated for you."

"Well, tell me what you found."

"Do you know a rehab patient named Rita?"

"No. Why?"

"Damon was in love with her. She was moved unexpectedly to another site, and Damon was searching for her."

"That old perv was known to take advantage of addicted women."

"I'm sure, but he was legitimately fond of Rita. Are you familiar with a sober home called The Shady Palms Apartments?"

He scratched his head. "Yeah, it's on my route. If I recall, the company that owns that place, Hopeful Recoveries, is good for a few hundred units a week."

"Units?"

"Of pee."

"Thanks for clarifying. Shady Palms is where Rita lived, along with a bunch of other patients who were taken away. Do you know of any sober home located on a ranch?"

"I know there are recovery places like that for rich people.

They ride horses and eat five-star meals. We don't have any clients like that."

"The patients at Shady Palms wouldn't get sent to a place like that?" I asked.

"Heck, no. Have you seen the kind of place Shady Palms is?"

"Not exactly. Tell me where it is."

"It's on the wrong side of town, and several miles below rock bottom."

# CHAPTER 8

## WELCOME TO SHADY PALMS

Buddy was right. The Shady Palms Apartments were where you went after you fell through the cracks of society and landed in the deepest pits of despair.

The two-story building with breezeways sat perpendicular to the street, right next to railroad tracks. It had probably been built in the 1960s for those of low-to-moderate income—an acceptable place for your first apartment. Before you made enough money to get the heck out of there.

Shady Palms was not shady. There were no trees around it, certainly no palms. Asphalt and concrete ruled.

The drug rehab company that owned it, Hopeful Recoveries, had cleaned up the property and slapped a fresh coat of paint on the building's walls and steel railings, but the place nevertheless reeked of desperation.

See, I did my homework and researched the company. No psychic abilities were needed, only the internet, which allowed me into the county's public records listings as well as the archives of *The San Marcos Record* newspaper.

I learned Hopeful Recoveries was owned by a shell company and had been slapped with several fines for allowing drug use on the property, as well as engaging in patient-brokering. This was the seedy practice of finding patients in recovery who had good insurance and offering them money, drugs, or free rent if they were admitted to your facility.

A doctor who referred patients to the company was under investigation for Medicare and insurance fraud. That signaled to me that Buddy and Damon were probably also under scrutiny for their unnecessary testing billed to insurance.

My car rolled past the building and parked on the street next door, in front of a disheveled duplex. The parking lot for Shady Palms was empty, except for a passenger van, but I didn't want to pull in there. It would attract too much attention. A picnic tent at the end of the building near the train tracks provided meager shade for a circle of plastic chairs, where a half dozen mostly young people sat around smoking.

I approached them. They stared at me like hungry dogs. Were they hoping I was a drug dealer? Or a street performer?

"Hi, my name is Darla. I've been looking for a long-lost friend who once lived here. Her name is Rita. Rita Morales. Any of you know her?"

I had forced Buddy to go through his drug testing records to find her last name.

"I kind of knew her," said an African American woman, the oldest of the group, old enough to be on Medicare.

"Would you know where she went?"

"Nah, she was part of a group they shipped out of here all of a sudden. I never saw her again after that, and I don't know where she went."

"Does that happen often—people getting shipped out of here?"

"It happens like every month. Management says they get kicked out and sent to another facility because they were caught using. What nonsense," the lady cackled. "The manager hands out drugs right and left to force people to stay here."

I looked at the faces staring at me. "You guys, too?"

"No way," said a young man with a shaved head. "We're serious about getting clean. And getting out of here for good."

"I'm happy to hear that," I said. "How long ago did Rita leave?"

"Just last month," the old woman said. "If you find her, tell her Linda says hi. Tell her I'm almost done with my therapy."

I thanked her and said I will.

"Oh, do you happen to remember which unit Rita lived in?"

"Two-oh-seven. Someone else is in there now."

Fortunately, the group was sitting at the end of the building near the railroad tracks and couldn't see me as I climbed the concrete stairs and walked down the breezeway to 207, the second unit from the street side.

Without having access to the apartment, I had little hope of finding any useful memories. But as a psychometrist, I would be negligent if I didn't at least try while I was here.

I hovered my hands near the door handle, not a promising place to look. Too many people handle this kind of hardware, and they hold it only briefly. Indeed, several tenants had cycled through this apartment in a short amount of time, along with their visitors.

I sensed something out of the ordinary: a memory of someone with authority and in an angry mood. It took severe concentration to isolate this memory before I touched the handle, and—

— *(Turn the passkey.) "Rita! You in here?" She better not be passed out. I can't stand when they use drugs right in my face and then end up*

*OD-ing, and we get paramedics crawling all over the place. Where is she? It's just a danged studio apartment. In the closet? Yeah, hiding. "Get out—*

— of the memory when he let go of the handle to march into the room.

Very interesting. I wish I could find a memory of Rita's. There was a brief one of someone opening the door, while someone else called Rita's name from down the breezeway. It was only two seconds long, but I focused on the psychic energy to familiarize myself with it and distinguish it from all the other people's memories on the handle.

Now, I could recognize other memories she left here. But none were useful. Was there anyplace else to look?

I turned, and the railing caught my eye. In Damon's memory, I had seen people hanging out, leaning on the railing. Did Rita ever do that?

On the railing directly across from her door, there was virtually no energy from anyone. Hovering my hand, I moved to the right, toward the street.

And bingo! Rita had stood here, at night, watching the street.

Waiting for Damon to arrive. Worrying because a security guard—a big, mean white guy—said something about Damon visiting too much outside of picking up the samples. And she was afraid of being sent away like her friend, Vickie, who lived on the first floor.

"Can I help you?"

It was a security guard below me in the parking lot. He wasn't the big, mean white guy, but an older Hispanic man wearing sunglasses. I didn't recognize him from Damon's memory of residents being rounded up. The memory included the big mean-looking white guy, I recalled.

"You're not a client here, are you?" he asked. "Our clients can't have visitors unless they get permission."

"Sorry. A friend of mine used to live here," I said, as I hurried down the breezeway to the stairs.

He waited for me at the bottom with a suspicious frown.

"I was wondering what happened to my friend, Rita Morales," I said. "I didn't realize she finished her therapy."

"Rita? No, she was sent to another place. You haven't heard from her at all?"

"No."

He shook his head. "Man, that's a shame."

"Where did she go?"

"I heard there's a ranch out in the country where the clients have no opportunity to backslide and start using again. But I have my doubts."

I glanced at this uniform. A patch said, "Becker Security."

"Do you work for Hopeful Recoveries?" I asked.

"No, lady, I'm just a contractor for this facility."

"Tell me what your doubts are."

He glanced behind him to make sure no one was there and removed his sunglasses. The skin around his eyes was heavily wrinkled. His eyes were dark brown and glittered with a hint of empathy.

"I heard from a guy on the night shift," he said, "that these clients, the ones who get taken to the ranch, they never come back."

"Maybe they recover and return to their normal lives."

"No, we've had their family members coming around here, asking for them. Those who still have a family after drugs took over their lives. No, these people are never seen again."

It took me a moment to digest this. "Are you telling me they're murdered?"

The guard shrugged and looked around again nervously.

"Who knows? The guy who told me this said he had to drive the druggy buggy out there one night. The place isn't a real ranch. There were no horses or cattle or anything. He told me there were guards there who led the clients into a barn. And before he even drove back down the driveway, the lights in the barn went out."

This sounded a lot like what Damon had seen. But neither he nor the night shift guy witnessed any sights or sounds of murders. It seemed like the recovery patients simply disappeared.

Knowing what I know, there are more ways to disappear than you'd think. There are the gateways whisking people and other creatures off to the In Between or other destinations.

And there's magic.

"Do you know where the ranch is?" I asked.

"State Road Nineteen, several miles southwest of town. I think it's called the Hard Ridge Ranch."

Don't even think of going there, Darla, you probably want to tell me.

Unfortunately, I'm not so good at listening.

ON THE DRIVE HOME, I CALLED BUDDY TO TELL HIM WHAT I had learned. I also called Samson and asked if there were any missing-persons reports related to the rehab patients. His keyboard clicked while he checked the system.

"At first glance, I don't see anything. But I'll need to look more thoroughly. Unfortunately, some patients who have long-term substance-abuse problems end up breaking ties with friends and family. So, there wouldn't be anyone to report them missing."

I thanked him, feeling like I'd done all I could.

There was plenty of time to set up for the Wine Hour when I returned to the inn. I uncorked a few extra bottles, just in case. More than half of our rooms were occupied tonight, which was a huge achievement for us. It was a good feeling to be gaining traction at last in the fickle small-inn market of this city that was filled with bed-and-breakfasts.

The worry-wart part of my brain had to ruin my satisfaction.

What about the Fae? it asked. What if the minotaur marauds through the town? How will the bookings be when the city is a battleground?

I shut off that part of my brain and poured myself a glass of wine.

Through the living room French doors, I saw Sophie and her friend, Imelda, hanging out in the courtyard by the pool. I passed through the living room and opened a door.

"Hi, ladies. Would you like to join me inside and kick off Wine Hour?"

I only just noticed now that they were frowning.

"It will cheer you up," I said.

"No, thanks," Imelda said.

"We're talking about matters you don't want your guests to hear about," Sophie said.

I stepped outside and grabbed a chair close to them.

"You remember Imelda is half-Alux?" Sophie asked.

I nodded. Imelda's family was from Mexico, of Mayan descent. Her father was an Alux, the Mayan version of the Fae, similar though distinct, with their own unique magic.

"There have been a lot of incursions by the Fae in these

lands," Imelda said. "They are disrupting the Aluxes who live here."

"I told her you've had run-ins with them," Sophie said.

Sophie knows only a fraction of what I've been through. I never told her how close I had come to being executed by one of their leaders. Nor did I tell her about participating on a raid at the Faerie Queene's palace. I wasn't simply trying to protect Sophie from needless anxiety; I also didn't want her trying to limit my future reckless activities.

"Have the Fae hurt or captured any Aluxes?" I asked.

"Not that I have heard," Imelda said. "It could happen, though. The Fae claim these lands have been theirs long before humans came along. They forget, though, that the Aluxes have been here long before the faeries showed up."

"I hope the Aluxes don't form an alliance with them."

"The Aluxes wouldn't want that. Unless we were threatened with harm."

"It would be wonderful if the Aluxes joined with us in defending against the Fae."

"Joined with the humans?"

"With the supernatural and paranormals of this area," I said. "We hope normal humans aren't drawn into this conflict."

"I will speak to my father and ask him to convey your message to the elders."

"Thank you." A strange line of thought came to me. "Forgive me if this question comes across as too personal, but why were your mother and father able to have you? The Fae can't produce children with humans."

Imelda giggled. "The Aluxes and the Fae are different. Not so much biologically, but in our magic. I'm told the reason the Fae can't mate with humans comes from their own prejudice. Thousands of years ago, they decided they didn't want to dilute their blood with that of non-magical humans. Their natural magic evolved to make this prohibition a biological law, and fertilization became impossible."

"You have something in mind, don't you?" Sophie asked me.

"The two of you know the Fae are suffering from a disease that harms their fertility, causing a population decline. They've been kidnapping human children to raise as their own. Before humans reach puberty, their DNA can be altered through Fae magic to make the children grow up as faeries. I was wondering if the Fae could use Alux magic to mate with humans and produce offspring, so they wouldn't have to kidnap children."

"You would have to ask the Elders if that could be possible," Imelda said. "Even if it could be, the Fae would have to lose their prejudice. And there's no magic in the world strong enough to erase prejudice."

"I wish there was."

A seedling caught my eye below my chair. Somehow, the little guy with five tiny leaves, had managed to squeeze between two paving stones. I was certain it wasn't there when I sat down. Having this propagating effect on plants and trees was very gratifying. My container gardens in the courtyard were doing wonders.

I only wish I had this effect on business profits.

# CHAPTER 9

# UNICORN IN AISLE THREE

I was examining the tomatoes at the grocery store when the unicorn galloped past the deli counter.

Sometimes, animals find their way into stores—deer, bears, dogs, birds, and such. In Florida, often it's alligators. It happens and provides great sharable video content for the internet and the local news. Not to my knowledge, has a unicorn ever done it.

The unicorn leaped over the refrigerator case holding the gourmet cheeses and thundered into the produce section, trampling a guy with a man bun, and accidentally skewering a large potato with its horn.

The dozen or so people in this section screamed and fled in all directions.

A young girl in a stroller delightedly squealed, "Unicorn!" Her mother was not delighted at all.

Then, the unicorn came at me.

I threw a large bag of apples at it, which it dodged. I scurried around the stand with the tomatoes and onions, knocking the produce in the beast's path. As it surged toward me, its hooves crushed the vegetables into a ratatouille, causing the unicorn to slip.

It blocked my path to the front of the store, so I sprinted from the produce section, turned a corner, and ran past the meats. The unicorn was right behind me.

A meat department guy, who was laying out hamburger packages in the display case, got speared by the unicorn's horn. The man was too astounded to scream, and the horn only punctured him slightly, thanks to the potato still impaled on it.

Did you know unicorns poop as much as horses do? I didn't, but now I do, right there in the meat section.

And they don't poop gumdrops or marshmallows. No, sir.

I went down the international foods aisle, tossing bottles of Thai chili sauce and cans of refried beans at my pursuer. He batted them away with his horn and potato, but they slowed him down a bit.

You know those annoying people who totally block an aisle by standing next to their carts? Well, one of them bought me valuable time. Being as petite as I am, I squeezed through the tight space between the cart and the shelves on my left. The shopper, who blocked the space between the cart and the shelves to my right, served as a speed bump for the unicorn. I hope she survived the trampling.

I headed toward the checkout lanes, the sunshine streaming through the exit doors signaling freedom.

The lane in front of me had only one customer. All her groceries had been scanned and bagged. I stopped running before I collided with her, knowing she would be moving out of my path.

But she waited until now to open her purse, as if she had forgotten she had to pay for these groceries. She carefully searched for her wallet. At last, she found it. Then, it was time to search in the wallet for her credit card.

Screams erupted all around us as the clatter of hooves on the floor approached. The lady in front of me still hadn't paid.

I jumped up onto the conveyor belt and climbed over the rack that displayed the tabloid newspapers and the magazines with holiday recipes.

The woman who finally found her credit card also found the unicorn freight train inches away from her.

I made it into the next checkout lane before I heard the collision. The lady's shopping cart, with her atop it, rolled by. I ducked down between the flabbergasted shoppers in front of and behind me.

The unicorn appeared at the end of our lane. It swung its head back and forth, the potato still stuck on its horn. Its nostrils flared. When he picked up my scent, he saw me crouching there, even though a fat guy and his cart were between us.

The unicorn dug at the floor with a hoof, preparing to charge.

Sirens came from outside. The unicorn, realizing his time was up, trotted the other way toward the rear of the store. He somehow escaped without being seen.

Later, after I'd calmed down and stopped shivering in my car in the parking lot, the news reports and social media postings began coming in.

Oddly, the incident was reported as a horse running amok in the store. The injuries to the humans were reported to be "non-life-threatening."

The brief clips of video, picked up by one shopper's phone and the store's security cameras, showed the blurred shots of the marauding unicorn. Except you couldn't see its horn, which was either by accident or through magic.

No one saw or knew that it was a unicorn, except for the young child in the produce department. And me.

THIS HAD GONE TOO FAR. WHEN I GOT HOME, I MARCHED into the front room and demanded that Archibald request a meeting of the Memory Guild. Of course, I had to demand this for nearly twenty minutes before the recalcitrant gargoyle awoke from this slumber and animated.

"You said a minotaur *and* a unicorn?" he asked.

"I did. I don't know if the Fae are simply trying to create panic before they attack, or if they're using these mythological creatures as their proxies. But this is only the beginning. It's going to get much worse if we don't stop them."

"I shall pass along your meeting request."

And before I could even register his sentence, I was soaring above an ocean.

No, it was the English Channel. And the endless convoys of ships below me were part of the Allied invasion of Normandy. The educational message of this journey was more on the nose than usual. And I hoped it was a good omen that it was the good guys who were doing the invading.

Oh, wait, now I flew over a seaside village getting sacked by Vikings. A bad omen, for sure.

The next thing I knew, I was in the Memory Guild meeting hall with Dr. Noordlun and the rest of the membership.

"Did Archibald fill you in?" I asked.

"The Executive Council of the Supernatural Guilds knew about the incidents in real time," our director said. "I find it fascinating that the shoppers in the store saw a horse, but not a unicorn. You're the only one who saw it?"

"And a toddler."

"It could be that only those who are paranormal or supernatural can see these creatures as they truly are. Perhaps, the child has the gift. Or perhaps, it's simply the innocence of childhood."

"When we were attacked by the minotaur," I said, "the gallery owner's assistant didn't see a minotaur, only a carnivorous bull. Who knows what its victim saw?"

"And the gallery owner?" Archibald asked.

"She said she saw the minotaur. I guess that means she's not a normal human. Interesting. What do you guys think is going on here? Are the Fae going to continue throwing mythological creatures at us, or are they going to come after us themselves?"

"That is what we need to determine," Dr. Noordlun said. "One would think at first they were attempting to panic the human population, but not if the humans don't see the monsters."

"One other thing," my fellow psychometrist, Laurel, said, "why are these creatures trying to kill Darla?"

"A most excellent question," I said. "The unicorn was interested only in me. The minotaur, though, wanted to eat everybody."

"The Fae worship their own version of Danu, the mother-earth goddess," Summer said. "Why aren't they sympathetic to Darla now that she has the goddess in her?"

"We have many questions to answer," Dr. Noordlun said. "I must leave now to attend an Executive Council meeting. Darla, you're going with me."

"I am? I'm only a junior member of the guild."

"The council wishes to question you on these matters."

"Really? That's—"

Suddenly, I was in a different space. I now knew the Executive Council used astral travel to attend their meetings virtually, just like the Memory Guild did. Their space had a lot less ambiance than our guild's stone chamber with flickering torchlight, though.

It was a modern conference room, the kind that a good percentage of the human population dreads spending time in but spends too much anyway. In the beginning of my career, when I worked for an insurance company, I learned that every minute you spend in a corporate meeting means two minutes taken from your life.

But this meeting was different. It was about saving humankind. The individuals sitting around the long conference table studied me curiously. I recognized Arch Mage Bob of the Magic Guild and the vampire Pedro, Duke of the Clan of the Eternal Night.

"Allow me to introduce you to Darla Chesswick, the newest member of our guild," Dr. Noordlun said. "You know Arch Mage Bob, and Pedro, who is the chair of the council."

He next went in clockwise order around the table: Rufus, Alpha of the Shifter Guild; Gaarg, Chief of the Troll and Gnome Alliance; Sybil, Queen of the Elven League; Timothy, President of the Union of Undead Flesh Eaters; Evelyn, Priestess of the Psychic Guild; and Baldric, Chief of the Guild of Fae and Wee People.

Dr. Noordlun explained Baldric's Guild represented the faeries, Aluxes, sprites, pixies, and similar creatures who have always called San Marcos home. The guild's membership had nothing to do with the Fae armies assembling to attack the city.

"As you can imagine, it has been exceedingly difficult for us of late," said Baldric, a faerie in human form, typically good-looking as they are. "Our loyalties are constantly questioned by both sides."

I nodded in sympathy.

"Darla," Dr. Noordlun said, "the Executive Council invited you today to recount your experiences with the mythological creatures. Please take all the time you need."

My nerves, so tight after all I'd been through, and from being put on the spot, got the best of me. I talked at a hundred miles an hour as I described discovering the sink-hole cavern beneath the art gallery and the minotaur who lived there. When I got to the unicorn story, I tried to make light of it, though the image of the creature's murderous eyes, as it tried to impale me, haunted me.

"I don't know what the purpose of these creatures is," I said. "I'm certain the Fae brought the minotaur to San Marcos and lowered him into the cavern. And I can only assume they're responsible for the unicorn, as well."

Feeling a little self-conscious in front of the group, I sat in a chair along the wall of the room. It was a virtual chair, and I was here only as an astral spirit, but it felt good to sit down. Psychologically, I mean.

"Are the Fae amassing creatures here to attack the city?" asked Pedro. "It seems rather inefficient compared to simply attacking with their armies. What do you think, Baldric?"

"I believe the Faerie Queene is doing it simply because she can. The Fae have a unique connection to the mythological since their history is interwoven with our myths. I believe she has torn open the veil to create panic among the human population."

"I'm hearing reports that normal humans don't see the mythological creatures as what they are," Dr. Noordlun said.

"Then the intention is to spread panic among us, the guilds," suggested Timothy, whose rotting zombie face was really distracting me.

"In one of our recent meetings, I heard a discussion of Ms. Chesswick's ascension to the role of a human manifestation of the Goddess Danu," said the shifter, Rufus. "Can these mythological creatures be related to this?"

"In what way, exactly?" Dr. Noordlun asked.

"To kill her."

The room was silent, and my breath was sucked away. But you know me—I'm never quiet for long.

"How could the minotaur be intended for me? I only stumbled upon it by accident, and three people were already offered to it. One of whom appears to have been eaten."

"Monsters need to eat," Rufus said. "Maybe you were on the menu for another day."

His comments made me wonder what the faeries I had seen coming up from the utility hole were up to. Were they leading me to the minotaur? And the unicorn was definitely out to get me and me alone.

"Like Pedro said, it seems inefficient."

"It requires a highly symbolized ritual to slay a goddess," Rufus said. "Since she is not in the Fae's custody and they can't perform the ceremony, the mythological creatures could do it in their stead."

"You're saying it takes a mythological creature to kill an ancient goddess?" asked Bob.

"Exactly."

All eyes were on me again, like they were when I first showed up here.

"Why would the Fae wish to kill a goddess they themselves worship?" Dr. Noordlun asked, repeating the question Summer had raised.

"The Fae, as a whole, would not," Baldric answered. "However, certain individuals or a breakaway sect might."

"I see," Dr. Noordlun said. "The thought of a rift among their army is intriguing. Until we learn more, we must finish shoring up our defenses. And then, go on attack. I propose we slay the minotaur and unicorn."

"We shall put it to a vote," said Pedro.

Everyone at the table raised their hand.

"It's unanimous. Let us begin planning the operations."

I was no longer in the conference room but back in the inn next to Archibald's fireplace.

"I'm sorry. I thought you were allowed to attend the council meetings," I said to him.

"This was a special meeting for interviewing you. I already heard your story. Besides, why would I possibly want to be in a meeting when I don't have to?"

"You hate meetings, too?"

"They're frightfully boring and a waste of precious time."

"Wait a minute. You're nearly a thousand years old and you spend most of your time as inanimate stone. How could you possibly experience boredom?"

"Oh, I am quite easily bored. Especially when I am forced to listen to inane chatter like this. Goodbye."

And back to inanimate stone he went.

# CHAPTER 10

# SHIFTERS AND THEIR TOYS

S amson showed up at the inn the next morning with someone unexpected. Jeff, a shifter and retired cop, loomed in the doorway. The biggest, baddest redneck I'd ever met helped Samson and me stop an executed murderer from being brought back to life by a necromancer.

"Jeff! Good to see you! What brings you here?"

"I'm telepathic," he said, stroking his bushy red beard. "Samson thought you'd want to communicate with me."

Noticing my puzzled expression, Samson said, "There's a raid going down today to kill the minotaur. The Shifter Guild is sending a team of its wolves and grizzly bears. I knew you'd want to be part of the team, and there's absolutely no way in the world that's going to happen."

"I just want to—"

"No," he said. "You love to do reckless things, but you would endanger not only you, but the entire team. You don't want to piss off these wolves and bears, believe me."

"Are you going?"

"As an active-duty cop, I can't go either."

"You guys need to know exactly how to find this cavern," I said, grasping for straws.

"We've already done recon, with the art gallery owner's help," Jeff said. "I'll stay connected with you."

*Like this,* he said in my head. *We'll be connected the entire time.*

I wouldn't be able to see what he's seeing, like my psychometry allows me to do with people's memories. But Jeff's narration would be good enough, I guess. It was more than I had any right to expect, to tell the truth.

*Thank you,* I said to Jeff telepathically.

"Thank you," I said to Samson out loud. "When is the raid?"

"This morning. I can't tell you when, for security reasons. But Jeff will connect with you as soon as they go in."

*Good luck,* I said to Jeff. *Be careful.*

He nodded.

"You realize how lucky you are that Jeff agreed to loop you in?" Samson asked.

"I do. And it was smart of you, Michael, to stave off any temptation I might have had of doing something stupid."

"You actually went into an underground cavern knowing that hostile faeries might be in there." Samson shook his head. "Lord knows what you will do next."

"Okay. Got the message."

I thanked them both again, and they left, Jeff giving me a casual salute.

It was nearly impossible to concentrate on preparing breakfast for my guests knowing the raid could happen at any moment. I didn't know if a raid was the best strategy, but it seemed like the only thing we could do at this point. We couldn't just sit around and let the Fae organize their invasion.

And, frankly, if it was true the minotaur was brought to San Marcos to get me, this seemed like the best plan in the world.

It was halfway through breakfast, and I was in the middle of adding fresh sausages to a chafing dish, when a prickling sensation ran through my head. And Jeff's voice appeared.

*We're in the cavern. There's no sign of the target. And no tunnels, either. I was told the target came from a large tunnel.*

*There are at least three openings,* I said. *They were disguised by magic when I first went down there. They appeared shortly afterward. How many shifters do you have?*

*There are sixteen of us in two squads. One squad is down here, and one is positioned upstairs.*

How are you going to kill it?

Jeff laughed. *We have all the best toys. In the Greek myths, Theseus killed the minotaur with a sword or club. Some say with his bare hands. I think grenade launchers and M-4 carbines will do just fine.*

*Do you have magic? I would feel better if you—*

*The Magic Guild gave us a wizard who put a protection spell on us. Anyway, how are we supposed to get the tunnels to appear?*

*I guess it's up to the Fae and their magic.*

Their magic worried me. Cory had successfully cast a protection spell that stopped the attack of a small group of faeries, but he used tons of energy from ley lines. Plus, his magic was boosted by the pearl the faerie had given me.

Was this wizard's magic strong enough to stop the Fae and their beast?

*We're manually checking the walls,* Jeff said.

*Be careful.*

*Yeah, yeah. Why is Wanda messing around with that rock?*

*What?*

*Sorry,* he said. *Didn't mean to send you all my random thoughts.*

"Do you have more honey?" said an audible voice.

I snapped my attention back to the here and now. The elderly lady in 201 from Gainesville stood in front of me, shaking the empty plastic honey bear bottle at me. She was shorter than even me.

"I always have honey on my biscuits," she said.

"I'm sorry. I'll grab another one. Be right back.

I hurried to the supply closet across from the kitchen and found a cardboard box I had to tear open to retrieve a new honey bottle.

*Tunnels just appeared!* Jeff's voice said excitedly. *And one of them is as big as a garage for an RV. Any guesses which one our target is in? Team, follow me.*

My heart raced as I carried the honey to the dining room and handed it to the woman.

*Something big is coming around the bend in the tunnel ahead of us.*

*Be careful, Jeff.*

*My squad is in defensive positions. We all have night-vision goggles, so we can—oh! Oh! Holy Moses! This is the real deal! He's so freaking big! He's huge. Open fire!*

Like I said before, telepathy allowed me to communicate with Jeff in our thoughts. I wasn't connected to his five senses, so I couldn't share in what he was experiencing. But I imagined the ear-pounding blasts of the shifters' weapons.

*Oh no! No, Wanda!*

*What's going on, Jeff? Are you okay?*

*Our weapons aren't stopping him. Neither is the protection spell. I'm radioing to the reserve squad to get down here.*

*Has anyone been hurt?*

*Team, shift now. Shift now! Now, now, now!*

Instead of Jeff's coherent thoughts, I got only random words and fragments of phrases, along with wordless animal impulses.

He was a wolf now. The others in his squad were wolves,

bears, and a panther. They were in a desperate fight with the giant man with the bull's head.

Jeff's thoughts were more animal than human: the savage snapping of jaws, the taste of blood, the urge to tear the flesh of the giant adversary. The primitive wolf impulses were directed by a human's knowledge of tactics.

As the fight raged, Jeff forgot completely about me. It was as if I witnessed the battle only by listening to a cellphone left unattended but still connected to a call.

Soon, Jeff's thinking turned dark as the tide turned against the shifters.

Fleeting thoughts came into my head of shifters bashed against the tunnel walls, necks bitten by bovine jaws, bones cracked, skulls crushed.

How could eight experienced fighters with powerful weapons —who were now savage carnivorous beasts—be defeated by a giant man with a bull's head?

What were the other eight members of the squad held in reserve doing?

A particularly vulgar expletive uttered by Jeff echoed through my head.

And my mind went quiet. My telepathic connection with Jeff was cut off.

"Do you have any more scones?" asked a voice in my dining room. A kindly middle-aged man stood beside me. Room 302, I believe. I hadn't even noticed him approach me.

"Um, let me check in the kitchen."

"Are you okay? You look like you've just had a terrible shock."

"I'm fine, thank you. I'll be right back."

It turned out the man in 302 had good timing. The second batch of scones was ready and in danger of being overdone as I yanked it from the oven. The warm, buttery smell did nothing to relax me. Transferring them to a tray, I carried them into the dining room, used tongs to serve the man the two he requested, and put the tray on the buffet.

I rushed back to the kitchen and called Samson.

"The raid is going badly," I practically shouted. "The minotaur was crushing the first squad when I lost my connection with Jeff."

"Oh, no. Let me make some calls, and if I hear anything, I'll call you back. Be careful. *Don't* go over there."

A sense of doom came over me. I prayed that none of the shifters had been killed, while knowing that several were badly injured. And how was I supposed to be careful? It wasn't as if the minotaur would come charging down Cadiz Street in broad daylight to get me. If the purpose of the minotaur was, truly, to kill me, it would eat me after the Fae captured me and tossed me into the sinkhole.

Being that faeries could shift to human form, I had to watch out for anyone I didn't recognize. Someone else would have to do my errands. I wasn't leaving the property until this was resolved.

Resolved. What a lame word. What I really meant was until the minotaur was killed. Or I was.

"Morning, Mom," Sophie said, coming into the kitchen and going straight for the coffee pots. The perennially late riser was just in time for cleaning up before I sent her to assist our housekeeper in the guest rooms.

"Morning, sweetheart."

"Mom, what's wrong? You look like someone just died."

"Some members of the Shifter Guild were attacking a monster the Fae have brought to town. I'm afraid it might have gone badly." I left out any mention of what the monster might do to me.

"A monster? This problem with the Fae sounds worse than you've been letting on. Is San Marcos in trouble?"

"I won't lie. It very well might be in trouble. The guilds are finally fighting back, but I don't know if they understand what we're up against."

"Don't shield me from the truth," Sophie said, looking me in the eye. "I'm not a child anymore. We're all going to need to fight, right? Including me with my magic."

"Not now. We need to learn more about what the pearl can do and how it can help us. It's the only special weapon we have at this point. You and Cory need to study it and discover how it can affect your magic. And you need to learn all you can about the Fae's magic."

"How can we learn about the Fae magic?"

"The pearl can help. What would help even more is if we had a faerie who can help us. I'll speak to Baldric from their guild and see if he can meet with you. And Arch Mage Bob, too."

Samson didn't call me back until hours later.

"The entire team of shifters is missing," he said in a grave voice.

"Are you serious?"

"There is no sign of them at the art gallery or the in the cavern below. No sign other than spent cartridges and blood. And no communication from them, either."

"Did they go into the tunnels?"

"There are no tunnels."

"They're hidden magically," I said.

"Right now, there are no tunnels for us to enter to search for the shifters. I was there myself and I inspected the cavern walls carefully. Have you had any communication with Jeff?"

"No. I tried several times to reach him telepathically but couldn't. Do you think he's dead?"

"Don't think like that. Let's hope they all went into the tunnels on their own accord, not as prisoners, and the openings simply closed behind them. We're going to keep sentries in the cavern at all times in case the tunnels appear again."

"I've been hearing more and more military terms," I said, "but do we really have an army? What are we going to do when the Fae attack us for real? There could be thousands of them. You should have seen how many there were in the woods next to the Gilleys' home."

"No, we don't have an army. We only have units made up of certain capable individuals scattered across the guilds."

"Well, we need one. If we don't want the actual Florida National Guard involved."

"You're preaching to the choir. Hopefully, the Executive Council is preparing more than they seem to be."

After the call, I returned to my simple world of inn keeping. It's work that I love—preserving the charm and history of this 300-year-old building, sharing it with guests, and helping them have a wonderful stay, with delightful memories of our inn and city.

Now that I've become a psychometrist, a priestess of memories, I've become amazed at their power. Often, memories mean more to us than actual real-time life. We speak about "being in the moment," which is all good, but the memories of these moments are stronger emotionally than the moments themselves. We can savor the memories—or suffer from them—for years to come.

So, when I complain about my mundane details of a day at

work, it's only to contrast them with the fantastical stuff I experience in the hidden supernatural world of San Marcos.

I don't mind these details, because they are part of the work that goes into creating pleasant memories for my guests. And for me, too.

Of course, all of that just went out the window later in the day when I broke my vow to not leave the property.

And paid the price big time.

# CHAPTER 11

# THIS IS COMPLETE BULL

I do not consider a parking garage the same thing as an underground labyrinth.

Apparently, the minotaur did. And as we know from the legends, labyrinths are where minotaurs hang out.

San Marcos is not big enough to have many parking garages. I can think of only two: the one at San Marcos College and a municipal garage popular with tourists at the edge of Old Town.

I was in the first one. It was cheaper than the municipal garage and was close to a bakery that I rely on for the inn. The college garage was fairly empty at this time of year, with the students away from school for the winter holidays. I found a spot on the deserted second deck, went downstairs, and crossed the street to the bakery.

When I returned to my car with a box of lemon tarts to serve at Teatime, I had an unpleasant surprise. A freakishly gigantic man was stooping down and peering into the driver's window.

His back faced me. It was shirtless, hairy, and rippled with muscles. His head had dark, short hair, and pointy ears. When he turned his head for a better angle to see inside my car, I saw the horns. Then I noticed the tail.

It was the minotaur.

I stopped dead in my tracks. He turned and saw me, raising his head and sniffing with flared nostrils.

Pretending to be calm, I pulled out my phone and called Cory. Thank goodness, he picked up.

"Get to the San Marcos College parking garage, second floor. Bring the pearl. And Sophie. Maybe if you could stop by the ley lines. . . Um, no. Scratch that. The minotaur just ID-ed me, and I have about thirty seconds to live."

"What the heck are you—"

I screamed and sprinted back toward the stairs as bellows of bovine rage echoed behind me.

Instead of the clopping hooves of a four-legged bull, the slap of naked human feet got louder as they grew closer.

Suddenly, there was a thud and a bellow of pain. I risked a glance behind me. The creature had hit his head on a low concrete ceiling beam. Now, he was even madder than before.

I was armed with nothing but lemon tarts. No, wait—Cory had made me put my pistol in my purse. Not exactly ready for quick-draw shooting.

The box of lemon tarts hit the minotaur squarely between the horns, the box bursting open and the tarts flying. It was such a waste of flaky crust and lemon goodness. Even the minotaur seemed flummoxed by being attacked with pastries. Too bad he was a carnivore.

There was no way Cory would get here in time to save me. I fumbled in my purse for the pistol, which slowed down my running. The minotaur, despite having the brain of a bull, sprinted around me, and cut off my route to the stairwell. He looked at me with his unreadable dark eyes and snorted. I took off running again.

The ramp down to the first deck was too close to where the minotaur stood, so I ran in the direction I had come from. I feinted toward my car, then angled away from it, sprinting as fast as my little legs could take me to the end of this deck and onto the ramp leading to the third.

A bright red sports car coming down the ramp almost hit me. When it passed the minotaur, his head swiveled to follow it. He ran after the car, then stopped abruptly and returned to chase me.

Of course, it was a *red* car. If only I had my red bullfighter's cape with me.

The minotaur's distraction allowed me to make it all the way up the ramp. A stairwell was right in front of me.

What the heck! The minotaur jumped in front of me and blocked the doorway again.

Why hadn't he simply grabbed me?

His massive chest heaved, and his bull nostrils quivered from the exertion of his chase.

I pulled out the pistol and dropped the purse, so I could hold the gun with two hands. I flicked off the safety and aimed with trembling hands.

The minotaur remained guarding the door to the stairwell. He stared at me calmly, breathing heavily. Despite his man's body from the neck down, he had a bull's tail that twitched as if swatting flies.

He must be completely unconcerned about my gun. After all, he had survived the attack of sixteen heavily armed shifters.

Why wasn't he charging me?

Then, to my surprise, I picked up his thoughts. They weren't the thoughts of a bull, but of a human.

*I don't want to kill her. She has the air of a goddess; I can sense the divine in her. She has room in her heart for the unnatural beasts of the world. I must kill her, though. It has been commanded of me. Must do it now.*

It was time to fire the gun. The report echoed in the concrete structure and made my ears ring. The recoil surprised me since it had been a while since I had shot at anything.

There was no sign of a wound on him. Oh, wait, the steel door above him was wounded.

I fired again. This time, his right shoulder twitched. He snorted, as if in pain, but there was no blood, only a hole in his flesh.

The garage echoed with my third shot. This time, I hit his right horn, breaking it in two, sending the broken part flying.

The minotaur whined desperately and bent over as if wracked with pain. The wound in the shoulder didn't bother him, but the horn without pain receptors caused this reaction?

Sympathy and empathy flooded me. The goddess in me he had sensed—the goddess who was mother to all of nature and the creatures who inhabited Earth—took over my mind.

Instinctively, I moved toward him, wanting to comfort and heal.

Don't do it! Darla, the sassy-tongued part of me warned. He's here to kill you. Let down your guard, and you'll be dead meat.

The minotaur sat upon the concrete floor, his bull muzzle held in his human hands. Tears oozed from his large black eyes down the blackish-brown fur. The creature was both unnatural and pitiful, the misbegotten product of a Greek god's petty anger.

I only wanted to heal him and stop his suffering.

Don't do it! Darla whispered in my brain. He took out a

special forces platoon of shifters. Do you really believe a broken horn would knock him down like this? It's a trap.

This was the first time the goddess in me went against the me in me. The love of the goddess was winning out. It was so much stronger than the self-preserving instinct of Darla.

I wanted to think of myself as a kind, caring person. Now, I realized my caring instincts only went so far. It was humbling to realize what true compassion was as the urge to heal and comfort took me over.

Through divine empathy. I had the realization that the minotaur's horns were the symbol of his strength, and the broken horn disabled him like the ancient Israelite hero, Samson, when his hair was shorn.

I approached the beast. He was so large that, when sitting on the floor, he was as tall as I was. I placed my hand on his forehead, the coarse hair atop a massive skull and the base of his horns. The agony within him flowed into my hand, and I realized I could extract it from him like sucking poison from a snakebite.

My other hand touched the broken end of his horn. He flinched at first, then relaxed.

Strange thoughts appeared in my brain, like ancient memories coming to life, of a time thousands of years ago when I, Danu, presided over the earth as its mother-goddess. I made water flow and flowers bloom. I made creatures reproduce and created food for them to eat. I healed all that was broken or ill.

*I, Danu, mother-goddess, heal your injured horn and restore your strength and will to live.*

The broken end of the horn in my left hand shifted as the horn grew into its curved shape, the jagged break smoothing over and narrowing into a sharpened tip.

The bull head tilted back so that one of its black eyes could gaze into mine.

*You healed me, mother-goddess.*

*Yes*, I said. *You are restored to your full self. And you will return to Crete in ancient times where you will live not in a labyrinth like your ancestor but will wander freely in fields and meadows.*

I sensed bewilderment.

*Don't worry. You'll figure it out when you get there.*

"Gateways, I humbly request you give this minotaur a ride to the In Between and then to Crete in the ancient era."

And, as easily as summoning a ride share with an app, a large disc of shimmering air appeared in the parking garage a dozen feet away.

*Go through that portal*, I told the minotaur.

He got to his feet, his head bent to avoid the concrete pillars above, and ambled into the gateway, disappearing.

I still had a divine warmth in me, kind of like the radiant feel of post-lovemaking, when the tires screeched on the ramp to this deck.

The car Cory and Sophie shared raced around the corner of the empty parking lot and stopped near me.

"Are you okay?" Sophie asked from her open window.

"Where's the minotaur?" Cory asked. "And why do you look so blissed-out?"

"I took care of him. Well, the goddess did."

"What do you mean?"

I walked over to the car and recounted the entire story. Their concerned expressions turned to bafflement and, then, disbelief.

"You've got to be making this up," Cory said.

"He was brought down by a broken horn?" Sophie asked. "Really?"

"Yeah. He's a mythological creature. Don't judge."

"And you didn't need the pearl to heal him." Cory said.

"No. It appears I have the ability all on my own."

"Does that mean we don't have to go to the doctor anymore?" Sophie asked.

"No. You need preventive care, and I wouldn't depend on my abilities to heal everything. Illness and death are natural parts of the world, and the goddess can't help me make you immune to it. Besides, we've spent a pretty penny to get healthcare coverage."

"Yeah, even a goddess can't heal our healthcare system," Cory muttered.

My divine glow had completely faded, and I felt like Darla again, back in the mundane human world.

"Give me a ride to my car on the deck below, and then follow me home," I said. "After I buy more lemon tarts."

I gathered my purse and got into the backseat, next to a large box of paper napkins for the inn from the wholesale club. Yeah, it would be nice to return to the nitty gritty of daily life and forget about mythological creatures and the impending Fae invasion.

It would have been nice. But then we got home and found the visitor waiting for us.

# CHAPTER 12

## SPECIAL REQUEST

When Sophie, Cory, and I strolled into the inn, I stopped short. A man stood in the foyer waiting. He wore a seersucker suit and held a Panama hat in his hands. He looked like a well-off tourist, because most tourists in San Marcos wear shorts and T-shirts, and the locals wouldn't dare wear seersucker in winter.

Cory and Sophie smiled and nodded to him while they went their different ways into the building.

I, however, knew he was not a tourist. He was a faerie.

"Mr. Jaekeree," I said. "Welcome. To what do I owe this pleasure?"

The dark, handsome faerie in human form smiled ironically.

"It's generous of you to welcome me so warmly, considering the recent tensions between my people and yours."

"Just minutes ago, I escaped death from one of the creatures your people have let loose on our town."

"You did, indeed." Jaekeree grinned with distinct pleasure. "I learned about what happened, and I'm very impressed."

"Enough of the fake pleasantries. Why are you here?"

"I come bearing a message from the Faerie Queene. She wishes a favor from you."

I snorted. "Nice. She tries to kill me and now wants a favor."

"We wish to make clear that the minotaur and unicorn were not authorized by the Queene. I'm embarrassed to say that there is a rogue faction of leaders who were most likely responsible for the attacks on you."

"I'm not interested in your internal politics. The Fae were responsible."

"There is an element among our people who worship Haarg, the God of War, above all other gods and goddesses. For them, Danu is out of favor. That is why they have hostility toward you. For that, I apologize."

"You're going to have to work this out among yourselves," I said.

"Let us speak of more pleasant topics. Ascending to goddess stature has apparently given you great healing powers."

"Thanks, I guess. I'm still trying to figure all that out."

"You healed the minotaur."

"Oh. Well, that was easy."

"Easy for you. It is because of your healing powers that I am here today. Her Majesty the Queene requests that you heal her."

I wasn't expecting this. "What's wrong with her?"

"She is gravely ill. And when she is ill, all the Fae suffer the illness."

"Is this the illness that affects fertility?"

He lowered his eyes. "I'm afraid so. That is but one of the many symptoms. It is a serious illness that could wipe out our people. We don't know where it came from, and whether it is natural or caused by evil magic. All we know is we must find a cure for it quickly. The priests have prophesied that you will be the one to heal us, beginning with the Queene."

"Wait a minute, why do you think I would help you? You guys keep trying to kill me."

"Yes, Dorn did," Jaekeree said gravely. "He was part of the rogue faction. He was put to death by order of Her Majesty. The minotaur and unicorn were summoned by the rogue faction, as well."

"Am I supposed to ignore that the Fae are preparing to conquer San Marcos and who knows where else? You've attacked the archives of my guild, the Memory Guild. Your people are my enemies. Why would I ever help you?"

"You are in debt to our people."

"Nonsense."

He smiled cruelly. "Oh, yes, you are. I've explained this already. When you accepted the pearl from me, you accepted a debt to us. You are under an obligation to give us something in return. That is what we ask of you now."

"I'm going to return the pearl, even if it hurts your feelings."

"You cannot return it. Even if you tried, magic would bring it right back to you. The pearl is yours, unless we ever decide to take it back. You have a debt. And we are calling for it to be repaid."

"Helping the Fae would betray my own people."

"Perhaps, it would improve relations between your people and mine."

"Perhaps, you're only using me for your own purposes."

Jaekeree shrugged and held out his hands.

"You can choose not to believe me. I should point out, however, that we could capture you and force you to help us. But we are not doing that. We wish to show our good faith. You were treated wrongly by Dorn and the ones who sent the monsters against you. The Queene is much more civilized than they are. You will be treated with respect. And honor. After all, you are the daughter of a goddess."

"It is difficult for me to trust you."

"I understand. But I hope my actions will reassure you. Will you help us?"

"I can't."

"The goddess is a healer. How can you refuse to help and deny her role? The goddess is above the petty conflicts of those who reside upon this earth. We are all her children. We are all under her care. She would want to heal us all."

I had to admit he had a point, but I wouldn't tell him that.

"Why are you so certain I have the power to heal the Queene? I'm not familiar with my powers. I'm not exactly sure what I did to heal the minotaur's horn, but that's a comparably minor ailment."

"You have the power," Jaekeree said, smiling warmly. "And you have the knowledge of how to use it deep in your blood. It will be revealed to you, when necessary. I am certain of it."

"I can't accept a request like this without speaking with my guild first."

"That is perfectly understandable. I will give you time to confer with the appropriate people. Then, I will return."

He gave a slight bow and strolled from the inn. Visible through the glass of the main door, he put his hat on and walked with a jaunty step down Cadiz Street. No human who saw him would guess that he was a faerie.

Wow. I was in a true conundrum. I needed to talk to Cory about this, though he would probably tell me not to help. I wouldn't blame him for being suspicious of Jaekeree. I also needed to speak with the Memory Guild. They would have a more strategic view of what I should do.

I wandered into the front room and was surprised to see Archibald already animated with no coaxing by me.

"Oh, you're awake," I said.

"Of course, I am. I awoke the moment I sensed the magic from a faerie entering our inn."

Note, he said "our" inn. I don't recall seeing his name on the mortgage paperwork.

"Did you hear what we talked about?"

"I did, and I'm outraged he would have the temerity to make such a request. Especially since you were attacked again this same day! Which you didn't tell me about, by the way."

"I didn't have the chance to. We got home to find the faerie here, waiting for us. Shouldn't we discuss this with the entire guild?"

"Absolutely. I've already arranged a meeting."

And just like that, I was standing in the meeting hall beneath the fake torchlight. There was no flying through history while receiving an educational message on this trip.

"We've gathered together today," Dr. Noordlun said, "to discuss a very interesting invitation Darla has received."

"Wait a moment, professor. How did you know about this already and get us here so quickly?"

"Archibald notified me, and I asked Diana to transport us all here."

"Are you and Archibald telepathic?"

"No. Well, not technically. It's the same as the way my wife and I know each other's thoughts. The oldest Memory Guild members have been together for so long, we have a similar bond."

I didn't know what surprised me more, the thought of Dr. Noordlun and Archibald being so connected to each other, or the realization that the professor was married. He'd never mentioned a spouse before, and he seemed too much like an Old Testament prophet to have one.

"Let us not get sentimental," Archibald said.

"Spoken by someone with a heart of stone," I said. No one laughed.

"Could you please give our members a summary of your conversation with the faerie?" asked Dr. Noordlun.

"Of course." I explained my debt to the Fae and their request that I heal the Faerie Queene.

"Heal her of what, exactly?" Diana asked.

"He didn't say, but indicated the ailment was the cause of the loss of fertility among their people."

"I think it's a trick," James said. "They want to siphon off your goddess powers."

"You're too cynical," Summer said.

"It is a perfect opportunity," Archibald said slyly, "for Darla to assassinate their monarch."

Everyone reacted in horror and outrage.

"Never mind."

"We could demand a peace treaty in return for healing the Queene," suggested Gloria.

"That is what I was thinking," said Dr. Noordlun. "In any event, I will have to bring this before the Executive Council."

"The bloody bureaucracy," Archibald said.

"We must include them. Their responsibility is to keep all of us safe."

"That didn't work out so well for the shifters," I said, which went over about as well as Archibald's assassination remark. "I'm hoping they're all well and will be rescued soon."

"Archibald, come with me," Dr. Noordlun said. "Let us gather the council together."

"Hey, what about me?" I asked. "I'm at the center of all this."

"Exactly. That is the problem."

"What do you mean?"

"I wish it wasn't a member of our guild who might have to be sacrificed to save the world."

Then, suddenly, I was back in the inn's front room. Archibald was there, too, in his stone form, though his spirit at the moment was actually in a conference room in an astral plane of existence, stuck in a meeting.

As I turned to leave the room, a familiar voice piped up.

"No decision yet," Archibald said. "The council wishes to delay your answer to the Fae, so they can continue preparing for war. They hope with stronger defenses, they can negotiate a better peace treaty in exchange for your healing of the Queene."

"Oh boy. I don't like being used as a pawn. If I truly have the power to heal her, I should be above the political maneuvering."

"You must not forget which side you are on in this war. Goddess or not, you still reside in a human body inside a historic inn, both of which could be damaged or destroyed by the Fae's army. Do you understand?"

"Got it. So, what's this about being 'sacrificed to save the world'?"

"Worst-case scenario. Do not let this thought trouble you at all."

Easier said than done.

# CHAPTER 13

## ATTORNEYS AT BRUNCH

"Why has it been so long since we did this?" I asked Jen at the outdoor cafe. It was on the edge of the most touristy part of town, a part I largely avoided. Still, the spot was a sentimental favorite for us since we'd been having brunch here together for years.

"You're always too busy, that's why," Jen said. "I know the inn demands a lot of your time. But now that you've admitted you're a psychic consultant to the police—I think that's where so much of your time goes."

If she only knew the full truth.

"And I was a virtual recluse for a while," Jen continued. "Well, as reclusive as a realtor can be."

I nodded, feeling a pang of regret for the trauma she went through when she was kidnapped by a psycho who had been brought back from the dead by a necromancer. I had worried about Jen being permanently scarred psychologically, but she seemed to have returned to her former vivacious self.

People can be good at faking it, though. They hide the trauma behind a veneer of normalcy.

"A toast," I said, "to good times again."

I clinked my Bloody Mary against her Mimosa. When we first started meeting here, during college breaks, the drinks never stopped flowing.

"And how is Cory holding up?" Jen asked, as if she'd read my mind about people dealing with trauma.

"To be honest, I believe he's suffering from PTSD after what we went through with the evil wizard."

Jen knew more about the supernatural goings-on in this town than most normal humans. When I first discovered my psychometry, I had kept it secret from her, but eventually I gave her a watered-down explanation of it.

I also had to explain why Cory went missing for over a year. That required discussing magic and a very basic outline of the In Between. She seemed to accept the existence of magic, but I don't think she bought the part about the In Between. That's okay.

Jen had no problem believing in the ghosts that haunted the Esperanza Inn. She didn't need to know a vampire and a living gargoyle made it their home. She also didn't need to know Sophie was developing as a witch, though Sophie was welcome to tell her if she wanted to.

The pending invasion by the Fae? I didn't want to go there. At least, not yet. If normal humans get dragged into this affair, I'll be sure Jen is the first to know. It might affect real estate prices, after all.

"Um, you said that Cory is a wizard, too?"

"A witch," I said. "The difference isn't important. He says he's not interested in magic anymore, though. I think it reminds him too much of his experience with the wizard. He says he wants to immerse himself in the day-to-day of running the inn. And to get back to his old passions, like photography. How's Marty doing?"

Marty was at least ten years older than Jen and had recently retired.

She laughed. "He wishes he didn't retire. So do I. He hasn't adjusted well to the empty-nest life, and he's handling retirement even more poorly. There's only so much golf you can play, after all. The rest of the time, he putters around the house. And let me tell you, he's not a good putterer."

There was a hidden strain behind her humor. My guess was their marriage was under some stress.

"And the kids?" I asked.

"Jackie decided she wants to specialize in emergency medicine and will begin internships next year. Mark still wants to run for Congress." She rolled her eyes. "When he and Marty talk politics, they're like oil and water."

Her home life perhaps wasn't ideal, but it sounded delightfully sane to me. At my house, dinner table conversations are about magic spells and being attacked by mythological creatures.

Jen's eyes darted to something behind me.

"Oh, Ron Dutton just walked in," she said. "Did he agree to take on Buddy's case?"

"No. He helped bail him out of jail and then said adios. He's only interested in high-profile cases or guaranteed slam-dunks."

"He sounds so cold-hearted. I thought defense attorneys are the ones with empathy."

"Not when you think of yourself as a celebrity. I agreed to help Buddy by poking around a little into his partner's life. Maybe if I find some evidence pointing toward someone else as the killer, Ron will take up the case. And do it for an affordable fee. If it gets him some publicity, that is."

"Are you, um, using your psychometry?"

"Of course. I'm not Sherlock Holmes. My paranormal abilities are all I have to offer."

"Plus, your winning personality. Wait, they're seating him just over there. Let me get his attention."

She waved frantically. Dutton, who was being seated with an elderly gentleman, looked over and smiled. He walked over to our table.

"Jen Howell," he said with a mischievous smile. "We must stop meeting like this."

"Ron, you remember Darla Chesswick?"

"Of course. Good to see you, Darla."

No more small talk. I opened the valve on my firehose.

"I don't know if Jen told you, but I'm Buddy Grimes' ex-wife. I really hope you'll consider taking on his case."

"Oh, that's right. I'm afraid my prices are too high for Mr. Grimes. A public defender would be a better bet for him."

"Their workloads are too high. The public defender will just tell him to plead out."

"Then I could refer you to another attorney. A more affordable one. In fact, I'm having brunch with a great one." He turned toward his table. "Jack, come over here and meet two fantastic women."

The tall, stooped man came over. He was thin and wore a pink dress shirt buttoned to the top. His tall forehead and thinning white hair gave him a scholarly look. Sunglasses were tucked in his shirt pocket. He appeared to be nearing retirement age.

"Jack Guarini, meet Jen Howell and Darla Chesswick. I went to high school with them."

"Pleased to meet you," he said in a gravelly voice with the trace of a European accent. He took each of our hands in a light handshake.

"Darla has a case she would like you to consider taking on. Her ex-husband has been charged with murder."

"How terrible. I'm sorry to hear that," Jack said. "I don't do much trial work anymore, I'm afraid to say."

"This is right up your alley," Ron said. "Her ex-husband was charged because his gun was used in the murder. The victim was his partner in a side hustle they had going, doing drug tests for recovery companies."

"Sleazy companies," I said, "that may have been involved in human trafficking. The victim's girlfriend was taken away, along with other patients, to a ranch outside of town and was never seen again. This could be important in finding out who the real killer is."

Everyone looked at me with surprise.

"I've been asking questions. Sort of."

"It's very kind of you to help your ex-husband like this," Jack said.

"He's the father of my daughter. Every time I see a 'Florida Man Does Something Stupid' headline in the news, I expect to see a photo of Buddy wearing handcuffs. But he's not a murderer. I can't allow him to be railroaded like this. Can you help us, Mr. Guarini?"

"Come on, Jack," Ron said, slapping him on the shoulder. "Just the other day, you were saying you were tired of corporate law and wanted to get back in the courtroom again."

Jack pulled a wallet from his back pocket and handed me a business card. "Have Buddy call my office, and we'll set up an appointment with him."

"Thank you," I said. "Thanks to both of you. You won't regret this."

After they returned to their table, I smiled at Jen. "Thank you, too."

"It's the least I could do after Ron let us down. I mean, is he really that high-and-mighty that he couldn't do some non-lucrative work for a former high-school classmate?"

"I don't think he believes Buddy is innocent," I said, taking a deep sip of my savory and spicy Bloody Mary. "Jack seems open to believing. He's a nice man."

"You won't say that if his rates are too high."

"Yeah. I guess you're right."

A COUPLE OF DAYS LATER, BUDDY CALLED ME. HE WAS IN VERY high spirits.

"Thanks for hooking me up with Jack Guarini," he said. "I thought I was going to have to wait forever for an appointment, but I met with him already today, and he's filing with the court as my attorney."

"That's excellent. Did you tell him about the Emerald Man?"

"No. No, I didn't get around to that."

"Buddy! I told you, I'm certain that's who the killer is."

"Look, I didn't want to explain about your psychic stuff, and maybe the vision you had wasn't accurate."

"It was."

"Mr. Guarini said he has a private investigator he'll hire to look into this very carefully. I don't want to get in his way with, you know, rumors and stuff."

"I told you what went through Damon's mind seconds before he was shot. He identified the Emerald Man pointing a familiar gun at him. I also had a vision of the Emerald Man at the ranch where the patients from Shady Palms went. Did you at least mention Shady Palms?"

"Yeah, yeah, I did. I mentioned the ranch, too. The P.I. will investigate all of that. Are you satisfied?"

"It's not about satisfying me. We're trying to keep you from being convicted for murder. You should have named the killer. You could have said you suspect him, if you didn't want to go into my psychic abilities."

"The Emerald Man is not the kind of name you drop in normal conversation. I'll be frank with you. It might be dangerous."

"If the investigator doesn't come up with him on his own, you need to bring it up."

"I will. I promise."

"Unless you don't mind going to prison for the rest of your life."

"Don't worry. I'm not an idiot."

Famous last words.

I WAS CROSSING THE COURTYARD, HEADED TO OUR COTTAGE, when I saw the photographic equipment. A camera sat on a tripod facing the fountain. Two white circular light reflectors on stands also faced the fountain.

When I entered the cottage, I found Cory rummaging through one of his camera bags.

"Who are you photographing?" I asked, pleased to see him returning to photography, his lifelong passion. "One of our guests? Selling portraits could be a profitable little side hustle."

"I'm photographing you. The sun is almost in the right position. Glad I didn't have to run around the inn searching for you."

"Me? Why?"

"Because I want to. Because you're beautiful."

"Oh, come on. What's the real reason?"

"I'm serious."

"Has the goddess effect changed my looks? To me, I look the same as I always have."

It was nice to get Cory's attention like this, but was it only because of the goddess?

"The goddess effect hasn't changed you in my eyes," Cory said. "It has inspired me somehow, though. I thought my artistic side was gone forever after I was enslaved by Texas Tom. Like it had been burned away by all the energy I was forced to channel from the ley lines. But now, it seems to be returning. Thanks to you. You're making my creativity come back to life."

He smiled as he selected a lens from his bag.

"Interesting," I said. "You're a nature photographer. You never did portraits."

"There's a force of nature inside you, my love. Your face inspires me as much as a flock of herons in the salt marshes at sunset."

"I *think* that was a compliment."

"It was. Now, come along. Let's get some shots of you before we lose the good light."

We went out into the courtyard, and Cory had me sit on the rock wall that ringed the fountain. He adjusted the light reflectors, then tinkered with his camera. Coming from behind the camera, he had me turn my body slightly and place my arms in a position he said looked more natural.

It didn't feel natural to me, but I'm just eye candy.

He returned to the tripod and began taking shots, each with the chunky clicking sound of the shutter.

"Good, good," he said. "I love this 85-millimeter lens. It softens your face."

"More than any skin lotion can achieve," I said.

"Now, don't look at the camera. Look as if you're staring at something behind me."

*Click, click, click.*

That's when I noticed Cory's aura. I'd never seen one before, though Diana from the guild sees them all the time. It was a cloud of pink and yellow light around his head. I think that means he's loving and creative, but I'd have to do some research on it.

Did I have the Goddess to thank for this new ability?

Cory moved the camera and tripod closer to me.

"Hey, not so close," I said. "I'm not wearing makeup."

"I know. I love it."

"You're going to have to do a lot of retouching work."

"Will you stop it, Darla? You look enchanting."

That sure was a loaded word coming from a witch. Anyway, soon Cory grumbled about how the light had changed, and our session ended.

Later that night, as he sat at the kitchen breakfast bar, he showed me the images on his laptop. His talent truly was evident, making me look pretty darned good. There was something about the images that took years off my age.

But when he got to the closeups, that's when I saw it. My own aura. It was white. Later, I looked up what that meant. The internet, which, you know, is never wrong, said a white aura means I'm spiritually advanced, and connected to a source of divine wisdom.

The Goddess effect has really changed me. Returning to a comfortably mundane life seemed even more out of the question.

# CHAPTER 14

# MORE MONSTER MISCHIEF

Mom called me to help her unload a new pile of junk— sorry, an assortment of antiques—from her SUV. Unlike high-end dealers, Mom scoured every potential source for inventory, from estate sales and individual items sold on the internet, to junk left by the curb on the night before bulk trash pickup day. Based on the condition of tonight's haul, I think it came from the curb, though she wouldn't admit it.

It was long past dark when I finished, and I zipped through Old Town on my motor scooter using shortcuts. The street where the faeries had climbed out of the utility hole was no longer blocked by construction. The utility hole was safely shut.

As I passed the art gallery, I was surprised to see lights on inside. I had thought Francis had closed it for an indefinite time. Coasting slowly past the windows, I saw Francis moving about inside, and I decided to pop in and say hello. The front door was locked, so I knocked.

"Oh, Darla. What brings you here?" She was far from over-joyed to see the woman who had saved her from the minotaur.

"I saw lights on and wanted to say hi. I thought the gallery would still be closed."

"It's not open to the public yet."

"Not to be insensitive, but I thought the building would be condemned because of the sinkhole beneath it."

"I have an appointment with a structural engineer to inspect it. I'm hoping beams can be installed beneath that part of the floor to shore it up."

I peered around her to look for the hole in the floor. The art installation had been moved back to its original position to cover the hole. This bothered me, because the team of shifters had disappeared down there and were presumably still beneath the city. But I didn't want to second-guess Francis.

"When I saw you in here, I just wanted to see how you're doing," I said. "The day we met was awfully traumatic."

"I'm holding up, thanks."

*Why is she here?* she thought. *They told me to stay away from her.*

I wondered who "they" were. The vibe here was getting really uncomfortable. I can tell when I'm not wanted.

"I sure hope you're able to reopen soon," I said. "Please let me know if there's anything I can do to help you. Even if you just need to talk about what we went through."

"I certainly will. Thank you." Her smile was strained.

I said goodnight and stepped out into the night, wondering what Francis was hiding and why.

My motor scooter had taken me only a block away when I had to slam on the brakes, almost going over the handlebars. An enormous creature had swooped in and stood in my path.

What. The. Heck. Is. This?

It stood about eight feet tall and had giant wings with hands protruding from about halfway down the wings. For a brief moment, I thought it was a hang glider who had experienced a technical malfunction.

But as my eyes adjusted to the darkness, I realized it wasn't human. It was completely black, with glowing red eyes, pointy ears, and needle-like teeth. What I had first thought were hands, were claws protruding from the front of its wings.

It was a giant bat, standing on two legs. And it gave me the distinct impression it planned to eat me.

I gunned my engine and launched my scooter at the creature, hoping to scare it away. It didn't work.

The bat flapped its wings and lifted off just enough to perch on my handlebars and grasp them with the claws of its feet. Its face peered down at me and fixed me with beady red eyes. I guess this kind of bat wasn't blind. And it was even uglier than your typical bat, with none of the rodent cuteness.

As if reading my thoughts, the creature snarled, showing more of those scary-sharp teeth. Saliva oozed out between them.

The wings flapped again, sending dust scattering across the cobblestones. The bat-like creature rose in the air, bringing my scooter—and me—with it.

I should have let go and slid off my scooter to the ground. But my first instinct was to hold on with all my might, my hands gripping the handlebars and my legs squeezing the base beneath the seat. In only a couple of seconds, I was already too far above the ground to survive a fall.

My hands were still squeezing the brake levers. No, Darla, the brakes will not stop you.

We had to be fifty feet or more in the air by now. The bat flapped mightily to the east across Old Town until we were over the marina and the bay. I assumed it was headed to its cave where it would feast on me, but I didn't know of any giant caves around here.

But there were sinkholes, all right. Yes, there sure were sinkholes beneath the ground filled with deadly creatures. Were there any on the barrier island we were about to fly above?

Suddenly, I was falling. The bat must have grown tired of carrying the heavy load. I looked down at the water zooming up at me and screamed, finally letting go of my scooter.

The scooter and I landed in the chilly water separately with giant splashes. After almost sinking to the bottom of the bay, I struggled to rise to the surface as my lungs screamed for air.

Finally, my head popped out, and I gulped in huge breaths.

Needless to say, my scooter did not pop up with me. This was the second time I'd lost my scooter in a supernatural attack, and it would also be the last. Insurance doesn't cover supernatural attacks. Believe me, I've looked into this.

The shore of Old Town was the nearest land, at a distance of about two Olympic-sized swimming pools. I set out paddling toward it, hampered by my drenched clothing, but no way would I remove it.

Giant wings flapped above me. I prayed it was a seagull, but knew it wasn't. A seagull's wings would not disturb the water like a helicopter's rotor.

Sharp claws raked my shoulders, seizing my jacket and top. And up I rose from the bay. As water trickled from me, I yelled for help. It wasn't that late at night. People would still be out and about along the waterfront, or the live-aboards would be awake in their boats. Anyone who looked up would see a sight worth calling 911 for. It's not often you see a giant bat flying with a woman dangling from its claws.

I guess no one looked up.

The creature rose in altitude, and soon we were above land and cruising over downtown. I almost cried when I saw my inn and courtyard sweep by below us. Screaming at the top of my lungs, I didn't stop until my throat was raw.

I was going to die, either from falling from this great height or being devoured when we landed. If I landed alive, how could I fight off this monster?

My handgun? It was in the storage bin beneath the seat of my scooter, now resting on the bottom of the bay.

I still had my phone in my pocket. Whether it was actually as water-resistant as the ads claimed was another story. The problem was the bat was gripping my clothing, causing it to hike up into my armpits and put my arms at weird angles. I couldn't reach into my pocket to extract my phone, not without risking tearing my clothing, sending me falling to my doom.

Even if I could reach my phone, chances were my shaking hands would drop it. I could do nothing but hang there at the bat's mercy.

We sailed over San Marcos, leaving behind the historic neighborhoods and passing over the gritty old outskirts, before reaching the shiny new suburbs.

My heart stopped as buttons popped off my jacket, and the clothing held by the claws shifted. Thank goodness I didn't fall. Yet.

Beneath the deafening flapping of the giant wings came the whirring of a small motor. A tiny white light appeared, coming towards us.

A drone! With a camera, I hoped. I waved to it as it approached.

"Help me, please!"

The bat and the drone flew toward each other. The light hit my face, then moved up to the bat. I could see the four little helicopter blades spinning above it.

"Help me!"

The bat bent downward and with a sickening crunch, snapped its jaws on the drone, crushing both it and my hopes for someone coming to my rescue.

We continued coursing through the night. I guessed we were pointed to the northwest. And our elevation was about—

My stomach lurched. Oh boy, I can't look down again. The homes are so tiny. We are way too high.

I still couldn't believe I was plucked from the middle of San Marcos, and no one saw us.

Did the bat have magic invisibility? Well, I could certainly see the bat. And the drone seemed to. I guess in today's world, people are so focused on their devices and their trivial lives that they can't notice the wonder around them.

Or the horror above them.

We were descending now. Below us was a large forest. The moonlight wasn't bright enough to reveal anything other than trees and shadows for miles.

Bats don't live in trees. Were caves, sinkholes, or abandoned barns hidden in this forest?

As we dropped closer to earth, a large clearing came into view. The bat circled and approached the ground. Then I saw it —the dark opening of a sinkhole.

Of all the ways to die, what could be stupider than being eaten by a giant bat-like creature that shouldn't exist?

And what could be more horrifying?

The monster hovered above the sinkhole, and its claws scraped against my shoulders as they released my clothing. I screamed as I dropped.

I landed on a pile of dirt that had slid down into the hole from its lip. My landing was blessedly soft, except for some sticks and stones mixed in the dirt. I definitely got a few bruises from them. Not that it would affect the taste of my flesh.

The bat landed nearby and folded its giant wings.

The only thing I could think to do was pull out my phone and use the flashlight, hoping to blind the creature's eyes, which must be sensitive enough to see in the dark. As I angled the phone toward the beast, the light beam raked across the pile of dirt I had landed on. The hard objects that had hurt me were not sticks and stones.

They were bones. Large mammalian bones.

And that skull over there was a human's.

Bats are supposed to eat insects. Yeah, right. There were also vampire bats. And, as I now knew, giant flesh-eating monster bats.

I shined my light into the monster's face and the yellowish teeth of its open jaws. The creature flinched and let out an anguished squeak as its glowing red eyes were clearly hurt by the bright beam. Good. But now what?

I ran deeper into the sinkhole, hoping to enter a tunnel or nook too small for the creature to follow me into. With luck, I wouldn't run into an even worse creature, or Fae warriors.

There was, in fact, a tunnel at the far end of the sinkhole. It was tight. I hesitated, as I would have to get on all fours to enter it.

Sharp claws raked my back. I dropped to my hands and knees, squeezing into the tunnel entrance.

My left ankle was seized, and my leg yanked behind me. My body slid backwards, even though I grabbed onto clumps of dirt and roots. I dug with my hands, trying to pull myself forward out of the claws of the creature, but it was too strong.

Slowly, it inched me backwards, closer to its jaws. I kicked at it with my free leg, to no effect.

Hands grabbed my wrists. What the heck?

The hands yanked my arms forward, and my elbows slid out

from under me. Face-down now in the dirt, I was pulled in the opposite direction from the bat monster.

But the bat didn't release me. It was too strong. Now, I felt like the rope in a tug-of-war contest, arms pulled ahead of me, a leg pulled behind me. If I ever got out of this, I'd probably be an inch or two taller.

The only thing keeping me from abject panic was the fact that the hands holding my wrists were humanoid. Small, but not unlike mine. I realized each of my wrists was held by two hands, meaning two individuals were pulling me.

And they were gradually winning the contest. Even though pain flared in all my joints, I was beginning to have hope that I would not be the bat's dinner.

Assuming, of course, that whoever was pulling my hands wouldn't eat me.

I whimpered as the claws dug deeper into my ankle, but my body lurched forward several inches. Then, several more.

The tunnel widened, and the individuals pulling me forward grabbed me by the elbows and armpits and moved me a good two feet ahead.

Finally, the claws on my ankle let go.

"Stay down," whispered a human voice with a heavy accent.

My two rescuers scrambled over me, heading toward the beast. Frantic scraping and scattering sounds came as the bat retreated up the tunnel with the two humanoids in pursuit.

I said humanoids because they were quite small. As in faerie sized. I hoped I hadn't escaped out of the frying pan and into the fire.

Several pops came from the tunnel behind me, the same noise made when faeries shoot darts with blowguns, as I remembered from a forest one night.

I had enough room to look behind me, seeing nothing in the

darkness. I reached for my phone and shined the flashlight. Two faerie-like creatures returned from the sinkhole toward me. They were smiling.

And they looked a little different from the faeries I knew. One was male, the other female, with darker skin, black hair, and dark almond-shaped eyes. The pointy ears and noses were as expected.

"What happened?" I asked in a quavering voice.

"We will explain," said the female. "Come with us so we can tend to your wounds."

The two faeries crawled over me again and headed deeper into the tunnel. The passage continued to grow larger until we entered a cavern of sorts where a small campfire burned. Smoke escaped through an opening in the roof that revealed the starry sky.

Sitting around the fire were four other faeries like the two who had rescued me, two males and two females. They wore green tunics and breeches, and were armed with blowguns, bows, and small swords strapped to their bodies. They looked up at me and smiled.

"Sit," the female from the tunnel said.

After I obeyed, she examined my bloody ankle. She washed the wounds the bat had caused with water from a gourd, then rubbed a spicy-smelling ointment upon it.

"Am I your prisoner?" I asked.

"You are our ally," the male from the tunnels said in that unfamiliar accent. "We are Aluxes, faeries native to the Americas. We are foes of the Fae armies that are coming to conquer these lands."

"Oh," I said, smiling with relief. "Do you know Imelda, who is half human?"

The Alux nodded. "Her father negotiated with our chiefs and

secured our alliance with the humans. Our numbers are small compared to the Fae armies, but we are happy to use our weapons and magic to help defeat the Fae."

"Thank you. And thank you for rescuing me from that bat-like thing."

"That was a camazotz, a monster from the jungles of the Yucatan. It will harm no one else now. I didn't know camazotzes have migrated this far north, but I'm not surprised. So many creatures, both natural and supernatural, have been disrupted in recent years."

"Why?" I asked.

"There have been changes in climate you are surely aware of. And a misalignment of our planet's spirits, its energies. The two are related. The spirits are affecting magic in many ways."

"Ways that none of us can repair," said my female rescuer.

"Does that have anything to do with why the Fae have become so aggressive?" I asked.

"It may. We see it as an illness that needs healing. The Fae priests interpret it as they wish. The evil ones wish to blame it on other creatures and claim that only war will solve it."

And so here we were with war about to break out.

The six Aluxes looked at me, expecting more questions.

"Are you guys from Florida, or did you travel here?"

"We have always lived around here but are only now assembling in war bands. More of our brethren can come from Mexico and Central America if we need more soldiers."

"Do these tunnels connect with the ones the Fae use?"

"No, these are our own, connecting our villages. We are very careful to guard them from the Fae."

The Alux people were important allies to have, I realized.

"Have you met with the leaders of the supernatural humans?" I asked.

They shook their heads in the negative.

"I will arrange a meeting for you."

"Thank you," said the woman.

She introduced herself as Izel, and the man who helped rescue me as Alfonso.

"Nice to meet you. I'm Darla. Thanks again for rescuing me and agreeing to help our people. Now, I need to get home and change into dry clothing."

Cory was very relieved to receive my call, waiting nervously for me to return from Mom's. I located where I was, using my mapping app, and asked him to pick me up.

He didn't ask why I was way out here and why I couldn't drive my scooter. I didn't volunteer to tell him.

This story would have to wait until we got home, and he was sitting down.

# CHAPTER 15

# GNOME WAY TO FIGHT A WAR

I trudged through the forest one morning, a column of weird creatures following me.

One thing you could say about the Fae invasion, and the migrations caused by the disturbances in the earth's energies, was that San Marcos had an abundance of weird creatures. Not including paranormals like me, we had too many supernatural and mythological beings to count. It seemed like every day I learned of new ones.

The Troll and Gnome Alliance was planning a reconnaissance mission into the tunnels to search for the missing shifters. The guild included other subterranean creatures besides the various kinds of trolls, like beach trolls and bridge trolls. No internet trolls, thankfully.

As its name states, the guild also had gnomes. Silly me, but I thought decorative garden gnomes were the only gnomes that existed. Little did I know that large numbers of them come to Florida for the winter from the Northern climes where they normally live. And, of course, many retire here.

Today, I was guiding a sizable contingent of native Floridian gnomes through the large forest next to the Gilley estate. When Gilley, AKA Dorn, lived here, I discovered there was an extensive network of tunnels and caverns in the limestone substratum beneath here that connected with other networks throughout the San Marcos area.

No human knew where to find these tunnels better than I did.

The tunnels had been seriously damaged by the roots of the trees in the forest (thanks to yours truly). I had no doubt that many of the tunnels remained intact. Too small for humans to navigate without magic, the tunnels were built for faeries who averaged two feet tall in their natural forms.

The gnomes, who were even smaller than that, would be ideal for exploring the tunnels. If they encountered hostile faeries, they could fight them with physical weapons, but would be outclassed by Fae magic. Gnome magic consisted mostly of warding spells to protect buried hordes of gems and precious metals.

A faerie loyal to the San Marcos guild accompanied them to provide defensive magic, if needed. Her name was Gorkee, and she agreed to use a spell to link herself to me telepathically in such a way I could also share her sense of sight and hearing. It would be much better than relying on the narration of her thoughts, as I had done with Jeff.

Simultaneously, trolls were in the sinkhole beneath Francis' art gallery attempting to sniff out a way to find and enter the magically blocked tunnels there.

We entered a pine hammock, the forest floor carpeted with needles from the longleaf pines towering above us. I knew there was a tunnel entrance nearby because our cat had escaped from it. The problem was it was hidden with magic.

"Gorkee," I said. "I believe there's a tunnel entrance near the base of those trees over there. It's disguised with Fae magic. Can you find it?"

At the moment, Gorkee was in human form, probably because she wanted to tower above the tiny gnomes to instill respect. When I turned my eyes back to her after pointing out the trees, she had already transformed into her natural faerie form. This made it easier for her to work with Fae magic.

She walked among the nearby pine trees, staring at the ground, then halted.

"There's an entrance right here." She pointed at her feet. "The problem is, it's locked."

"How is it locked?"

"The magic that hides, opens, and closes it, requires a specific spell to work. Sort of like a password. The Fae who use the tunnel are probably the only ones who know it."

"So, we came all the way out here for nothing?"

"That's not what I'm saying." Her squeaky voice became indignant. "I located it. We simply need to open it manually."

"How?"

"We dig a hole until we reach the tunnel. The entrance is probably very close to the surface. Let's put these guys to work."

She was referring to the gnomes. Most of them carried tiny shovels in addition to their weapons, which only goes to show how well-prepared gnomes are. They're not the silly creatures you think they are.

"All we have to do is dig?" I asked. "I thought the magic would be more protective than that."

"There are probably several other entrances, and it would take too much power to put impenetrable magic on all of them. As it is now, no one would even know where to dig."

I shrugged, and Gorkee ordered four gnomes to dig. The

little guys were quick with their shovels. Only about a foot beneath the forest floor, they came upon a piece of plywood, which they splintered apart with their shovel blades.

"I hope the noise doesn't attract attention," I muttered. Gorkee ignored me.

"Gnomes, follow me," Gorkee ordered. "The shifters will be held in a large cavern or open space. They are too big to travel through the tunnels. You will need my magic to transport them to the surface, so don't stray too far from me."

She gestured for me to bend down to her level, then she placed her hands on each of my temples, blinked three times, and removed her hands.

Vertigo swept through me, and I almost fell. I realized I was looking at myself through Gorkee's eyes.

"It's working," I said, sitting and leaning against the base of a tree. "I hope we'll be looking at our shifters soon."

Gorkee climbed into the hole, followed by the dozen gnomes.

I would have a long wait here. We were several miles away from San Marcos and the sinkhole where the shifters had disappeared. But this was a place I knew, without a doubt, had Fae tunnels, and I suspected the network of them was more expansive than anyone imagined. We had to begin searching somewhere, and this was a good place to do it.

In the meantime, I would sit back and enjoy the mental footage sent to me magically from Gorkee's point of view. Good thing faeries can see in the dark.

I watched as Gorkee proceeded along a gently sloping tunnel. Soon, openings to smaller tunnels appeared. At each one, she entered for a short distance, but then retreated to the main passage. The party would become hopelessly lost if they followed every tunnel that branched off from this one.

An opening to the right caught her interest. She turned into a short passageway that climbed sharply before expanding into a cavern of limestone and dirt walls. It was abandoned and heavily damaged, its roof cleaved open by the giant roots of trees.

Indirectly, this was my handiwork, from when I commanded the trees to help free their mother-goddess Danu.

Gorkee returned to the main passage and led the party as the tunnel meandered vaguely eastward. Being connected to her hearing, as well, I heard the gurgling of running water become louder. Up ahead was a rocky outcropping with a small waterfall pouring down from a hole in the roof into a large natural basin in the rock. Stacks of wooden buckets sat beside it.

Nearby, the tunnel widened significantly, leading into a giant open space. My breath caught as I realized it was living quarters.

The limestone walls looked like a honeycomb, with scores of identical round openings at regular intervals. Gorkee got closer. The openings were a combination of natural features in the limestone and those bored into the rock by faeries. Inside of each, the rock was polished smooth and contained mattress pads and blankets. Each one was the right size to comfortably fit a faerie in their natural form.

The gnomes milled about the tables and chairs that took up the center of the space. A blackened hearth was in the far end. Gorkee reached inside and touched the stones.

"Cold," she said aloud. "No fires recently."

She glanced at the rounded ceiling. Shafts of sunlight streamed through fissures in the rock and earth. Roots hung down into the space like vines, many of which showed signs of having been severed by blades.

One gnome jabbered excitedly to Gorkee, in a language I couldn't understand, and pointed to a nearby table. Gorkee went over there, and the gnome showed her a plate of half-eaten food —bread and beans.

"It is still fresh," Gorkee said. "Someone has been here."

Another gnome spoke, pointing out a rack on the wall that held dozens of spears. Half were missing.

"I had thought this place was abandoned, but it seems some faeries are still around," Gorkee said aloud in English for my benefit.

She spoke to the first gnome, who went to the entrance to the space and stood out of view at the edge. Gorkee led the others toward a smaller opening in the opposite wall. Here, the tunnel continued.

They moved along the tunnel that meandered as before, with occasional smaller passages branching off it. Gorkee made cursory checks of each one, either finding empty caverns at their ends, or giving up before going down those that seemed to extend forever.

"We will check these branch tunnels another time," she said. "For now, we must continue moving closer to San Marcos."

Moments later, she stopped dead in her tracks. She'd heard a high-pitched whistle that human ears could not register.

She barked orders in the gnome language, and the party turned around and rushed back the way they had come.

When they entered the cavern with the living quarters, the gnome stationed at its entrance motioned for them to hide. The gnomes crouched beneath the wooden tables while Gorkee rushed to the entrance and pressed against the inner wall next to the sentinel gnome.

Multiple sets of footsteps clattered down the tunnel toward the entrance. Voices in the Fae language drifted into the room.

And then, the party of faeries entered. About twenty of them, all soldiers, most likely scouts, they filed into the room without stopping. They wore knit caps with slots for their pointed ears, had bows slung over their shoulders atop their folded wings, and carried spears.

They would have seemed diminutive to me, but from Gorkee's perspective, they were frightening. They were her own species, but she was in a guild allied with humans. Would she remain loyal to us?

As soon as the last faerie entered the room, Gorkee shouted a Gnomish word and stepped from her hiding spot to block the entrance. The gnomes launched a volley of darts from their blowguns and leaped out from under the tables, brandishing their spears.

The gnomes were outnumbered, but their darts must have been coated with poison or a drug, because half of the faeries dropped to the floor with darts protruding from their skin.

The rest of the faeries met the rush of the gnomes and fought them, spear parrying spear. Though the gnomes were slightly smaller than the faeries, their spears were about the same length as those of their adversaries. The gnomes were also fast-moving and savage.

Forget your garden gnomes; the real things were frightening warriors. Their technique was to parry the faerie spear thrusts with their own spears, trying to get in close enough to plunge their daggers into the faeries. Many were skewered by the faerie spears before they could do so.

Gorkee pushed her way into the fray, slaying two faeries before her spear broke. She drew a short sword I hadn't noticed before and hacked away at the faerie spears until they shattered. She went in for the kill.

Casualties were heavy on both sides, but Gorkee and the gnomes were winning.

A strange buzzing filled the air as the faeries' dragonfly-like wings carried the survivors aloft. The ceiling of the cavern wasn't high, but just enough to keep the faeries above the melee, so they could draw their bows.

Before they could shoot more than a few arrows, the gnomes fired another volley of darts, dropping all but one faerie.

He aimed his arrow at Gorkee.

Gorkee rushed toward him and threw her sword. The arrow narrowly missed her head at the same time the faerie fell to the floor, the sword protruding from his chest.

Out of Gorkee's dozen gnomes, only six were not dead or seriously wounded. All the faeries were down, but some of those hit with darts were showing signs of stirring.

Gorkee recited words in the Fae tongue and moved her hands through the air in an intricate pattern. The wounded faeries stopped moving, frozen by the magic. Gorkee knelt beside one of them and held a dagger to his throat, shouting at him.

The wounded faerie mumbled something, and Gorkee nodded.

"We must bring out our dead and wounded, along with the prisoners," Gorkee said aloud to me. "The one I interrogated said he had seen no captured shifters in this area."

*Thank you for what you did here today,* I told her telepathically. *I am thankful you survived.*

The war between the Fae and the guilds of San Marco was well underway.

## CHAPTER 16

## BYE-BYE BUDDY

"Why do you do this to yourself?" Cory asked me while we took a rare moment of relaxation on the couch, watching movies.

"Do what?"

"Take on all these responsibilities you don't need. You're getting more and more sucked into this nonsense with the Fae."

"Nonsense? You think a hostile supernatural species taking over our city is nonsense?"

"Not when you put it that way. But I don't see any evidence of all this. I mean, I'm a witch, right? I've applied for membership in the Magic Guild. But no one has said anything to me about a war. Except you."

I sighed. This was partly my fault for shielding him from so much of the craziness in my life. He knew about the minotaur but hadn't seen it. But he most definitely didn't know that a bat-like monster had plucked me from the streets of Old Town and taken me to a sinkhole to devour.

They say communication is the key to a good marriage. But

tell your spouse something like that, and you'll never be allowed out of the house again.

"I'm not taking a leadership role in the war," I said. "I'm just interested in what's going on, helping where I can."

And no, I did not tell him about guiding a party of gnomes to the tunnels of the Fae, who then had a pitched battle underground. I will, though. Eventually.

"It's time to concentrate on what affects us directly. Like running the inn. We need to work on our marketing to drive bookings up."

"Cory, do you really think we'll have guests when San Marcos is ravaged in a supernatural war?"

"I don't know. Maybe, if only supernaturals are involved, it won't matter to anyone else."

It mattered to Francis and her assistant. They were offered as sacrifices to the minotaur, and they're humans as far as I knew. But I kept my mouth shut.

"Let's follow your advice and stop discussing it. Please pour me more wine, and we'll enjoy the movie."

"Now you're talking."

When he got up to refill my glass, my phone buzzed.

"Ms. Chesswick, it's Jack Guarini. Have you talked to Buddy in the last couple of days?"

"No. Why?"

"I can't reach him. He missed an appointment with me the other day and hasn't answered any of my calls. We have a hearing before a judge tomorrow, and we can't miss it. If he's not there, they'll revoke his bail and throw him back in jail."

"Oh, no! I'll tell Buddy to call you immediately if I hear from him."

"Thank you."

This worried me. Buddy was very irresponsible, but even he wasn't stupid enough to miss a court hearing. Or was he?

Cory stood in front of the couch with two glasses of wine and a giant frown.

"And you're trying to exonerate your ex-husband at the same time you're fighting a supernatural war." He shook his head. "Do you really need to help Buddy now that you've gotten him a lawyer?"

"If my psychometry can be of any help, I must offer it. I told you I read his partner's memory right before being shot, and Buddy didn't do it."

"Right. And now the police can look for the shooter."

"They're not doing a good job of it. And now Buddy's missing."

"Are you sure he's not on a bender or something?"

"He has a court hearing tomorrow he can't miss. I have a bad feeling about this."

Cory handed me my wineglass and sat beside me.

"I think Damon was killed because he knew stuff he wasn't supposed to know," I said. "The murderer might think Buddy knows the stuff, too."

Cory opened his mouth to say something but thought better of it. Talking about your wife's ex-husband is walking on thin ice, especially when it comes to life-and-death matters.

He remained silent and watched the movie. I pretended to watch it while my mind whirled with strategies for finding Buddy.

"YOU WANT ME TO DO *WHAT*?" SOPHIE ASKED IN THE KITCHEN the next morning. She was upset to learn her father was missing.

"If you can't get him on the phone, go to his house and go through his paperwork. I'm looking for a schedule of when he makes his urine pickups each week so I can trace his movements. You get along with Cindy, right? She won't mind if you look through his stuff."

Cindy was Buddy's latest girlfriend and payer of his monthly mortgage bill. No matter whom he had a relationship with, they always ended up footing most of his bills. It was a remarkable talent of his, really.

"Yeah, yeah. I get it. Sorry, but I'm kind of freaked out about this news."

"I hope he had to go out of town for something. But I want to look for him if he doesn't contact us."

"Okay. I'll go to Cindy's when we're done with breakfast service. I think she works nights now, so she should be home."

"Thank you."

I grabbed a chafing dish filled with fresh slices of French toast. When I carried it from the kitchen, I got a nasty surprise.

Detective Siwicki stood in the foyer.

"You got a moment?" he asked.

"Let me drop this off, and I'll be right back."

I carried the steel dish into the dining room, placed it in the rack on the buffet table, and lit the butane burner beneath it. Then, I reluctantly returned to Siwicki.

"How can I help you?"

"Have you seen Buddy Grimes? We had some questions for him, but his attorney said he went AWOL. He's not at his house. Has he contacted you?"

"No. His attorney called me last night, and I'm very worried about him."

"Where should I look for him?"

"I don't know. But I do know this: Buddy did not shoot his partner."

Siwicki smirked.

"You should believe me. I had a vision of Damon Borgia's death—of a man I didn't recognize shooting him from another car. I would have thought Buddy's attorney had told you. If Buddy told him, that is."

"Sure, they're cooking up an elaborate fairy tale. Are you telling me you got this from that kooky psychic nonsense you did in his car?"

"Yes. I read Damon's memories. I'm a psychometrist. That's a real thing. You can look it up on the internet if you can figure out how to spell it."

"So, you 'saw' some guy shoot him?"

"Yes. In Damon's mind, he referred to him as the Emerald Man. Does that name ring a bell with you?"

"If it did, I wouldn't tell you because of your association with the defendant."

"Looks like I'm more generous of a person than you are. I'll also share with you that Damon had a girlfriend who was a patient at a sober home called The Shady Palms Apartments. Management took her away to some ranch outside of town. I think it's called Hard Ridge Ranch. Turns out, they take a lot of their patients to this ranch, and no one ever sees them again. Is this also news to you?"

He smirked again. But he also jotted down some notes on a small memo pad.

"I'm just a kooky psychic, but it seems to me that if Shady Palms is doing something illegal with those patients, and Damon knew about it, then they might want to make sure he didn't talk."

"Something illegal? Like what?"

I shrugged. "I'm not a detective."

The truth was, I didn't have a theory about what happened to the patients. Maybe they were killed, but I couldn't think of a reason why.

Siwicki stuffed the notepad back into his pocket.

"Thank you for your unusual information. If you hear from Mr. Grimes, please let me know."

I smirked in return before he turned to walk out the door.

Was Siwicki going to follow up on any of the information I gave him? Fat chance. Cops are overworked already without having to do extra work to prove their primary suspect is innocent. That's the defense attorney's job.

In a fit of pique, I called Jack Guarini.

"Please tell me you heard from Buddy," he said when he answered.

"No, but Detective Siwicki was here minutes ago, asking the same thing. And he claims he has heard nothing about what Buddy and I told you regarding the Emerald Man, Shady Palms, and the missing therapy patients. Did Buddy relay this information to you?"

"Yes, he did."

"Why didn't you tell the police?"

He laughed. "That's not how it works. We don't hand-feed them our defense strategy. When it's time for pre-trial discovery, we'll give them the absolute minimum. The rest will come out in front of a jury."

"Oh. Right," I said, feeling stupid. "I didn't trust Buddy to keep you in the loop."

"It sounds like you wish you had more control over the situation. That's perfectly normal. You need to be patient and talk to me if you have any information to share, or any questions."

"Okay, thanks."

I guess he was right about feeling in control. Once I put time and effort into something, I want to make sure it's completed properly. This probably explains why I get so deep into dangerous affairs, instead of trusting Samson or the Memory Guild to handle them.

Did I need counseling? It could reduce my prevalence of near-death situations.

Maybe someday. As soon as I tracked down Buddy, exonerated him, and ended the threat of the Fae. That's all.

SOPHIE BROUGHT ME A DISORGANIZED STACK OF PAPERS FROM Buddy's house. Each had long rows of dates, numbers, and people's names. I had to assume they were inventory lists for the urine samples Buddy has been picking up from the sober homes and delivering to the testing lab since Damon died.

Some sheets had the name of the recovery company on top. Others only had an address. I needed to check my notes to match the address of Shady Palms. The other names and addresses, I didn't recognize.

By comparing the dates to my calendar, I concluded which days of the week Buddy went to each facility. The last day anyone had heard from Buddy was Monday of this week.

One facility he regularly visited on Mondays was Shady Palms.

Before I gave serious thought to what I was doing, I ended up in my car, headed to the sober home.

People call me reckless and impulsive. I describe myself as spontaneous because it sounds like a good thing. Whatever you call it, it gets me into trouble all the time.

At least, I planned ahead enough to bring a handgun with me

—a new one that replaced the one on the bottom of the Intra-
coastal Waterway with my poor, beloved motor scooter. It will
be a while before I can replace that.

By the time I pulled in front of Shady Palms, the only plan I
had devised was to ask anyone I encountered if they had seen
Buddy on Monday and if anything weird had happened. I figured
calling the company that ran the place would be a waste of time.
Only an honest, non-scripted answer from someone here would
be helpful.

A few residents, three young men, sat beneath the picnic
tent smoking. I ambled over, noting they weren't the same
people I had spoken to before.

"Hi," I said. "I was wondering if any of you saw a friend of
mine on Monday. His name is Buddy Grimes, and he's with the
company that handles the drug testing." I went on to describe
his appearance.

The three men shook their heads no.

"He drives a white Ford SUV," I added.

"Funny you say that," said a strung-out skinny guy with a
shaved head and lots of piercings. "There was a white Ford SUV
in our parking lot, which I remember because practically no one
parks here."

"Did you see the driver leave in it?"

"It was towed away Monday night."

My heart missed a beat. If it was Buddy's SUV he saw towed,
this was really, really bad news.

What happened to Buddy?

"Who would order the SUV to be towed?" I asked.

"That would be me," said a deep voice behind me.

I turned to find a large man standing there, hands on hips,
giving off the air of barely repressed violence. He wore a T-shirt
and tight jeans. His hair was white and closely cropped. His

muscles stretched the black T-shirt he wore. Surprisingly, considering his buff body, his face was wrinkled and craggy.

It was the same guy from Damon's memory, the big mean one who had brandished the rifle when the residents were roused from their apartments and taken away.

"And who would be you?" I asked.

His eyes squinted with anger. He didn't like my attitude.

"I work for Hopeful Recoveries. And you're trespassing on our property."

"Sorry, but my ex-husband is missing, and it sounds like he was abducted from your property."

The man snorted with ridicule. "Is he a patient?"

"No, he's a business partner with your company."

"Business partner?"

"He handles the drug testing for you."

"Ah, the Pee-Pee Man scamming the insurance companies."

"Yeah, like you guys are squeaky clean."

He moved closer to me, just inches away, trying to intimidate me with his size. Sure, he was like two Darlas tall, and his pecs were bigger than my first apartment. He smelled of cheap after-shave. Do guys still wear aftershave?

I bit my tongue before I revealed how much I knew about them and that I suspected they were trafficking patients for some nefarious purpose.

"I haven't seen your ex-husband in weeks," the man said. "And the word 'ex' means you have no legal connection with him."

"Prefix."

"What?"

"'Ex' is a prefix in your usage, not a word."

He looked like he was going to take a swing at me. It would

shatter my skull, but would put this jerk behind bars where he belonged.

"Sorry, lady, but I have to ask you to leave our property now," he said, moving closer and trying to herd me with his pecs.

The patients under the tent were hoping this confrontation turned violent to add a little excitement to their boring day.

"You haven't seen the last of me," I said as I walked out of the parking lot. I had too much self-respect to flip him the bird, though I wanted to so badly.

Contrary to my supposed need to have control of the situation, I called Siwicki and told him that a witness described an SUV like Buddy's being towed away from here. Samson received a call from me, too. You know, share with everyone.

When I returned home, I told Cory, but not Sophie. No sense in freaking her out when I wasn't sure if it was really Buddy's SUV.

"Detective Siwicki said he'd call around and find out which towing company took the vehicle and get the VIN number to confirm if it was Buddy's," I told Cory in the privacy of our cottage.

"And what if it is?"

"I trust they'll look for him."

But that was a lie. I wouldn't trust the police to take this as seriously as I would. Yep, I had control issues.

"And you'll let the police look for him?" Cory asked. "Promise me you won't go off and do something reckless?"

Ah, that feeling when you realize you found the perfect man who truly understands you. Though that might mean he gets in your way.

"Reckless? Me?"

Cory chuckled while shaking his head.

"Not at all. And you never face off against terrible monsters, either. Tell me, who was worse, this bad dude with the white hair, or the minotaur?"

"The minotaur could have easily eaten the bad dude. But the minotaur wasn't evil like him."

"Wow. That's really saying something."

"Yep."

Please let it be noted that I did not promise Cory I wouldn't go off and do something reckless. That's the secret to a great marriage: don't make promises you can't keep.

# CHAPTER 17

# HER MAJESTY'S TRAVESTY

There was no telephone listing for the Hard Ridge Ranch, nor any mention on the internet. I had to rely on my recollection of Damon's memories to help me find it, with only four hours to do so until I had to prepare for teatime.

Yeah, I was taking the risk and going there myself. If Buddy had been shot, his body would have been dumped somewhere, and I wouldn't be able to find it. It would be too late.

If he was alive, though, they could have taken him anywhere. I really doubted he'd be tied up in a room at the Shady Palms. Or in the big, mean guy's utility room.

No, they would take him far from Shady Palms. The only place I knew where they took people was the Hard Ridge Ranch. Where the people disappeared.

So, I studied Damon's memories, compared them to my own of driving the country roads outside town, then cross-referenced maps. I ended up narrowing down the ranch's probable location to three roads. I tried each of them, driving away from San

Marcos into the countryside for several miles, keeping my eyes peeled for a sign or a driveway that looked familiar.

Nothing caught my eye on my first route, and I had to decide arbitrarily when I had driven far enough. Then I turned around and returned to town. This was the case for the second route, as well.

However, on my return trip, passing through a heavily wooded stretch, I saw the hand-painted sign on raw plywood.

"Hard Ridge Ranch. No trespassing," it said in sloppy lettering. Because of the thick foliage, the sign hadn't been visible when I came from the other direction.

I stopped on the shoulder of the road. What was my plan? As usual, I had none. It was risky to go snooping around during the day, so I convinced myself that this was merely a reconnoitering mission. I would simply check out the property, pretending I was lost.

No fence or chain blocked the driveway, so I drove into it. The narrow, sandy lane winded slightly uphill through pine trees that quickly gave way to pastureland blocked off with barbed-wire fencing. No farm animals were visible, and the grass in the fields was overgrown.

Small outbuildings came into view in the distance. I went around a bend, and before me was a modest two-story house and a nearby barn that was the height of a two-story building. Presumably, *the* barn. No vehicles were visible.

Should I take advantage of this opportunity to snoop? You bet.

There was a sandy area on the far side of the barn where I parked out of view of someone coming up the driveway. Getting out of my car, I stood for a moment and listened. All I heard were the distant songs of birds and the faint rumble of a truck passing on the road, unseen behind the trees.

I peered into the nearest window of the barn. The glass was dirty, and the interior was dark, so I saw nothing. I checked another window, and it was the same. I mustered the courage to walk around to the front of the barn.

Here, there were two large roll-up doors. Maybe this was more of a garage for farm equipment than a barn for animals. Beside it was a normal door. It was unlocked.

I glanced around behind me to double-check that no one was around. Then, I opened the door and slipped inside, closing it behind me.

The interior was murky despite the four windows. After my eyes adjusted to the low light, I walked around. The large space was mostly empty, with the feel of a property abandoned long ago.

A rusty mower, the kind towed behind a tractor, sat covered with cobwebs in the far corner. Bags of feed were stacked opposite it, several of which had been gnawed open by rats with feed spilled onto the floor. On the left wall, beneath two of the windows, was a workbench with tools hanging from a nearby rack on the wall. On the far end, where the shadows were deeper, were wooden crates and cardboard boxes scattered about.

The building was simply a big, rectangular space. I saw no closets or separate rooms. The only exterior doors were those in the front. That meant the patients hadn't left from the rear of the building unseen by Damon or the security guard I'd spoken to.

Where had the patients who had been brought here gone?

The obvious guess would be a tunnel or some sort of basement. And unlike the faerie tunnels, the passageway must be large enough for humans.

I wandered the floor, looking for seams or cracks that would indicate a trap door. The floor was dirty with scattered oil stains but was smooth concrete with no visible cracks.

Any opening to a tunnel or basement would have to be beneath the boxes at the far end, or under the stack of feed bags.

No, probably not the feed bags. As I examined them, it was clear the bags hadn't been moved in a long time. The spilled feed was old and mildewed, the bottom bags appeared to be stuck to the floor due to water intrusion.

I walked over to the cardboard boxes. I pushed aside a large one that was mostly empty. Nothing was beneath it. Another box was too heavy for me to move. Three additional ones were stacked too high for me to reach the top one. As for the wooden crates, pushing with my back against one moved it a few inches, which was enough to reveal nothing beneath it. The other two crates were packed with something heavy and were unmovable.

What if they weren't filled with anything and were attached to the floor? I went to the workbench and found a crowbar. Fitting the flat end beneath the lid of the first crate, I slammed down the other end repeatedly until I had loosened enough nails to get the lid partially open. The crate was filled with rusting machine parts.

The same was true with the second crate. I was out of ideas.

I made a half-hearted attempt to close the crates, and turned to return the crowbar to the workbench.

"Nice try," said a familiar voice behind me.

I jumped almost out of my shoes. Jaekeree stood there in human form.

"Are you trying to give me a heart attack?" I asked between deep breaths. "What are you doing here? How did you get inside without me hearing you?"

"You were correct that there are tunnels here. You apparently thought they were dug by humans, not by us. By now, you should have learned humans need magic to enter and fit through our tunnels."

"There were several humans brought to this building who disappeared. Were the Fae responsible?"

"We did not bring them here. They were sold to us."

"*Sold* to you? What did you do with them?"

"We put them to work, so that our laborers could become soldiers."

"You enslaved them?"

"Of course. Humans are of lower status than the Fae. Everyone knows that."

"That's not true!"

"Not for you, of course, Daughter of Danu. But it's true for the rest of your species."

"What about my ex-husband? Did you enslave him, too?"

Jaekeree laughed. "How would I know?"

"He would have been delivered to the ranch this past Monday night or Tuesday morning."

"I am sorry, but we have not received a new group of slaves for two weeks."

He moved his hands through the air in a complicated pattern.

"Wait a minute," I said. "No magic. I don't want—"

He clapped his hands.

I was suddenly inside a cavern lit by glowing lights on the walls. It had your typical craggy limestone walls and ceiling, but the floor was covered by an expensive-looking carpet with intricate designs that seemed otherworldly. At one end was an extremely large chair of dark wood, carved with similar designs. It was the only furniture in here but was large even for a faerie in human form. I approached it.

"No. You don't want to sit there," said Jaekeree, now in his tiny faerie form, pointy nose, ears, and all. "It's the Faerie Queene's."

"Her throne?"

"No, it's a chair. Her thrones are at her palaces."

"You mean in Palm Beach?"

"That is her winter palace, which she is not using at the moment because of security issues. The Queene is here in the San Marcos area to accompany the invasion force. And you are here to heal her."

"I haven't received permission yet from my guild."

"That does not matter," he said sternly. In his natural form, his voice was high-pitched, like he'd just inhaled helium. It was hard to take him seriously with a voice like that.

As if he had read my mind, Jaekeree transformed into human form so quickly my eyes couldn't register the process. He was even fully dressed in human clothes. This kind of morphing was completely magical, unlike the way werewolves shift, which was a physical process that looked painful.

"We cannot wait any longer," he said. "The Queene is gravely ill and needs your healing powers."

"But I don't know how to do it."

"The goddess will come to you and guide you. She would never refuse a request to heal."

"Right, but please wait a moment. You said I have to help her because I'm in debt to the Fae. But a pearl for the life of your Queene—is that a fair exchange?"

"It is not about monetary values."

"No," I insisted, "it's about generosity and good acts. Bring me someone who can negotiate in the name of the Queene."

He frowned. "I have the power to do so. You might think I'm a mere messenger, but I'm a High Lord of the Fae, the top advisor to Her Majesty. You are not here to negotiate whether you will heal her."

"Yes, I am. I'm the human manifestation of the Goddess, and I am subject to the ills of all mortal humans. I cannot heal the Queene if your people are going to inflict misery on my people. It's not fair. It's not right."

He gave the type of smile that made me nervous.

"Surely, you cannot expect us to call off the invasion?"

"I expect a temporary peace, at the very least. Perhaps the Queene will feel more benevolent after she is healed and would want better relations between the Fae and humans."

"Perhaps. But there are powerful lords and generals who are in favor of the invasion."

"They are subject to her will. Is she conscious and able to communicate?"

He nodded.

"Tell her I will heal her in exchange for a pause in the war and peace talks between our people. Also, the return of the prisoners you have taken."

"We're not giving back our slaves. We paid dearly for them."

"I meant a group of shifters who went underground to fight the minotaur. Oh, and my ex-husband, too."

Jaekeree frowned again. "I cannot guarantee your last demand. I do not know if any of those shifters survived, and where they might be. Or what happened to your ex-husband. But I shall inquire."

Then, in the blink of an eye, he had returned to faerie form and strode from the cavern into a tiny tunnel.

I wanted to sit down but didn't dare try the giant chair. I settled down on the luxurious carpet to wait for Jaekeree to return. Several minutes passed, and I yawned.

Before my yawn was finished, I was in another cavern—a

giant one, larger than any of the Fae's underground world I had seen. My mind struggled to comprehend what I was seeing.

Lying atop a raised platform was a vaguely humanoid creature, her body a gigantic rounded, oblong shape covered in pleats of multicolored silks and satins. Her head looked like the typical faerie in natural form, with pointy ears and nose. Her hair was piled atop her head in a bun adorned with strings of gems.

Her limbs were tiny compared to her massive body. How could she move on her own power?

She wasn't moving; she merely lay on her back while hundreds of faeries thronged around her on their knees and on top of each other, all touching her with one hand. The scene looked like a queen ant thronged by smaller worker ants.

As she breathed, so did they, all in unison. She and her minions were like a single organism.

"What are they doing?" I whispered to Jaekeree, who had appeared in human form beside me.

"They are drinking in Her Majesty's energies. That is how we all maintain our magical powers—by absorbing them from her. Now, you should be able to understand that when she is ill, we all are."

The thought crossed my mind that if I allowed her to die, the Fae would weaken to the point they couldn't threaten us anymore.

The thought quickly disappeared as the goddess' love surged through me.

"Did she accept my offer to be healed in return for peace?"

"Yes," Jaekeree said. "For a cessation of hostilities and the beginning of peace talks."

"May I approach her?"

He nodded. "Allow me to assist you."

Taking my arm, he pushed through the horde of faeries who were on the periphery, waiting to touch the Queene. Next came the more arduous task of getting through the piles of bodies, who reached out for at least their fingertips to graze her.

I got near enough to touch her forehead with my left hand. Her skin burned with a fever.

A change was happening inside of me. My senses were heightened, a warm glow filled me, and I felt detached from my sense of self.

It was as if I had become one with the multi-creature organism of the Queene and her subjects. My rate of breathing matched theirs. My love for the Queene matched theirs. My worries for her matched theirs, as well.

But I did not thirst for her energies. Instead, I prepared to share mine with her.

Words came from my mouth that I didn't know. I was speaking the Fae's language, as if another mind had taken over mine.

"What is your ailment, Your Majesty?" I asked in the Fae tongue.

"It is not an illness that had a biological cause," she replied. "It came from a curse. Magic of some sort created this disease and caused it to spread from me to my people."

She turned her head with great effort to look me in the eye. "You are the Daughter of Danu, no?"

"I am."

"If you cure me, I will honor our agreement for peace."

"Thank you, Your Majesty. You must understand that I can cure your disease and rid it from your body. I cannot control the magic that created it. Whoever gave you the curse could do so again."

"My priests are trying to find out who that is. And destroy them."

I shuddered at the ruthlessness of her last sentence. And at the fact I just promised a queen I could heal her and had no idea how. This would be much more complicated than mending a broken minotaur horn.

The Goddess knew how to heal her, however. I was only the ignorant human vessel of her power. She was taking over my mind and body, and I would simply go along for the ride.

I sang a song I had never heard before. Its melody was ancient and timeless. The words were not in English or in the Fae lexicon, and I sensed they came from the earliest days of language.

I placed my other hand on her head, too.

It was almost as if I had closed an electrical circuit. My hands tingled and a blue-white current flowed between my hands, encasing her head.

The hundreds of faeries around us uttered a collective gasp and removed their hands from the Queene.

The power flowing through me intensified until I was no longer in my body. I floated above it, near the ceiling of the cavern, looking down upon the scene and the light crackling around the royal head.

And then, I was in a primeval forest, with thick, towering tree trunks, leaves so lush they were almost bursting with life, and the feeling of boundless fertility and everlasting life.

I was the Goddess now and no one else. The laws of physics and the rules of time did not apply to me. I was immortal and ever-present, yet secret and invisible.

There were other beings just like me here, gods and goddesses. I couldn't see them, but knew they were here.

They told me I had to go now but could return later.

Suddenly, the feeling of vertigo as I fell a million miles from the heavens, past the stars, into our atmosphere, and then deep into the ground.

The electricity stopped flowing from my hands and through the Queene's head. My vision grayed and my legs gave out beneath me.

Just before I lost consciousness, a roar filled my ears. It was the collective cheer of happiness from the hundreds of faeries around me.

The Queene was well again.

# CHAPTER 18

## NOT THE REAL DEAL

I awoke in a really uncomfortable position on the concrete floor of the barn. My watch couldn't tell me what time it was because the Fae magic had fried it. I'd already been through three watches thanks to these creatures and their darn magic.

My phone was off but appeared to be capable of restarting.

The light coming through the dirty windows was dimmer than it had been before. I worried that I had missed teatime.

I got to my feet painfully and almost tripped on a small but heavy metal box. It was shiny black with embossed decorations that were similar to those on the carpet in the underground cavern where I had waited. Bending to examine the box, I removed a small but thick piece of parchment protruding from beneath it. A message was written in flowery cursive in black ink.

*The Queene insists you accept this gift from her in gratitude for your service. The box will remain locked until you are sent the key and are instructed to open it.*

The box was ridiculously heavy, more so than solid cast iron.

I wondered if the shiny, smooth metal was the same that created the key to Pandora's Box, a substance said to have come from somewhere other than earth.

Unbeknown to the Fae, I had a copy of the key. And based upon a memory I had read from the artisan who had installed the lock on the jar known as Pandora's Box, the key might work for this box, too. The person who left the memory had hoped the lock would divert attention to the jar and away from this box.

Why? Just like Pandora, I would be nagged with curiosity about what was inside this box I was commanded not to open.

Although I wasn't in a safe place, I searched the box for memories. But there was very little psychic energy on it. Perhaps the rare metal didn't retain the energy. There were fleeting thoughts from Jaekeree, negative ones I couldn't isolate and decipher. Other than his, nothing.

Which aroused my curiosity even more.

I had too many other problems to deal with now, however. I walked to the door of the building and opened it just a crack to allow a glimpse of the house. Thankfully, no cars were there. Slipping out, I ran to my car with the heavy box and jumped in.

When I started the car, the clock on the dashboard said it was an hour and a half past teatime.

I sure hoped Sophie and Cory handled it in place of me.

Before I shifted into drive, I felt something in my back pocket. I reached down and pulled out a piece of parchment like the one beneath the box. In the same flowery handwriting was the message: *The prisoners are at the art gallery.*

So far, the Faerie Queene and Jaekeree were good to their word.

My phone had restarted, and I called Cory.

"Are you okay?" he asked breathlessly. "You had us in a panic."

"I'm sorry I missed teatime."

"It's not just that. Whenever you're late, it usually involves something dangerous."

"I had some goddess business to attend to, which I'll explain later. Right now, I'm heading to the art gallery on Seville Street. I've been told our missing shifters are there."

"Do you need me to go there?"

"I'll be okay. Please set up for the Wine Hour. I'll let you know when I'm coming home."

Next, I called Dr. Noordlun, telling him the shifters were at the gallery, and he needed to pass along to the Executive Council details about my encounter with the Faerie Queene. Maybe it was because I had the Goddess in me, but Dr. Noordlun was a lot better about taking my calls these days.

"You actually met the Faerie Queene?" he asked. "The council asked you to wait before you agreed."

"Yes. I had no choice. I was abducted and taken there. You have to understand, the Goddess wanted me to heal her, and I had to do as she wished. She has no interest in the conflicts between species. The good news is I got the Queene to agree to a ceasefire and to hold peace talks with the council. Also, the captured shifters were released, and I'm on my way now to the art gallery where they entered the sinkhole."

When I arrived at the gallery, Francis and her assistant were there, but there were no shifters in sight. In fact, it looked like a normal evening with two customers browsing the art. Francis was surprised to see me walking in.

"I'm happy to see the building department didn't close down your business," I said.

"The engineers are still looking at the structure, but it passed the initial safety inspection. Um, can I help you with anything this evening?"

I lowered my voice so her assistant wouldn't hear.

"I was told the prisoners who were taken during the attack against the minotaur have been freed. They're supposedly down there." I pointed to the floor.

"Oh. I had no idea. Help me move the art installation out of the way."

We hurried to the bizarre sphere sprouting lawn tool. Its price, in case you were wondering, was $25,000. As we pushed its wheeled base, the opening in the floor was revealed.

We looked at each other as if to say, now what?

I got down on all fours with my head above the opening.

"Hello? Anybody down there?"

No answer.

I shined my phone's flashlight into the hole. It wasn't strong enough to reveal much more than the steel ladder and a small portion of the earthen floor. I had expected to see a group of the shifters standing there, ideally the entire group that had initially come down here.

No one came into view.

A feeling of unease gnawed at my stomach, but I convinced myself that the shifters were in the process of being released and would appear in the sinkhole soon.

I decided to go down and make sure no one was there. I began easing myself down the ladder.

"Are you sure you should go down there alone?" Francis asked.

"The minotaur is gone. It should be safe."

She was correct, though. Some members of the guilds were surely on their way here, and it would be wise to wait for them.

Yeah. You know me better than that. I continued descending the ladder.

"Hello?" I called out again. My bad feeling was only getting worse.

Shining my light around me revealed no one. I pointed the light at the limestone walls of the cavern and saw no tunnel openings.

Please, open and let our people out.

The tunnels didn't hear me.

I looked up when I heard the thud of shoes on the ladder rungs. A man was descending.

It was Samson.

"Hey, Mike."

"Darla. The owner told me you were down here. The Shifter Guild contacted me because they knew I'd be the fastest to arrive." He shined his heavy-duty police flashlight around the space. "There's no one here."

"Right. I'm hoping they're on their way."

"Maybe the Fae reneged on their promise."

"I was told the Faerie Queene agreed to my demand."

Samson shrugged. "You can't trust anyone during a war. Even though I was told you healed her."

I hoped he was wrong.

I pointed my light at the largest wall. "That's where the tunnels were. They open and close magically."

"So, we simply wait here until they open, and our shifters walk out?"

"We have to," I said. "Even though Jaekeree, the faerie I've been communicating with, left me a note that said the released prisoners *are* here, not *will* be coming here."

"I guess he had the wrong information. Or the Fae reneged."

"Don't be so pessimistic. With the Queene healed, they all

should be rejoicing. Her health affects every single one of them. They must be very grateful to the Goddess."

"It also means they're all stronger now. And less inclined to negotiate."

"Jaekeree said the Queene promised. You don't have to stay here and wait if you don't have time."

"We don't know how long we'll have to wait. Or if the prisoners will be released at all." Samson stuck the flashlight in his belt. "I say we post someone at the top of the ladder day and night, and they can alert us if the prisoners show up."

"When they show up. I can take the first shift if you find someone to relieve me before too long."

Samson glanced around in the darkness again. He looked as uneasy as I did, though I was trying to hide it.

"Maybe it wasn't such a good idea to heal the Faerie Queene," he said.

"I had no choice. I was held captive by the Fae. Besides, the Goddess insisted on doing it. That's her thing, you know."

Samson took his flashlight from his belt and swiveled his beam around the sinkhole again. "My wolf instincts are really bugging me. Something isn't right."

He walked into the portion of the cavern where the ceiling was lower and shined his light at the small alcove where Francis and Bebe had been hiding.

"Is that a tunnel entrance there?"

"No," I said. "It's just a nook. A dead end."

He approached it and shined his light inside.

"Oh, no," he whispered.

His light revealed a pair of boots with the toes pointing upward. We both hurried over to the alcove.

There, in the harsh, unforgiving light, lay Jeff on his back. His hands were bound.

And he was dead. Samson bent down and touched the side of his neck to make sure.

"Why?" I asked, crying. "Are they sending a message? Are they threatening to kill the other prisoners?"

"Something tells me Jeff was the only prisoner. And they did deliver him here as promised. I think the peace negotiations aren't going to happen."

"Jaekeree!" I screamed with all my might. "Why did you lie to me?"

It was a while past midnight, but I didn't check the actual time. I didn't want to know. I sat in a wooden deck chair in the courtyard, sipping another glass of wine that I would regret imbibing. Samson had left hours ago. Cory and Sophie had finally gone to bed recently. The phone calls and texts from various guild members stopped coming.

I needed time alone in the quiet darkness to think.

Everyone was grieving for Jeff and the shifters. Several guild members believed other prisoners were still alive. Some theorized Jeff had been the only prisoner, the only survivor of the battle. Others darkly declared that there had been several survivors, and the Fae executed them.

It was impossible for anyone to know.

One thing was certain: everyone was mad at me for healing the Faerie Queene. They didn't understand the Goddess is compelled to heal the life on earth she cares for.

And frankly, I thought it was a smart move diplomatically—the show of generosity toward the Fae. I didn't realize how strong their hate and animus were. None of us had known they were enslaving humans. Innocent people sold out by sleazy people. Our species is just as lousy as the Fae.

If only I hadn't gone to the ranch to poke around. It was because Buddy was missing, not anything to do with the Fae. But I realized even if I hadn't been near their tunnels, they would have captured me, anyway. They know where I live.

Of course, just as I was thinking this, I heard someone clear their throat. I turned my head to see Wilference, a priest of the Fae. He was in human form, dressed in the drab woolen robes the Fae priests wear regardless of which form they take.

"Good morning, Daughter of Danu."

"Morning?" I looked at my watch. "Good heavens, why am I still awake?"

"I come to you for two reasons, one of which is to thank you for healing our Queene."

"We had a deal. The Fae were supposed to release the shifters you took prisoner."

Wilference looked down and fidgeted. "Which brings me to the second reason I am here. The Queene's wishes were not obeyed, because there has been a palace coup."

"Are you kidding me?"

"I wish I was. There is a group of radical nobles and generals who are responsible for making the Fae hate humans and pushing us into war. Dorn, whom you knew as Dick Gilley, was one of them. They are led by Jaekeree—"

"What? He serves as the Queene's messenger to me."

"That was his duty as her top advisor. However, when the Queene accepted your terms, Jaekeree rebelled against her."

"If he was against what I offered, why did he pass it along to her?"

"It was his sacred obligation. Should she ever discover he didn't pass messages to her, he would lose his position."

"Is the Queene still alive?"

"Her Majesty is alive. Her health is good, thanks to you. But she is now being held in captivity. No one knows this except for the members of her court."

"So, her people can't touch her, like I witnessed them doing?"

"No, they cannot. However, her improved health has already positively affected the community."

Great, I thought. Now the soldiers attacking us will be stronger.

"Why did you come here to tell me this, Wilference?"

"I am a loyal subject to Her Majesty, the Faerie Queene. And a devout worshipper of Danu. Jaekeree and his coterie are traitors who are leading the Fae down an evil path. If he knew I am speaking to you like this, he would have me killed. But I felt I must warn you. Jaekeree sent the monsters against you, and he will send more. The only gods he worships are Haarg, the God of War, and Aastacki, the Father of Lies. In honor of Danu, I wish to protect her daughter, even if you are a human."

"Thank you."

"I must go now. I am putting myself at tremendous risk by coming here to share information with you. My advice to you is to not be distracted by the threat of the Fae armies. An armed conflict is not how Jaekeree and his generals will ultimately subjugate your people."

"Can you tell me more?"

He shook his head. "This is all I know."

"Answer me this question, please, before you go. Jaekeree said I was indebted to the Fae because I accepted his gift of an enchanted pearl. He said I was obligated to heal your Queene, and that is what I did. Has my debt been repaid?"

Wilference smiled bitterly. "Jaekeree never retires a debt."

# CHAPTER 19

# THUNGUS AMONG US

Ever get the feeling you were a pariah? That would be me, now that the Executive Council of the Guilds of San Marcos decided I screwed up. My quasi-goddess stature didn't add any points in my favor, it seemed. By "assisting the enemy" and healing the Faerie Queene, I was nearly a traitor in their eyes.

So, I was frozen out of all discussions about defending the city and the guilds. Moving forward, I was just like the other non-supernatural humans who plodded through their daily lives, unaware of the existential threat to us posed by the Fae.

And you know what? I was fine with that. I was tired of all the anxiety and heartbreak, the waking up in underground caverns, and the good-looking men who turned out to be ugly little faeries.

I was also sick of being attacked by mythological monsters. Who wouldn't be? The problem was Jaekeree, and those who summoned them to kill me, wouldn't know I'd been sidelined from the war. Meaning I could still be attacked.

In the meantime, I would concentrate on my true occupation of running an inn and trying to make a profit.

Well, no, there was more unfinished business.

My missing ex-husband who was accused of murder.

The buzzing of the doorbell and pounding on the door at the main entrance at 5:30 a.m. brought that back onto the front burner.

Our security system locks all exterior doors of the inn overnight so that only guests with a card key can gain entrance. The doors are unlocked at 6:00 a.m., or when I come in from the cottage to make breakfast, whichever is sooner.

I had to rush into the inn from my bedroom to find out what the ruckus was. It was a burly guy in a black baseball cap.

"Can I help you?" I asked through the glass before I opened the door.

He held a business card up to the glass for me to read. It was an appointment reminder for a psychologist.

"But I don't need a psychologist," I said. "I mean, I probably do, but I've never heard of one banging on my door to give me therapy. Am I that bad off?"

The man looked at the card and stuck it back in his pocket with frustration. He produced another card and pressed it against the glass.

*Ralph Thungus, Registered Bounty Hunter.*

Bounty hunter?

"What do you want?" I asked.

"Please let me in. I'm looking for Buddy Grimes."

"He's not here. He's missing."

"I know he's missing. I'm trying to find him. His bail bondsman hired me. Can I come in, please?"

My first urge was to refuse, out of an instinct to help Buddy.

But as far as I knew, Buddy hadn't left town to avoid prosecution. I feared he'd been killed or taken by bad guys, namely the Emerald Man. I wanted him to be found alive and then exonerated.

"Okay." I unlocked the door and stepped aside as Ralph Thungus entered the foyer. The man looked formidably muscular, but he also had an ostentatious black handlebar mustache, each side curving down and then up, ending in a sharp point. There was serious mustache wax holding this thing in place. It made him look like a goofy silent-film villain.

His mustache was in the major leagues, compared to Siwicki's.

"Why do you have a semi-automatic rifle strapped to your back?" I asked cautiously.

"It's a dangerous field I'm in."

"But why would you want to shoot someone you're trying to bring in?"

"If they don't want to come in, they could shoot me."

"But you're not a Federal Marshal going after an escaped prisoner. You get paid if you make sure your guy shows up in court. If you kill him, you won't get paid."

Mr. Thungus thought about it for a moment. "Good point. I guess I carry this to look like a bad boy."

Then maybe he should lose the mustache, I thought.

"When was the last time you saw Buddy Grimes?" he asked.

"Last week."

"Do you have any thoughts about where he would have gone?"

"No. If I did, I would have looked there already. I'm very concerned that he's been killed or kidnapped by the same people who killed his partner."

"I thought *he* killed his partner."

"No. He's wrongly accused, and they'll drop the charges against him."

"Whatever." He pulled a notecard from his back pocket and studied it. "Where is his favorite vacation spot?"

"He usually likes to rent a place at a nearby beach."

"Does he have relatives he can stay with?"

"I already called all of them. They haven't seen him."

"I'll need to check for myself, in case they're lying to you."

"His mother lives in San Diego. You better get going. It's a long flight." I turned away and started for the kitchen, hoping he'd get the hint.

"Wait, I have more questions for you." He studied the notecard.

"Are you new at bounty hunting?" I asked.

"Kind of. I used to be an actor, but there isn't much work in San Marcos, besides low-budget commercials. I'm also a re-enactor at the fort, playing a Spanish soldier. But they don't pay me."

"Do you fire the cannon?"

"No, I walk around with a musket and pose for selfies with the tourists."

Maybe this explained the handlebar mustache.

"I wish I could help you," I said, "but I don't believe Buddy went into hiding. I'm worried the bad guys did something to him. Before you go to San Diego, will you please stop by The Shady Palms Apartments? It's a sober home run by a sleazy company, and I fear they did something to Buddy because he knows of their criminal activities."

"I could go there," he said, smiling, eager to please.

"Be careful, though. There are some *real* bad boys there."

When he left, Mr. Thungus almost got hit by a car on Cadiz Street. This guy should stick to low-budget TV commercials. I hoped I hadn't sent him on a mission that would leave him injured despite being heavily armed.

I should have told him to visit the office of Hopeful Recoveries, too.

Then it occurred to me: why don't I visit their office one day this week? I had plenty of questions to ask. You know, leave no stone unturned, and all that.

THE BUILDING USED TO BE DENTAL OFFICES. NOW, INSTEAD OF fixing cavities, the business restored lives. Or so they said to their clients and their clients' insurance providers.

Hopeful Recoveries had a wooden sign out front engraved with a rising sun and a seagull flying above it. The parking lot was half full of cars and passenger vans. In a shady area of the parking lot, a picnic table stood. Several patio chairs were lined up behind the building with industrial-size outdoor ashtrays. Two young women and a man chatted while they smoked, ignoring me as I entered the building.

As usual, I didn't have a plan. You'll be relieved to know I did some additional research prior to showing up here. Although a shell company was listed to hide the company's ownership, I uncovered the details that Hopeful Recoveries was owned by Grady Williams and Dr. Ernesto Vasquez. Both of them had a habit of showing up in newspaper articles involving Medicare fraud, patient brokering, and other schemes.

I had to give Hopeful Recoveries credit for their marketing. The company website was colorful and modern, with lots of stock photos of happy, presumably recovered, people enjoying the Florida sunshine. Their building had shed all its dental gear and featured a lovely group therapy room with pastel colors and rattan furniture. It was occupied at the moment by a session.

The place had the feel of a boutique hotel on the beach. It was meant to attract folks who'd have no problem dropping tens of thousands of dollars to spend a month or three getting clean and starting over. If your budget was tight, you'd end up living at Shady Palms. If you had better insurance and more money in the bank, you'd have more upscale digs that looked like this office and the photos on their website.

I strode directly to the door past the lobby that said "private." Unfortunately for them, it wasn't locked.

I walked into a small reception area. A young woman wearing a phone headset looked at me warily.

"Is Mr. Williams in?" I asked.

"He's in a meeting. Is he expecting you?"

No one expects me, they dread me. That's what I wanted to say. Instead, I shook my head.

"I have a quick question about my daughter, who's a client."

The receptionist looked worried. "Someone else can help you."

"My daughter is a very happy client. I wanted to ask Mr. Williams about enrolling in follow-up programs."

This seemed to mollify her. "If you'll take a seat, I'll let him know you're here. And your name is?"

"Darla Morales." I hated to lie, but it was part of the game.

The telephone sales pitches of a man and woman in cubicles behind the receptionist entertained me for several minutes until a man in his early sixties finally emerged from a hallway behind the cubicles. He wore a tight black silk shirt, that barely held his prodigious gut in check, and a gold chain hanging atop a hairy chest. His gray hair was slicked back, and he sported an earring and several rings.

He was not a people person, I could tell.

"I'm Grady Williams," he said. "How can I help you?"

"My daughter is a client of yours, and I haven't been able to reach her. I'm very worried."

His face was impassive. "I'm sorry to hear that. Wendy here will have the appropriate counselor reach out to you."

"My daughter's name is Rita Morales. She used to live in The Shady Palms Apartments. Do you know what happened to her?"

His face remained impassive. He obviously didn't recognize the name or didn't care.

"Sorry, I don't know. She probably ran away. Her counselor will reach out—"

"I heard you guys sent her somewhere else."

Now his face showed some emotion. Namely, annoyance.

"I'm sorry for your situation and hope it will be straightened out." He turned to go.

"She was dating Damon Borgia," I blurted out. "He was murdered. Do you know who killed him?"

"Get her out of here," Grady said to the receptionist, who pressed a button on her desk.

Two men quickly entered the office area. They wore white polo shirts with Hopeful Recoveries logos. They scanned the space, confused. I guessed they were used to subduing violent patients in withdrawal, not petite, middle-aged innkeepers.

The receptionist pointed to me and cleared up the confusion.

"You'll have to leave the premises," the beefier guy said to me, placing his slab of a hand on my back.

"Thank you all for your time," I said. "I'll be going. Tell your goon to take his paw off my back."

On my way out, I noticed a red Ferrari parked beneath a canopy. Who else could it belong to other than Grady Williams?

When I got into my car, I reflected that this visit didn't yield any information. But I got the undeniable feeling that Grady Williams was up to no good. Maybe even murder.

Chalk it up to mother's intuition.

# CHAPTER 20

## BAD HAIR DAY

In the middle of Wine Hour, a young woman entered the main door and stopped short when she saw the half dozen guests and me chatting in the foyer with glasses of wine.

I didn't recognize her as a guest, and she was memorable. Tall, thin, wearing a sundress with colorful, exotic designs and a knitted cap holding all her hair like Rastafarians use to cover their dreadlocks.

"Hello," I said. "Come on in. Are you visiting a guest?"

"Do you have any rooms available?" she asked.

"I believe so. Let me check." Of course, I had rooms available. I'm never fully booked. But I didn't want to seem desperate.

I cut through the gathering of wine drinkers to get to the desk at the rear of the foyer. Clicking through the booking software, I saw that three rooms were available. Not as pitiful as I had thought.

"Yes, I have a vacancy. Would you like to book it for tonight?"

As strange as it may seem in today's world of e-commerce, we do occasionally get walk-ins like this. Tourists wander by and are intrigued by the colonial architecture and the historic landmarks plaque out front. Sometimes, they decide to extend their stay in our fair city, and why not do it here?

"I would," the woman said. There was something glassy and hypnotic about her eyes, like she was on drugs. My instinct was to look away. As I stared at my computer, I got that chill in my solar plexus that told me magic was present.

Was this woman a witch?

"The inn is so charming I decided I absolutely must stay here. How old is it?" she asked, trying to engage me in conversation while I tried to avoid her eyes. My gut told me not to look.

"It was built in seventeen thirty-six." I gave her the room rate. "Can I have your name and address?"

As she rattled off the hard-to-believe name of Jane Smith with an Orlando address, I kept my eyes on the computer screen.

"Can I please have your ID and credit card?"

"Of course. Here they are."

She didn't reach to hand them to me, instead holding them in the air near her head. I suspected she wanted me to look into her eyes. Was she an agent of the Fae attacking me?

Get a grip on the paranoia, Darla.

I turned toward her and reached for the cards, keeping my eyes on her chin. My eyes detected movement, and I couldn't help but look at the top of her head. I thought her cap had moved. Weird.

I took the cards without looking her in the eyes. After checking the ID and running the credit card, I handed them to her. But before she took the cards, she did something unexpected. She removed her knit cap.

And revealed her hair. Only, it wasn't hair. It was a writhing nest of snakes hissing, showing their fangs.

What the heck? Is Jane Smith a gorgon like Medusa? No wonder my instincts told me to avoid her eyes. Otherwise, I'd be turned to stone.

I wished the Fae would knock it off already with the monster attacks. This was getting really old. And the problem this time was that I had guests gathered only a couple dozen feet away.

I jumped up to put myself between Ms. Jane Smith of Orlando and the guests. The snakes snapped at me as I moved past.

"Can you cover your hair, please? My guests are normal humans who shouldn't be involved in this."

"I have a secret for you."

"I'm sure you have lots of secrets. Like how you style your hair. Please put the hat on."

"Look at me."

"I'm going to cancel your booking. I don't think this is going to work out. Your snakes will find our pillows too firm."

"Hey, Darla, I have a question."

Oh no, it was Henry from 201. I shifted my position to block his view of Medusa.

Too late.

"Oh, wow," he said. "Freaky. It's not Halloween, is it? Ma'am, your wig is—"

Henry was stone-faced. I mean, he was stone for real. His clothes remained as they were, but his flesh was immobile and rock-solid like a statue's. More like concrete than marble, to be specific. His stone hand still held a wine glass filled with Chardonnay, which was now in no danger of spilling.

Thank heavens Henry's wife was upstairs now. I prayed no more guests wandered over here.

What was I going to do with Medusa? If I remember my Greek mythology, Perseus beheaded Medusa and carried her head around as a weapon to turn enemies to stone. I wasn't going to cut off any heads tonight.

On the wall at the end of the hall was a fire alarm. I was required to have it by law. I leaped over and pulled it.

My guests complained amid the ear-splitting cheeping.

"Sorry about that," I said. "Just a mandatory drill. Let's take this party out into the courtyard."

I called the Fire Department and told them it was a false alarm. The guests were still milling about in the foyer, and I went to herd them outside and away from the monster. But she tried to block me, snakes hissing and lunging.

I punched her a good uppercut to the jaw. Though I avoided her eyes, I could tell she was stunned. Whether the blow stunned her, or the fact a petite middle-aged woman landed it, I did not know. So, I punched her again, the snakes' teeth narrowly missing my hand.

Then, for good measure, I grabbed the brass lamp from the desk and nailed her in the temple. She went down, her head knocking against the stone knee of Henry.

She was out cold. The snakes appeared stunned, too.

*I could make short work of the reptiles,* said Cervantes in his slight Spanish accent. He had crept up to us unnoticed.

"They're freaking *snakes,* and they look poisonous. You're just a cat."

*I'll have you know I killed a deadly coral snake just the other day. You wouldn't want a guest to be bitten by one of them.*

"Oh. Thank you."

*Now, if you don't mind, I'll take care of these nasty creatures. It will be easy with them stunned like this.*

I didn't want to watch the carnage, so I rushed to a nearby

utility closet to turn off the alarm. Finally, the painful cheeping ended. Next, I hurried to the front room.

"Archibald, please wake up. I need you very, very badly. I have a guest who's been turned to stone, and maybe, as a stone-speaker, you can help."

You'd think the crotchety gargoyle would respond to an emergency like this, but no.

"Cervantes, when you're done with the snakes, I need you to smack Archibald's face and get the old grump to wake up."

"No need for that," Archibald said as he animated from stone to flesh. "I hate that four-legged demon."

"The feeling is mutual, I'm sure. Did you hear my request?"

"I was asleep."

I repeated my entreaty.

"Are there any guests nearby?" he asked.

"Not at the moment. The guest is right outside this door."

Suddenly, Archibald was gone from the mantel. I left the room and found him mounted to the end of the main hallway, near the fire alarm, close enough to Henry to touch him.

"Oh, my," he said, studying my petrified guest.

"Exactly."

"The good news is the human was turned to stone magically," Archibald said, "so he's not true stone. His human DNA is probably still in there somewhere. Allow me to commune with the stone and attempt to coax the magic away."

I stood with my arms crossed, tapping my feet. Medusa still lay unconscious on the floor, and the snakes were now no longer in the land of the living. I replaced the knit cap to cover her head. Then, I texted Cory to come here and get her out of the inn before she woke up.

"Henry? Where are you? Is there a fire? You left me all alone upstairs."

Uh-oh. It was Henry's wife. I couldn't let her find him turned into stone.

"Hen-*ry?*"

Mrs. Battleax (I couldn't remember her name) was twice the size of Henry. She looked strong enough to carry the stone version of her husband upstairs easily. In fact, she could have taken Medusa out more quickly than I had.

"Hi," I said as I headed her off from coming into view of her husband. "Everyone needs to step outside now."

"Is there a fire? Where's Henry?"

"No, just a drill, but the Fire Department wants everyone to go outside like in an actual fire. Just head through that door on your left to the courtyard. Henry is probably out there."

"Oh, okay, if you say so."

She wandered past the kitchen and dining room toward the doors leading to the courtyard.

I ran back to the front room.

"Any luck reversing the spell?"

"If I could have a little silence in which to concentrate," Archibald said crossly. He still had both hands on Henry like a faith-healing preacher.

"His wife will be back inside any moment now."

"That is your problem, not mine." He sighed with frustration. "The gorgon's magic is crude, but quite strong. I'm trying to convince the stone that it is not meant to be stone, and it's being stubborn. Stones tend to be that way."

"I wouldn't expect anything else."

I left Archibald to his work and headed toward the courtyard. Henry's wife burst back inside and almost bowled me over.

"Henry is not out there."

"He must have gone out the main entrance. Let's look for him out there."

I moved her through the foyer, away from her petrified husband, and toward the door. If I could only get her out onto Cadiz Street, I could kill several minutes as we searched up and down the block for the man who wasn't there.

But just as we were exiting, a shriek came from the end of the hallway behind us. It was a man's shriek, but so high-pitched you would think he was having prostate surgery without anesthesia.

"That's Henry's voice!" his wife proclaimed, knocking me aside and storming back into the foyer.

There was no stopping her. She passed the staircase and went into the rear hallway where the Henry statue was.

Spoiler: he wasn't a statue anymore. Whatever Archibald had done saved the day.

"What is wrong, my sweetie?" Henry's wife gushed as she swept him into her arms and lifted him into the air.

"An evil creature had its hands on me!" he said in a voice that was still high-pitched. "A loathsome, reptilian, demonic, monster. He's right there!"

He shrieked again. Actually, it was more of a squeal. He pointed at Archibald. My gargoyle housemate had returned to stone and protruded from the wall like a misplaced decorative figure.

"That's a gargoyle, my love," his wife said. "To be precise, it's called a grotesque, since it doesn't spout water."

"It was groping me," Henry said.

I wanted to argue with him, but wisely kept my mouth shut.

"I think the fire alarm set off your blood sugar level, dear. And the wine you drank without me. Let's go upstairs."

She led her diminutive husband to the elevator and out of my hair. I was relieved to notice Ms. Medusa was out of sight. Cory must have taken her away. Wine Hour had been a disaster, but I survived another monster attack. Now, I had several half-full bottles of wine to put away.

Put away in the kitchen, I mean. Well, one or two might not make it that far.

"Darla, the most interesting thing happened," Cory said, having appeared in the foyer.

"Thank you for getting rid of Ms. Snakehair. What did you do with her?"

"I started dragging her to the utility room, and she simply dissolved."

"Dissolved?"

"Yeah, I had her by the ankles, and suddenly my hands were empty, and she wasn't there anymore."

"That's bizarre," I said, my mind running through possible explanations. "I wonder if the Fae's magic is weakening, making it more difficult to sustain these mythological creatures they're summoning."

"I wouldn't count on it. I would get ready for even worse attacks from their magic."

"Okay, Mr. Optimist."

"And I want to be with you more of the time. I'm sick of worrying about you when you're late coming home. Half the time, I find out you've been attacked by a monster. Don't think I'm unaware there's lots of dangerous stuff you do that you don't even tell me about."

"I'm sorry, you're right. I'll be less secretive. But I will not put you in danger."

"Right, because you're not going to rush into dangerous situations anymore."

Wouldn't it be nice to think so?

# CHAPTER 21

# BOX OF BAD

I drove along the winding country road until I saw the sign, "Birken Metal Works. Custom fabrication and artwork." I turned onto the dirt road through cow pastures to James' house.

The barbed-wire fence that kept the cattle out of the road was adorned with metallic artwork of animals and strange stick-figure humans. It showed true creativity you wouldn't expect if you only saw James working at the historical reenactment village, hammering iron rods on an anvil to entertain tourists.

James lived in an unassuming double-wide manufactured home on his giant tract of land. Behind it was his metalworking studio, his "real" version of the recreated colonial smithy in Old Town.

Yes, there was a forge with bellows and an anvil for striking things; but he also had extensive welding equipment and a crucible for melting metal before pouring it into molds. Nearby were grinding and polishing tools, along with precision spray-painting equipment.

When I arrived, James was sitting on his front porch reading a novel, a Western.

"Would you like some coffee?" he asked after we greeted each other.

"No thanks. I've been trying to cut back on the caffeine. I get enough excitement just trying to survive. Are you ready to interrogate the subject?"

He nodded, and I handed him the sturdy tote bag that held the box. I sat down in a chair near his.

"Whoa, this thing is heavy!" he said, setting the bag down between his feet and slipping the box out. "Remarkably beautiful."

He placed the box on a wooden table in between our two chairs. "Man, I wish I knew what kind of metal this is." He stroked his beard as he peered closely at the surface of the box. "Any idea what these engraved symbols mean?"

"Nope."

"I don't believe any of my tools could engrave this metal. It's so hard. And the sheen it has seems natural, not polished. Have you tried your key to see if it fits?"

"No. I'm too afraid. Like I told you when I called, I was warned not to open the box. You know, kind of a Pandora situation. But I've since learned that the faerie who gave it to me is treacherous, and I'm afraid he had an ulterior motive. So, if I opened it, something would escape that might harm humankind. I didn't even want to put the key in the keyhole for fear of the box accidentally opening."

"I see." He stared at the box.

"Do you think you'll get a feel for what's inside?"

"Hard to say. If the contents are powerful enough, I might." He glanced at me with a smile. "I admit I'm procrastinating. When I read the key you brought me before, which I believe is of the same metal, it really blew my mind. I'm a little nervous to metal-speak with a larger amount of the same material."

"Take your time," I said. "I don't want you to be uncomfortable."

He turned his attention to the side table and placed both hands on the box, closing his eyes. Minutes ticked by while he sat silent and immobile, except for his lips moving slightly and his breaths getting deeper.

A nasal hum came from him. He had made the same sound when reading the key. This time, it was louder. This time, his hands trembled, and the tremors spread up his arms and throughout his entire body. I was concerned he was having a seizure.

But I knew better. When James spoke with metal, he picked up on all the impressions the metal received over the years and burrowed down to the atomic level, connecting to the electrons themselves. With an ordinary piece of iron, it was an easy experience. Rare metals like this put him through a turbulent journey.

Sweat poured from his face. His head tilted backwards, and his eyes opened, revealing the whites of his rolled-back eyeballs.

Okay. Now I was worried.

"James?" I whispered. I hated to disturb his session, but I didn't want him to get hurt, either.

His humming ceased. His mouth dropped open, and he emitted a deep rumbling sound from the back of his throat, an "ah" that rattled like a roulette wheel. It sounded demonic.

Could he have become possessed? I wouldn't put it past Jaekeree to give me a box with a demon inside.

Now, James' voice went up an octave. Then another. He was singing a long, sustained note like a soprano now. I placed my hand atop his and instantly pulled it back as a painful shock went from his hand to mine.

"James?"

His singing turned to screaming. Distant cows in a field looked over at us.

Suddenly, James yanked his hands from the box and slumped lifelessly in his chair. I jumped up and checked his neck for a pulse. Yep, he was alive, and his heart was racing. I went inside to his kitchen, wet a dishtowel with cold water, then wiped his face, holding the cloth against his forehead.

His eyes opened. He looked at me, confused, and pulled himself upright in the chair.

"That was a doozy." His words were slurred, as if he'd been aroused from the deepest sleep. "It was almost as if the metal possessed me."

"I was worried about the same thing, about a demon taking you over."

"No, but I got a taste of some serious evil."

"Tell me what you learned."

"The metal is from someplace other than the earth. It wasn't from an asteroid that hit earth and was harvested by a human. The box was actually fabricated in this other world. And the metal refused to speak with me like the metals on earth do. It was almost as if it wouldn't acknowledge me. A human did not create this box. Neither did a faerie or any other creature we're familiar with. A different kind of being made this."

I remained silent as he struggled to make sense of his experience.

"As to what is inside it, I don't know," he continued. "But it's something bad. No, there's not a demon inside the box, but I can't say demons weren't involved."

"Did they create the box?" I asked.

He shook his head. "Not demons as we think of them. A physical creature or creatures made the box, individuals who knew the craft like me. But were they half-demon? I know it doesn't make sense. But that was what I felt. And a different individual, aside from the box's creator, filled it with something. It's disease or pathogen—not a virus or bacteria, but a form of magic. Extremely dangerous."

"I'm glad I didn't open the box," I said. "What I don't understand is why someone would fill a box with a substance like that. This box is not simply a container for transporting the contents. It's been decorated to make the box itself valuable, a display piece."

"A Trojan Horse," James said. "I think your suspicions of the faerie are correct. The box is meant to be a gift that an unwary recipient would open, releasing this toxic substance."

"A poison gas to kill?"

"No, to corrupt and turn others evil. Like Pandora's box sent the ills of human existence out into the world, this substance, I think, is meant to do something even worse."

"Maybe it would be the Fae's secret weapon, like chemical warfare, to defeat all the humans without a fight."

"If the Fae didn't create it, why did they have it?" James asked. "Were the creators of it under orders of the Fae, who were wise enough not to open the box?"

"Maybe the creators wanted to defeat them. Or convert them to a different mindset and make them obey. I wonder if we should use it against the Fae ourselves. No, that would be evil. We can't stoop to their level. I guess I should tell Dr. Noordlun and the Executive Council about the box."

James looked at me seriously. "Do you trust them?"

"Dr. Noordlun, yes. I can't say for sure about all of them."

"I think you should keep it and hide it."

"I don't want that kind of responsibility. You and I don't know what's best for the guilds."

"I suppose you're right."

"Will you keep it here temporarily?" I asked. "All my enemies know where I live, and there's too much risk it will be stolen from the inn."

"Temporarily," he said. "This thing scares me too much. I don't want to keep it here any longer than I have to."

THE MEETING OF THE MEMORY GUILD WASN'T HELD virtually this time. Instead, we gathered in person at James' home after dark. The box, temporarily buried in the backyard in the meantime, had been placed back on the same table on James' front porch. Members of the guild filed past it, looking down at it, like mourners passing the casket at a wake.

Diana, our astral witch, was the only one who touched and studied it closely.

"Can you get a read on the magic it contains?" Dr. Noordlun asked her.

"All I can say is it's not of human origin. Not from the Fae, either, though I sense some Fae magic may have been added to it. I agree that it's evil. But I can't tell what its function is."

"I'm certain Jaekeree wanted us to open it," I said. "He told me to wait until I was told to open it, and a key would be sent to me. But he might suspect I already have a duplicate key. He planted the seed of curiosity in my mind, like Pandora, but I won't succumb."

"We need to hide it, but not here," James said. "What about in the Hall of Records?"

"No," Dr. Noordlun said. "Nothing dangerous like this should be where it could possibly harm the Tugara."

"Entomb it underground beneath concrete," Archibald said.

"Darla, you said we should never use this as a weapon," Diego said. "But I believe we shouldn't rule it out."

Exclamations of disgust came from the group.

"Allow me to explain. We might discover more about the magic inside the box. And we might find ourselves in a dire situation where it would be appropriate to use it."

"I don't think so," I said.

"You don't know what it does. All I am proposing is we don't put it somewhere that's impossible to get to if we need it. I know a place where we can bury it. It's on someone else's land, but the land can't be developed right now because of the graves discovered there."

I gasped. "Are you talking about on the grounds of the sanatorium? Where you slept when you were possessed by the spirit of the evil inquisitor."

Diego smiled with irony. "Yes. I know the place well. No one is allowed to go there. I was thinking specifically of the destroyed crypt of the Inquisitor. If the Fae wanted to steal the box back, they would search all our properties, but would never know where it was."

"Is it a good idea to put something evil in an evil place?"

Diego laughed. "Better than in a holy place, wouldn't you say?"

Everyone murmured with unease, but we eventually agreed it had to go somewhere not associated with us.

"I also think it's best not to inform the Executive Council about this," I said.

"As much as I would prefer not to, we must," Dr. Noordlun said. "I am obligated by oath to share such information. It's the whole point of the council and of the guilds in general. We must stick together and share information in order to survive and thrive. I won't tell them the hiding place, however."

The words "survive and thrive" didn't go together at all with the idea of this box.

In the end, we agreed to hide the box in the destroyed crypt where the possessed Diego had taken refuge during the day. What finally convinced us all was the fact that there were no Fae tunnels known to be anywhere near the grounds of the former sanatorium.

The same night, Diego, James, Diana, and I rode in James' pickup truck to the property. There was lots of yellow tape and several no-trespassing signs warning us to stay out, which made our hiding place seem like an even better idea.

I led the way to the location of the crypt, which had been destroyed decades ago when the former official of the Spanish Inquisition, a vampire for centuries, had been staked by local farmers.

None of us knew the crypt better than I did, since I had fallen into by accident. No way would I go into that hole again.

Diego volunteered to go down there with the box and bury it. His vampire strength and agility made getting in and out of the deep grave easy.

I hoped the box would stay there forever. That's why Diana came with us. As an astral witch, she didn't know many earth-based spells. She couldn't encase the box inside a magic barrier, for instance. Instead, she cast a stasis spell upon the buried box. It would set off an alarm in her head if the stasis was disturbed. In other words, if the box were moved from its current position.

Having done all we could do, I told myself to forget about the box and move on.

I never listen to anyone, even myself.

# CHAPTER 22

# UNBOXING

I rarely received phone calls from Diana. So, when she rang me in the middle of the night, I was frightened.

"Darla, it's Diana." Her voice was tense.

"Is everything okay? Did something happen to one of our guild members?"

"No, thankfully. Do you remember the stasis spell I cast on the black box we buried? I was just notified that the box was removed."

"That's not good. Just out of curiosity, how were you notified? Did you hear alarm bells in your head?"

"I was awaked by an image of the box being uncovered by a shovel and removed from the hole." She was not amused by my stupid question.

"I was asking to see if you would know who did it."

"No, only that the stasis was disturbed."

"Thanks for letting me know. Will you tell Dr. Noordlun?"

"I already did."

We said goodnight. I didn't know the significance of this

news. How did the thief know where the box was? The members of the Memory Guild were the only ones who knew. Dr. Noordlun had assured us he wouldn't give the location to the Executive Council when he reported the box's existence.

My only relief was that whoever stole the box didn't have the key. The Fae had the original key, and I had the copy. It was cleverly hidden beneath stones in my courtyard fountain because faeries have an aversion to running water.

The key *was* there, right? Of course, it was.

Anxiety seeped into my stomach. I raced from the bedroom and into the courtyard. Plunging my hands into the fountain's basin, I reached for the stones in question, lifted them, and felt for the key.

It wasn't there.

Panic surged through me while tears of frustration dripped into the pool of water. Reaching for the hidden control box behind thick ivy on the coquina wall, I turned on the fountain lights.

The bottom of the fountain was perfectly illuminated. I turned over all the stones in vain. The key was gone.

No one knew its hiding place except for Cory and me. Even Sophie didn't know.

Who could have stolen it?

Very few people knew I had the key. The members of the Memory Guild. Arch Mage Bob. Dorothy Gilley had known, but she was dead. That was all. Some of the Fae had suspected I had it but didn't know for sure.

Wait, the Caste of Vampire Thieves knew. When they raided the Faerie Queene's Winter Palace for Pandora's Box, I had insisted on holding onto the key.

The vampire thieves didn't know where I kept the key. But if anyone could find a secret hiding place, it would be them.

Pedro, the head of the vampire guild, was on the Executive Council and thus knew about the box. He could have sent the thieves on a mission to find the key.

I returned to the cottage, so guests wouldn't hear me, and called Diego, who, of course, would be awake at this hour.

"No offense, Darla, but you sound rather paranoid."

"Both the box and the key were stolen. How am I supposed to sound?"

"I find it unfair for you to accuse us vampires."

"I'm not accusing you. I'm accusing Pedro and the Vampire Thieves."

"How would Pedro know where the box was buried?"

"He's familiar with the property where the crypt was. Maybe he read your mind."

"I don't know. It sounds far-fetched. Also, why would he want the box in the first place?"

"You tell me. He might know something about the demonic nature of it we don't know."

"There are many other potential suspects," Diego said, a bit too patronizingly for my taste. "The other members of the Executive Council. Perhaps even one of us in the Memory Guild."

"We can scrutinize all of them. But can you at least keep an eye on Pedro? We can't let him open the box."

"I don't believe he has it."

I sighed. "Please, watch for signs of something amiss among your fellow vampires."

I said goodbye and clicked off before he could make me angrier.

"The box *and* the key are missing?" Cory asked from the doorway to the bedroom. He wore only boxer shorts and still looked as hot as he had when we married. Maybe a bit too thin, though. Got to work on that.

"Yes. It had to be the vampire thieves who found the key. They're professionals who have been doing this for centuries. There is no clever hiding spot that they wouldn't know about."

"From what you've told me, no one knows what's inside the box. Everyone has their theories."

"James and Diana are certain it's evil magic."

"I'm just saying things might not be so dire."

"Tell that to Pandora."

SITTING IN MY LIVING ROOM WAS THE LAST PERSON I WANTED to see here. Make that the last individual, since "person" wasn't accurate.

"You get up early for a human," said Jaekeree in human form, one leg crossed over the other as he lounged on the couch. He wore a black sport coat, black pants, and a black button-down shirt. The faerie had the air of a handsome hipster hanging out at an exclusive nightclub.

"I couldn't sleep. Too many worries, many of which are caused by you guys. It's only a couple of hours before I normally get up to make breakfast for the guests. I'm surprised you have the gall to show up after you reneged on our deal."

"My apologies," he said insincerely. "I didn't have the authority to make such an offer without the other lords and generals agreeing to it."

"Why are you here today?"

"I'm making good on a promise I made." He reached into the breast pocket of his coat and retrieved a small key, like the one I had.

"What is that?" I asked, playing dumb.

"The key to the black box the Faerie Queene gave you after

you healed her. You may open it now, if you wish. However, my magic tells me it's not on the premises."

"No. I was afraid it would be stolen. Too many uninvited creatures show up here. Including the Fae."

He smiled at my barb. "Nevertheless, now you have the key." He placed it on the coffee table.

"What is inside the box?"

"Magic. Wonderful magic. It will help the humans see with greater clarity and add strength to your convictions. It reveals truths. Since you are a member of the Memory Guild, one would think you would support the spread of truth among your people."

"Yes, one would."

"There are said to be additional gifts in the box, but no one knows for sure, as it has been locked for generations."

"Why would you give this to humans?"

"To thank you for healing the Queene, of course. It's a good-will gesture."

"But you see humans as your enemies."

"We hope the magic will help you see the Fae more accurately, so we can be your friends."

Fat chance, I thought.

"What if we don't open the box?"

"That is entirely up to you. All the gifts the box contains will only be revealed if it is opened. If you decide not to, then so be it. The box could simply serve as a decorative object. It would look splendid on this table, no?"

"No. I'm sticking to early American antiques."

He laughed. "So I see." Standing up, he made ready to leave.

"What would happen if someone other than a human opened the box?" I asked.

"You mean another species?"

"Yeah. A supernatural one."

"I cannot say. Except to guess that the benefits of the magic would be enjoyed only by that species. Which would be a shame for you."

"Such a shame."

"Seriously. Humans are known for their misguided beliefs and warped realities. The magic would be such a benefit for you."

"I agree. The truth would be a benefit."

"Excellent. I must go now. Thank you for not treating me with hostility."

"Humans are gracious by nature."

"I am not so sure of that," he said, sauntering from the room, the hipster on his way to a trendier spot than this one.

When he reached the foyer, he stopped abruptly.

"That's odd," he said. "Did you give the box to someone else?"

"I did not give it to anyone. Why?"

"My magic tells me it has just been opened. But that would be impossible without the key."

"I guess there's a duplicate key out there."

He stared at me, eyes narrowed with suspicion. "Then the rumors are true—the key for Pandora's Box also works on this one. And you had the duplicate," he shook his head sadly. "You said you hid the box for its protection."

"I did."

"Then who could have opened it?"

"I guess I didn't do a good job in hiding it."

"This is why you asked me about other species. You know who opened it, don't you?"

"No, I don't. I wish I did." Technically, it wasn't a lie because I didn't know for sure a vampire opened it.

"It would take curiosity and greed to get humans to open the box. Supernaturals, though, can sense the magic inside and lust after it. We shall see what happens."

He strolled down the foyer and out into the pre-dawn darkness.

I texted Diana and asked her to spread the word to everyone that the box has been opened.

# CHAPTER 23

## FAMILIAR FACE

The parking lot of Hopeful Recoveries was full of cars and passenger vans. No one was outside smoking. Everyone must be in therapy sessions right now.

My hopes were buoyed when I saw the red Ferrari from last time. Grady Williams was in today, so my visit would not be in vain. Even after I'm thrown out, which I completely expect.

Then, why did I come here, you ask?

To be honest, it's because I'm losing my mind with worry over Buddy. Also, I wanted to see Williams sweat.

I believed he killed Damon or hired the killer. And the more Williams sweated, the more likely he would be to make a mistake and get caught. There was a massive chasm between the sweating part and the getting caught part, though.

I walked in the front door. Voices came from the main meeting room and from the hall that went past it. There must be another meeting room down there.

No one stopped me, so I went through the door labeled Private.

The same receptionist was there. She was in the middle of a phone call and her mouth dropped open in dismay when I marched right past her, through the cubicles, and toward the window offices where I hoped to find Williams.

Two offices were empty. A third had its door closed.

It's unlocked! How lovely, I thought as I barged in.

A thin guy with a backpack stood in front of the desk. Williams was sitting behind it, examining a large prescription bottle full of pills. Small baggies were arranged atop the desk, containing pills and powders.

"What are you doing? Get out!" His face was beet red as he shouted at me.

"What did you do with Buddy Grimes?" I demanded.

"Get out!"

"I'm going to report you for killing Buddy, just like you killed his partner, Damon."

"Get out of here, you nutcase. I haven't seen Buddy for weeks. And I'm going to call the police and report you for trespassing."

"Better hide all those drugs before you do that." I ducked out of the room, dodged the receptionist's attempted tackle, and hurried out of the place.

I got into my car, turned it on, and tried to cool down in the air conditioning. My heart was racing. It was time to get out of here in case Williams called the police.

Laughing out loud, I replayed the confrontation in my mind. Williams really did sweat when he saw me and heard my accusations. Beads of it were running down the edge of his scalp.

As I put the car in reverse, it beeped a warning. A car was passing through the parking lot behind me. After it parked, I continued to back out of my spot.

I happened to glance at the driver leaving the car and

heading into the recovery center. He looked familiar, so I looked again.

Holy cannoli! It was Buddy's lawyer, Jack Guarini.

What on earth was he doing here?

I exited the parking lot and headed down the street. Was Jack a patient in recovery?

Not that there's anything wrong with that. If he's turning his life around, I'm happy for him.

But it sure was a coincidence that he would be a client of the same company that was Buddy's client, without Buddy knowing it.

The other possibility was that Williams was a client of Jack's.

These thoughts nagged me the entire journey home. After I finished with teatime, I sat at the desk in our cottage's second bedroom and opened my laptop. It had a folder filled with stories I had saved about Hopeful Recoveries and their brushes with the law.

There were plenty of investigations of the company and others like it, but Grady Williams was never indicted. I went through article after article until I finally found the quote I was looking for:

"Mr. Williams claims the investigation is politically motivated, said *his attorney, Jack Guarini.*"

His freaking *attorney*?

I was getting angry and tried to talk some sense to myself. Okay, I was suspicious of Hopeful Recoveries because Damon was killed after he discovered patients were being trafficked from Shady Palms. Little did he know they were sent to the Fae.

I had no proof Williams had Damon killed. It wasn't necessarily a conflict that Jack had him as a client as well as Buddy. Maybe Shady Palms was solely responsible for the trafficking, and Williams didn't know about it.

Still, this was messed up.

On a whim, I called the phone number at the bottom of the article, hoping to speak to the reporter who wrote it, Lidia Posa. I left a voicemail, and she called me right back.

"Lidia, thanks for calling me back. I was hoping you could give me some scuttlebutt about Grady Williams. I've read your stories about him."

"Um, I guess. Why?"

"My ex-husband hired Jack Guarini as a defense attorney for a murder charge. But my ex provided drug testing to a bunch of recovery companies, and I didn't realize, until reading your story, that Guarini had ties to the industry."

"That's putting it lightly," she said. "He's doesn't just represent them in court, but he's also on retainer, drawing up business contracts for them and stuff like that. Can I ask your ex-husband's name?"

"Buddy Grimes."

"Oh, yeah, the murder of Damon Borgia. I did some reporting on that."

"Well, I know for a fact Buddy did not do it."

"I understand you used to be married to him. Do you have any actual evidence to prove his innocence?"

She was being sincere, not sarcastic. But I couldn't tell her about my psychometry.

"No, not any material evidence," I said.

"The police have no leads on anyone else. I understand the murder weapon was your ex-husband's gun?"

"Yeah, but Buddy lent it to Damon for self defense."

"It does seem a little too obvious that the gun was left at the scene. We need to find out if Damon lent it to someone or if it was stolen from him."

She said *we* need to? Well, I could definitely use some help if she'd be willing to team up with me.

"I was told the police will get the gun back from the FBI ballistics lab soon," I said. "Hopefully, we'll learn something then."

"I've never had much luck getting forensics evidence from the police."

We won't need it, I thought, if I can read the gun successfully. But it was a big "if," assuming the shooter left incriminating memories on the weapon.

The sound of a keyboard clicking came over the phone.

"Can you give me a quote about your dealings with Jack Guarini?" she asked.

"Sorry. Not now. I can't antagonize him while he represents my ex-husband. Now, it's my turn for questions. Do you think Grady Williams would murder someone to cover up crimes?"

She laughed. "You mean kill Damon Borgia to cover up getting kickbacks for urine testing? He's a bad person, but that seems pretty extreme for a criminal like Williams."

"What if he has bigger crimes to cover up?"

"Do you know something I don't?"

I weighed how much to tell her. The fact is, I needed help in finding out who the Emerald Man was and proving he shot Damon. Detective Siwicki had no interest in helping me. Samson would, but he couldn't interfere with Siwicki's investigation. Lidia was my best shot.

As long as I left out any mention of the Fae.

"Damon believed Hopeful Recoveries was involved in human trafficking," I said.

"Are you serious?"

"Some of their most troubled patients—those with no family or community ties—were fed drugs to keep them addicted. They were then moved out of a sober home with no notice and sent to an abandoned ranch and never seen again. Damon's girlfriend was one of them."

"Trafficked for sex or labor?"

"Labor," I said. "Unfortunately, I don't have proof, but I spoke to a security contractor who can confirm they were sent to the ranch where they disappeared."

"Wow. This is gigantic. I'll talk to some sources I have in the recovery industry. I'll need to call you from time to time for additional information."

"Please do. And I have one more question for you. Have you ever heard of a guy called the Emerald Man?"

"No. How does he fit into this?"

"I believe he's the killer of Damon Borgia. I can't explain why I believe this right now, but it could be helpful if you ask your sources if they know of him."

"I will. I'm totally intrigued right now. Can I ask you a personal question, off the record?"

"Yes," I said reluctantly.

"I understand why you'd still feel affection for your ex, but why are you working so hard to exonerate him?"

"He's the father of my daughter, and I promised her I'd help him. To be perfectly honest, though, Buddy isn't bright enough to get himself out of this mess. Left to his own devices, he'll end up convicted. And I know in the core of my being that he's innocent of murder."

"I admire your dedication," she said. "I wouldn't do the same thing for my ex-husband."

"I'm doing this for my daughter, remember? I'm not a saint."

Actually, I was the daughter of a goddess. Not that I would ever mention that.

# CHAPTER 24

# A GUN STORY

"Siwicki says he doesn't want or need help from a psychic," Samson told me in the elevator at the police department. "So, I had to get creative."

"You're the most creative werewolf-shifter detective I know," I said.

He frowned. "I don't believe that's a compliment."

"It was a joke. How are you getting us access to the gun?"

"I'm stretching the truth a little, saying I need to show it to a witness for a shooting I'm investigating. No one will mind."

"Even Siwicki?" I asked.

"Don't worry about him."

"Michael, I really appreciate this."

"Don't get your hopes up for having a big payday with the memories."

"I know. It all depends on what went through the killer's mind while he held the gun. If this guy is a pro, he probably didn't think about himself when he pulled the trigger."

Samson nodded and led the way from the elevator to the

evidence room. Tommy was happy to see me, and his beard was free of crumbs today—wait, I spoke too soon. What I had thought was premature graying turned out to be powdered sugar from a donut.

Samson handed him a slip of paper, and Tommy disappeared into the stacks to get the gun. He returned with a heavy-duty plastic bag containing the pistol. Samson and I both signed a form, and I took the bag to a table in the corner.

I tuned out the small talk between the two men while I removed the gun from the bag. It had a yellow plastic tag with numbers on it hooked around the trigger guard. Right away, I sensed a paltry amount of psychic energy on the weapon. That's to be expected with one that was not held regularly for target practice and cleaning. Or killing.

I held my fingers close to the steel and surveyed what was here. Memories from Buddy, mostly. Lot of memories of examining and fondling it when he first brought it home, like a grownup boy with the best toy ever. Some memories firing it at a shooting range.

I came upon one powerful, poignant memory of Buddy's. I placed both hands on the weapon, on the handle and barrel, like Buddy when—

*—I put it on Damon's kitchen counter. "You need this," I say. "I get the feeling you're involved in some crap you're not telling me about that could blow up in your face. You need some protection." Damon gives me a hug that surprises me, even though we're both hammered from Happy Hour. "I'm protecting you," he says. "You gotta trust me." I want to hug him back—*

—He lifted his hands from the gun. This fits into the narrative I had, but there's nothing new here. I scanned the gun further, looking for another memory to dive into. There's very little energy from Damon on the weapon.

There was something here from an unknown person, a man. He laughs—

—*as I grab the weapon off Borgia's passenger seat and remove it from the car through the open window. "You can't leave your gun in the open like this," I say. "I don't care what kind of permit you have. There are drug addicts living here, man. Are you an idiot? You leave it out like that to impress your girlfriend, or something? She's not even allowed to have visitors after hours. I'm doing you a big favor, man, letting you see her. I'm gonna hang onto your piece for safekeeping." Stick it in the back of my pants—*

—and the energy from his back isn't focused like the energy from his hand, so I received nothing more that was useful.

That memory was obviously from a security guard, but he didn't provide clues to his identity. When he removed the gun from the car, his hand was briefly visible, revealing that he was a Caucasian. But that's all I had.

Was he the one who killed Damon? I had to find the memory of the actual shooting. I was nervous, hoping to have the payday Samson warned me not to expect.

And there it was—a man's intense memory. I couldn't tell if it was the security guard or a different person. He was perfectly focused on—

—*pulling the piece from under the seat, rolling down the window. Glare in my eyes from the sunlight reflecting from Borgia's window. These Ray-Ban polarized shades really help with that. Good shooting glasses. He's looking at me with food stuffed in his mouth. The pig. Smooth pull. Retort and recoil—nailed him right between the eyes. Another one in his mouth with all the food. My ears are ringing. Wipe the piece and toss it—*

—I was practically hyperventilating. It felt as if I had just shot Damon. That I, Darla, fired those bullets into his head. I experienced all the sensory inputs of shooting: the feel of the pistol kicking in my hand, the loud bangs, the smell of cordite. But what really got to me was the cold lack of emotion as the shooter saw the bullet hole flower in Damon's forehead, and the corn dog spray from his mouth.

Totally cold, without an ounce of empathy or revulsion or guilt. It was inhuman. And it was probably the mindset of a good number of the murderers out there in the world.

I wanted to be as far away from this gun as possible, *right now*, but I forced myself to scan it for any memories I had missed.

There were none. I managed to get it back into the bag with a minimal of skin contact.

"Tommy, can you take this gun?" I called to him.

Before he ended his conversation, Samson drew his thumb and forefinger across his mouth as if he were zipping his lips. Tommy nodded.

As I walked to the elevator, Samson asked if I had any luck.

"No, only a soul-crushing experience."

"Yeah, you look like you just killed someone."

"I feel exactly like I did."

"I HAVE SOME NUGGETS OF INFORMATION," I SAID WHEN I called Lidia. "I'm pretty certain that a security guard at the Shady Palms confiscated Buddy's gun from Damon at the sober home. So, either the security guard was the shooter, or he gave the gun to the shooter."

"How do you know this?"

"I can't explain at the moment," I said, trying to invent a reason why I can't. "I promised not to divulge my source. Also, the killer was wearing a pair of Ray-Bans with green shades. I'm not sure if those are his shooting glasses or if he wears them all the time. Please mention this when you ask your sources about the Emerald Man."

"Do you think he's called Emerald Man because of the green sunglasses?"

"The possibility crossed my mind. At first, I thought it was a guy who wears emerald jewelry, but you never know."

Speaking of things that cross your mind, and then settle in your gut, I had a hunch. And it nagged me too much to ignore.

I started with internet searches, not just name searches, but also scouring professional directories. I even checked the county's public records database. I came up with nothing.

So, I resorted to visiting the only other place I knew where I might have good luck. I drove there a couple of times a day for five days in a row with no results. I even went on a Sunday, when offices are closed, but facilities like this might be open.

Yes, the parking lot of Hopeful Recoveries was busy on a Sunday. I sat there for two hours until the person I wouldn't expect to see here on a weekend showed up after all.

I started my car and moved it to intercept him before he reached the building.

Jack Guarini looked good, sporting his Ray-Bans with green lenses. He also looked surprised as heck when I lowered my window and said hello.

"Ms. Chesswick? What are you doing here?"

"I could ask you the same thing. I saw you here recently and wanted to ask you if this was a conflict of interest. But, you know, I couldn't find where your office is. It's not listed anywhere. Buddy has your business card, but he's missing. As you know."

My telepathy was picking up alarm bells going off in Jack's head, but I wasn't hearing any coherent words. He came right up to my window and crouched, hands on the bottom of my opened window, pretending to be relaxed and intimate.

"No, it's not a conflict of interest. It's good for Buddy that I work with clients like this. You've seen the commercials for the personal injury attorneys who used to work for insurance companies, giving them inside knowledge? It's just like that."

*What does she know? Why is she here?*

After those words appeared in my head, along with powerful feelings of hostility, I did something impulsive. I know you're thinking, what, Darla doing something impulsive?

Yeah, impulsive and dangerous.

"Nice shades," I said. "I've never seen green lenses before."

"Thank you," he replied, relief pouring off him like heat. "Green polarized lenses are great for outdoor sports. They really cut out the glare of bright sunshine."

"Really? Let me see."

I reached out and plucked the glasses right from his face.

Then hit the gas and sped out of the parking lot.

# CHAPTER 25

# SHADES OF GREEN

You might think eyeglasses and sunglasses are ideal subjects for psychometrists, but that's not the case. Yes, you wear them on your face, but the only significant contact they have with you is the bridge of your nose and the cartilage of your ears —not the most sensitive of areas.

Glasses are worn for hours on end, which means we psychometrists have tons and tons of memories to sift through, most of which are low in psychic energy. Eyeglasses are the opposite of binoculars, which you hold in two hands while intently focused on something. Trying to glean memories from glasses that spend entire days perched on your nose is almost a waste of time.

Why did I steal them from Jack, then? Because I was desperate to get any insights I could. It's not like I'll ever have access to read his car or home.

And there's an exception to the caveats I mentioned above: when people are holding their glasses with their fingers. It could be grasping the arms when putting glasses on or off. It could be while you're cleaning the lenses, which often prompts introspective moods.

Some people, when they take off their glasses, like to play or fidget with them, often when their attention is centered elsewhere.

I truly hoped Jack did some serious thinking when he touched his glasses. Though I dreaded the hours of searching it would take to find the memories.

As soon as I returned to the inn, I told Cory what I was up to, although I edited the story to make me look like less of a lunatic. I took the shades after Jack had placed them on a table at the recovery center. Yeah, that's what happened.

I locked myself in the spare bedroom of the cottage, sat at the desk, and went to work on the sunglasses. I doubted Jack would show up here to demand his glasses back, but you never know. Cory promised to be my sentry.

If Jack knew about my psychometry, I could be a dead woman. But there's no way he would know.

Gulp. Unless Buddy told him. You couldn't rule out Buddy doing something stupid like that. But there was nothing I could do about it if he had.

Focus, Darla, focus.

The first thing I looked for were memories of Damon's murder. I needed to confirm my hunch about Jack. But boy, there were a lot of memories on these glasses. Jack wore them constantly.

Which is why he earned the nickname Emerald Man, as his memories confirmed. When he wasn't performing duties as an attorney, he refused to use his name among the recovery companies' lower-level employees and their patients. That's why they gave him a nickname.

I picked up memory fragments of violence and intimidation, mostly against patients, but also with employees.

Why was someone with a law degree working as a soldier for these criminals? It struck me as being below his education level, plus he was putting himself at risk of being disbarred. The impression I got was he'd had a rough upbringing, and criminal enterprises were not foreign to him.

The more I studied his memories, the more I concluded he was involved at the highest level with the scams and fraud the companies perpetuated. And he profited mightily from them.

Please understand that I came to these conclusions by piecing together brief fragments of memories from the arms of the sunglasses when he handled them, as well as faint, dull impressions left on the curved parts that rest on the ears and on the nose pads of the bridge.

Below layers of trivial memories, I found something. A memory of—

*—looking at my reflection on the glass door of the bank as I approach it and remove my shades. Looking good in my designer suit. I've come far for a changeling. Stolen from human parents I don't remember anymore, but old enough to realize the faeries who took me were using magic to make me one of them. But I didn't have enough Fae in me to satisfy the snobs, as I discovered later. They called me a changeling, a hybrid. Not pure enough for them, they teased. Well, look at me now. Raking in big bucks for myself while supplying the Fae with hundreds of human slaves. Show me a faerie who could get slaves this way, cleanly and undetected. Those idiots who try to kidnap humans by force only bring unwanted attention to us.*

*Ah, the bank manager is coming to greet me like I'm his best customer. Two million in cash to deposit from the gem sales, even after the quarter mil to the recovery sleazeoids for more slaves. (Slipping shades into inside breast pocket.)—*

—Wow. There's a lot to unpack in that memory. Not only does he confirm he ran the human trafficking, but he also reveals he's a faerie converted from a human.

And the reference to gems—it sounds like that's how the Fae raise their cash. I wonder where they get the gems? Could there be emeralds among them?

I returned to studying the sunglasses. The shooter's memory of killing Damon was on the gun, but it wasn't clear whose memory it was. Also, I wanted a bit more context to establish intent. Not that my findings were admissible in court, but I wanted to be absolutely certain so I could convince the police to find conventional evidence that backed up what I already knew.

Jack hadn't owned this pair of glasses for long. I found memory fragments of him trying on the frames. He told the salesperson he wanted polarized green lenses. That was all he ever wore. He mentioned they were great for outdoor activities, while he thought to himself they were perfect for shooting.

There were memories of shooting someone else, even though the glasses were recent. He put on the glasses one day at sunset, walking toward the car owned by a drug dealer who was selling at a sober home I didn't recognize. His gun weighed heavily in his side pocket. He knew that only Hopeful Recoveries sells on their properties. Anyone else must stay away or face the consequences.

I jumped out of that memory, not wanting to see what happened. Scanning through the psychic energy on the arms of the glasses, I skipped memory after memory of Jack putting on his glasses or taking them off in completely mundane circumstances. Until I—

—*take my sunglasses out of my pocket and buckle the seatbelt. George backs the Lexus out of my driveway. The big lug keeps volunteering to take on some of my assignments, but I don't trust him yet. He's just a violent meathead without a drop of intelligence or finesse. I need to be convinced he won't get caught. Okay, pull the piece from my waist and place it on the floor mat. There's Borgia's car up ahead, making its rounds. He's pulling into the Mega-Mart parking lot.*

"We're going to do it here," I say. *This is long overdue, with all he knows. Should have done it weeks ago when he showed up at the ranch. And after him, we'll do his partner. His car is parked all by itself. Slip on these lovely shooting shades, and away we go—*

—I drop the shades onto the desk. He was planning to kill Buddy, too. All the while, he was serving, or pretending to serve, as his defense attorney. It would be so easy to get Buddy alone somewhere to confer on his case and kill him.

And Buddy is missing now. It's my fault, too. Buddy probably knew nothing about the human trafficking until I told him to pass on the information to Jack about the patients disappearing at the ranch. I signed my ex-husband's death warrant.

How could Ron Dutton have referred this monster to us? At the restaurant that day, he had said to Jack that this case was "right up your alley." I guess he knew Jack worked with recovery companies. But he didn't know the ghastly extent of Jack's services.

I called Samson.

"I found out who killed Damon Borgia, and I think he killed Buddy, too. As usual, a lot of what I know came from my psychometry. Please, please help me find a way to get Siwicki on board."

He sighed. "It's not going to be easy. I would need at least one solid piece of evidence that would change Siwicki's mind and get him to look for more evidence that would be admissible in court. Tell me more about the case."

It had been a while since I downloaded Samson on my findings. So, I rattled off everything I knew, beginning with Guarini and even including the crazy Fae stuff. It took a while, until my mouth grew tired of talking. And that's saying something for me.

"Buried in all the unbelievable stuff, there are some concrete building blocks for a case," Samson said. "Out of all the missing patients, there will be some people who knew them and are wondering what happened to them. They can be interviewed. We can subpoena the security camera tapes at the Shady Palms. I'm sure they exist and will show patients being rounded up and sent away, plus, hopefully, the guard taking the weapon away from Damon."

"Good."

"The big, violent-looking guard you saw through memories is someone we need to bring in. You said Guarini's memory had him driving the car to the murder. That means he's an accessory. Even if we have no proof, we can lean on him and see if he gives up Guarini. And we can interview the security contractor you spoke to. All these create a foundation we can build upon to find additional evidence."

"Will Siwicki cooperate?" I asked.

"He will once he sees the evidence. I'll do some of the work myself, just enough not to overstep my boundaries. And your ex has been gone long enough to file a missing-persons report. That will add some urgency for Siwicki."

"Thank you," I said.

"Don't thank me yet. There's a lot of work to do."

And meanwhile, Jack knows I'm onto him.

IT WAS SURPRISING I HADN'T THOUGHT OF THIS SOONER, BUT recent developments reminded me that I still had the Druid Disc. This prehistoric stone, polished by millennia in the running water of a stream, had been engraved with a triskelion symbol centuries ago, when Danu was actively worshipped by the Celtic peoples of Ireland and across Europe.

A wizard had given it to a woman I had once helped, and she told me to keep it. I climbed up the stepladder and found the shoebox on the top shelf in the back of our bedroom closet. I had mostly forgotten about it, even though the woman had encouraged me to use it.

You see, this small, flat rock that easily fit in the palm of one's hand had a rare power.

The power of truth.

The stone had been carved and imbued with magic by the Tuatha Dé Danann, ancient people of Ireland who were called the Children of Danu. The stone was passed around among the ancient Druids of Britain and Ireland, who claimed it could tell you if someone was lying.

It was said that Merlin himself used it to determine if Arthur was worthy of becoming king.

The stone also had the power to undo black magic. Unlike white magic, that could permanently alter the physical world, black magic was based more upon illusion—tricking your senses to believe something has been altered.

In short, black magic was a form of falsehood. And the Druid Disc could undo it. With it, I had successfully broken the spells of a necromancer who had brought executed killers back to life. But that is a story for another time.

I confess I had forgotten about the stone because it hadn't been relevant to my work as a psychometrist. People's memories are usually genuine, if slightly biased. I hadn't come across anyone who was such a liar that their own thoughts and emotions were lies.

Yet, I had never before faced the direct influence of the

Father of Lies, as we did now with his influence over the rogue factions of the Fae.

I found the sandy-colored stone inside a felt jewelry sack that was swaddled with tissues in a shoebox. The three curls of the triskelion were still pronounced. The stone was not a perfect circle, though maybe it had been long ago before the elements took their toll on it. It didn't feel powerful in my hand, but I knew it was. I slipped it into my pocket, vowing to always keep it with me.

I decided to carry the enchanted pearl with me, as well. The gem had been useful in amplifying the magic of the witches in my family, though I didn't know if it would be useful with the Goddess-imbued gifts I now had. Yet, it couldn't hurt to have it, just in case.

## CHAPTER 26

# FIENDISH INFECTION

I was walking through the main hallway of the inn when I heard a familiar English accent coming from the front parlor.

"Oh, Darla? I wish to have a word with you."

No guests were around, so it was perfectly okay to chat with an animated gargoyle. I entered the room.

"Did you hear about the vampires?" he asked, about to burst with the gossip he wished to share.

"No, I didn't. You're aware that no one shares any news with me. I'm always the last to know."

"It is as you feared. Diego reports that Pedro opened the box and released the magic. It is a black-magic spell of some sort that has infected the vampires of San Marcos and surrounding environs."

"How does it affect them?"

"That remains to be seen. Thus far, they have pledged their allegiance to the Fae. In truth, it's more as if they bent the knee to the Faerie Queene, agreeing to be ruled by her. They have broken their ties to the other guilds."

"That's terrible!"

"It's as if the Fae have conquered a major proportion of our city's supernaturals without a battle."

"Was Diego infected, too?"

"Thankfully, no. He was not with any vampires when this happened. Somehow, he learned about it, then fled his home. I hear he broke into Arch Mage Bob's surf shop overnight and has taken refuge there. Bob is developing a spell that will protect Diego from the infection."

"Has anyone else been affected, aside from the vampires?" I asked.

"We don't know yet. I'm guessing the spell adapts to attack a specific species or race and will affect similar creatures. I'm concerned that other undead creatures will catch it, too, such as zombies and ghouls."

"Zombies and ghouls aren't the sharpest tools in the shed. It wouldn't take much to convince them to follow the Fae."

"And that's the way it will work," Archibald said. "Piece by piece, the Fae will peel the guilds away from the others until they rule the entire region."

"I would like to speak with Diego."

"It has already been arranged. Our guild is meeting at Bob's shop tonight after dark."

"I'm always the last to know."

PAGAN SURF SHOP STAYS OPEN LATE TO MILK EVERY DROP OUT OF the tourists who hang out in San Marcos' beach area. Actual surfers are a minority of the clientele. The members of the Memory Guild include several fuddy-duddies like me who don't like to stay up too late, so we crowded into the back room of the shop with our vampire comrade while tourists were still browsing the T-shirts up front.

Diego looked haunted. The gorgeous, young vampire of African descent looked pale and anemic, like he hadn't feasted on blood for some time while simultaneously being frightened to his core.

Since Diego had been possessed by an evil spirit before, I assumed he was especially vulnerable to magic like this. And especially eager to avoid being controlled again.

We watched while Bob finished casting his anti-infective spell, which involved clouds of foul incense and a great deal of loud chanting. Bob's assistant complained through the closed door that the smell was chasing customers away. Bob's own parrot, Florence, complained loudly from her perch beside his desk.

"So, dude, are you sure you haven't been infected at all?" Bob asked after it was done.

"I believe I have been spared so far," Diego said.

"You're gonna need to stay away from other vampires."

Diego nodded sadly.

"Tell us all you know," Dr. Noordlun said.

"Ever since Pedro learned about the box at the Executive Council meeting, he talked incessantly about it. I don't know why he was so fascinated. I suspect he sensed the power of the magic once the box was brought up from the Fae's underground world. He mentioned it in the last meeting of the Clan of the Eternal Night. He said we must find it. The magic is too powerful for humans to handle, but we, being superior creatures, could harness it to become even more powerful. I had my doubts, but he ordered the Vampire Thieves to find it and its key."

"Steal it, is more accurate," I said.

"What is done is done."

"How did they find the box? It was associated with me—that's how they found the key. But what about the box?"

Diego turned to Dr. Noordlun. "I'm sorry, professor. Pedro learned its location from you. At some point, he visited and mesmerized you. He made you divulge the hiding place and then wiped out your memory of his visit."

Dr. Noordlun groaned and rubbed his eyes.

"I am good friends with Pedro's human housekeeper. Well, much more than friends," Diego said with a smile. "She told me what happened next. Once the box and key were found, Pedro, the thieves, and his inner circle gathered at his estate for an unboxing party. It did not go well."

"That is why we're here," Archibald muttered.

"My friend told me when the box was opened, it was empty. No cloud of gas or spraying of dust came forth from it. Pedro assured everyone not to worry, because the magic was invisible, of course. The rest of the night was spent sipping champagne and the blood of an unfortunate gang of teenagers who had been looking for a house to rob."

Diego shuddered as if he were ill. "Are you certain your spell will protect me?" he asked Bob.

Bob shrugged. "As certain as I can be trying to guard you against a spell no one has ever encountered before. We don't even know who created it. It wasn't the Fae, that's for sure. I can sense some of their magic has been added to it, but they didn't create the main spell."

"Okay. That makes sense. The spell of which we speak is so insidious because you can't tell you're enchanted. Pedro's guests were complaining, as if they had hoped to get high and didn't.

Suddenly, a faerie showed up. That's what my friend believes he was, though he was in human form. And the moment he appeared, all the vampires in the house dropped to the floor and prostrated themselves before him. Even Pedro."

"That does not sound like Pedro," I said. Or, I thought, any of those arrogant vampires.

"The faerie commanded that they swear their allegiance to the Faerie Queene and to the god Aastacki."

"Oh no," I said. "Aastacki is the Fae version of The Father of Lies."

"Maybe that's who created the spell," Diana said.

"This does not bode well," Dr. Noordlun said.

"The faerie told our vampires that the Fae are the supreme beings of the earth. Just below them are the vampires. And every other creature is inferior—humans, other supernaturals, paranormals, everyone—and no better than animals. You have no rights whatsoever and exist solely for the benefit and pleasure of the Fae and the vampires, with the Fae being the ruler of us all."

The room was silent as all this sank in.

"The Executive Council has gathered intelligence about the Fae's armies," Dr. Noordlun said. "It's possible we have been overestimating the size of their forces, based on intel about their movements here from all across Florida and the Southeastern United States. There is no doubt the number of faeries here has increased, but we haven't seen evidence of large armies—even under the assumption they're hiding underground."

"What are you implying?" James asked.

"I'm not implying anything. I'm theorizing the Fae have never planned to wage massive, pitched battles against us— which would be impossible to conceal from the human population. What if their plan was simply to convert all the guilds into their supplicants? They would then rule all the supernaturals and be able to influence the humans indirectly. They'd be the puppeteers of us all, while hiding out of view."

"It's a good theory," I said. "After all, they now control the vampires. But how are they going to convert the rest of us? Can the same box infect us, too?"

Screams and shouts came from the front of the shop.

"What the heck?" Bob headed for the office door.

"Wait!" Diego shouted. "It's a vampire attack. They have the entire Memory Guild and the Arch Mage of the Magic Guild all in one place. Let's not make it easy for them to turn you."

Of course, if we were all bitten and turned, we would serve the vampires that made us and, thus, the Fae whom they served. The vampires could go on to turn the Shifter Guild, Magic Guild, and the others. I didn't know if trolls and gnomes could be turned into vampires, but there would be a way to put them in thrall to the Fae without a military battle.

"I have to go out there," Bob said. "Those are innocent humans. With big, fat credit lines they were hoping to spend in my store."

"I doubt the vampires will kill them," Diego said. "And the humans can be mesmerized to make them forget all of this."

"And maybe still buy some bikinis and sunglasses," I muttered. Everyone ignored my sarcasm.

Diego continued, "We must stick together and stay in here. Bob, can you cast a protection spell?"

"Already working on it, dude." Bob sat cross-legged on the floor, his back against the door. He silently mouthed incantations while moving his hands in intricate patterns. It seems that each witch I know has different techniques for casting spells.

"What happens if the vampires get in here?" Summer asked.

"We must fashion makeshift stakes from the tools in the surfboard workshop," Diego said.

"You would stake your fellow vampires?"

"They're not my fellow vampires anymore. They're nothing but slaves, enthralled by magic to the Fae. And if you think they would hesitate before destroying me, you're naïve. Whereas you humans, you have no idea how quickly you can be drained to death, and how painful it is to be brought back into existence as one of the undead."

"I'm told once you get through the transition, you lot have quite a merry time," Archibald said. "Hot tub parties at the Alhambra Hotel? Really?"

"Obviously, *you* can't be turned, only destroyed," Diego replied crossly.

After Bob finished casting his protection spell, Diana began working on her own version of one. Things were heating up far too quickly, though.

The customers' screams from the front of the store had faded and snarling vampires threw themselves against the door. Bob had had the foresight, when Diego first showed up, to close the hurricane shutters covering the windows of the office and workshop. Vampires were already at the back of the building, attempting to tear away the aluminum folding shutters and batter through the rear door with brute force.

Meanwhile, my fellow guild members were gathering every cylindrical object—metal, wood, or plastic—that could be turned into a stake and sharpening each one with Bob's files and sanders. The situation looked grim, with no one knowing how many vampires were trying to get in, and no one to rescue us. We couldn't call 911, after all. I hoped none of the humans had been able to call for help. I didn't want first responders to be attacked by the vampires.

"I can summon a gateway to get us out of here," I said. I was met with expressions of fear because most of the guild members had never passed through the mysterious portals before.

"We can't simply run away," Diego said. "We must drive them from the property, otherwise it will forever belong to the vampires. Regardless of whose name is on the deed."

"Really?" Bob asked, turning as pale as a vampire.

"Yes."

"Is your protection spell going to keep them from breaching the doors?" Dr. Noordlun asked Bob.

"The perimeter of the protection bubble is attached to the outside surfaces of these doors and walls. They can bang on the door all they freaking want, but I'm pretty sure they can't get in. If you guys will give me some space to think, I'll work on a warding spell to drive them away."

One of the aluminum shutters tore away with a horrible screech.

A surfboard smashed through the window glass and flew into the room, hitting Bob in the belly.

"I said I was *pretty* sure," he gasped.

A male vampire clad in black appeared on the windowsill. Before he could jump into the room, James charged, roaring, and thrust a metal rod upward into its abdomen. The vampire screamed. Black goo poured from the wound as the creature fell backwards from the windowsill into the parking lot.

"Wow," James said, peering from the broken window. "He's shriveling up and turning to ash. Oh, crap—"

Another black-clad figure leaped toward the opening. James speared him with the same rod.

"Need a little help here," James said, panic in his voice.

"Chill, dudes," Bob said. "I'm repairing the holes in the protection bubble. The vamps must be using Fae magic."

"As if they weren't dangerous enough," Archibald grumbled.

"Just speaking for myself," Diana said, "but human magic is nothing against Fae magic."

"How many vampires are in your guild?" James asked Diego.

"More than a hundred."

"I think they're all here tonight."

Two more vampires rushed to the window. James fought one, which was attempting to wrest the rod away from him. Diego savagely attacked the other one, swinging his hands with elongated claws like scythes. He made quick work of his opponent, then turned his attention to James' foe.

The inside door to the store shuddered as vampires threw themselves against it. I wondered how long it would hold.

I think it was clear to all that the tide was turning against us. I would have to call a gateway, like a rescue helicopter, to get us out of here, and let Bob deal with having a vampire landlord.

But Summer put her hand on my shoulder and whispered into my ear,

"Remember, you have the goddess in you. You are the Daughter of Danu."

So what? I wanted to say but didn't. The vampires don't consider me their deity, and I'm not a warrior goddess throwing thunderbolts. All I am is the mortal manifestation of a mother goddess, an earth goddess. I create and heal. I don't knock off vampires.

*Yes, ye can heal*, said a voice in my head. I recognized it as Birog's, the druid who schooled me on what Danu would want from me. *And ye can bring peace to a conflict. These bloodsuckers are controlled by a magic that comes of hate and lies and the disease of rot and pollution. That's the opposite of what ye stand for as a goddess. It's what ye fight against in yer guild.*

It dawned on me that the magic controlling the vampires

really must have come from the Father of Lies himself, he who has been polluting the minds of the Fae.

*A little slow on the uptake, aren't ye?*

I ignored her, and all the chaos erupting around me, trying to focus, hoping to draw upon the goddess' power.

What's a goddess to do?

A vision walloped me, just as strong as when I have a reverie from my psychometry.

I was standing in a dense, ancient forest, with moss-covered tree trunks and a thousand shades of green surrounding me. The water of a stream tinkled nearby. The birds sang of happiness that I was here, and the root systems of the trees beneath me merrily exchanged messages about their pleasure, as well.

This is the world The Father of Lies had been banished from. It is a world of purity and goodness, and even as the birds feed upon insects, the deaths are necessary for sustenance. They are not deaths resulting from greed or hatred. They were part of the Creator's plan.

Yes, nature can be brutal, but it was inherently beautiful and good. Nothing is wasted. It is all about life, survival, expanding the numbers of the living. Being fruitful and multiplying.

Vampirism appears to go against the laws of nature, but only at first glance. Vampires have their own rules based on biology and physics, with plenty of the supernatural mixed in. Vampires, too, are the children of God, not of Satan. For Satan can only create demons.

As I stood in the forest among the innocent creatures that lived there, I realized the magic that enthralled the vampires to The Father of Lies was itself based on lies, on illusions.

Nature is the opposite of lies and illusions.

I had to convince the vampires that they were enslaved to

falsehoods. To do so, I had to dip into the goddess powers I have acquired but didn't yet know or understand.

I didn't believe I had the power to break the spell that infected them. At least, not yet. But I believed I could put it on pause.

My vision faded as I returned to the back room of Pagan Surf Shop. Vampires still raged and fought to enter the room through all its doors and windows so they could drain us, turn us into vampires, and rule us.

My companions' faces were tight with desperation as they barricaded the doors and fought the vampires at the breached window. Bob struggled to fortify his protection spell that had been overcome by the Fae magic the vampires used. Diana, too, was casting a spell, but didn't look confident it would help.

I, however, felt at peace now, the love of the Goddess filling me with joy and resolve. It was time to act, but I didn't know what to do.

*Just run with it*, Birog said in my head.

I sang. Yeah, it was like this action-adventure movie turned into a Broadway musical as I broke into song. The startled looks on my companion's faces showed they were equally surprised by the musical interlude.

I had no choice. It simply came to me—the rush of melody and emotion that poured out of my heart and into my lungs. I'd never heard the song before, but somehow, I knew the ancient, timeless tune. The words were in a language I didn't understand, but they flowed from me fluently.

What also flowed from me was a tremendous power. It didn't belong to me, but was simply channeled through me. I was the vessel for the Goddess' healing magic.

For that's what I realized I must do: heal the vampires, even if only temporarily. Wash away the hatred and lies that infected them, like one would cleanse bacteria from a wound. Then, in time, the wound would heal itself.

My song grew louder, with more volume than I thought possible from this set of lungs. Everyone still looked at me with shock, but no one covered their ears, at least. Maybe I can carry a tune better than I had believed from my drunken karaoke incidents.

Another vampire jumped up on the outside windowsill. He, too, appeared confused by my singing. He even seemed to like it. His fangs protruded over the beginnings of a smile.

Until James impaled him with the metal rod.

Stunning the enemy is not the purpose of the song, I wanted to say to James, but the music wouldn't allow me.

My volume increased, well past operatic levels, past rock-band amplification levels, even. The song vibrated throughout my body, from my skull to my toes and fingertips. The walls, floor, and ceiling drummed with the rhythm.

Bob's parrot picked up the tune at a higher octave. We were now a duet in harmony.

Finally, the pounding on the inner and outer doors ceased. So did the rending sounds of the aluminum hurricane shutters. It was as if the vampires were lulled into inaction or had left the property. I continued singing for a little longer, just in case.

I stopped and felt the Goddess' powers dissipate from me.

"What the heck was that?" Laurel asked.

"Oh, the Goddess," I replied.

"I believe that was ancient Gaelic," Dr. Noordlun said.

"What matters is what it did to the spell," Bob said. "Did the song break the spell?"

"I don't know," I said.

"The vampires are gone," Diego said. "I don't believe they

have been freed from the spell completely, but this is a promising beginning.

I explained the realization I'd had about The Father of Lies being the creator of the spell, as Diana had questioned earlier.

"That makes sense," Dr. Noordlun said. "It's clear that whatever powers the Goddess gives you will be instrumental in breaking the spell for good."

"And defeating The Father of Lies for good," James said, still panting from the fight.

"I don't know if it's possible to defeat him permanently. Though we can lessen his hold on the Fae.

"I really wonder where the black box came from," I said.

"The Father of Lie's lair," Dr. Noordlun said. "Or Hell itself."

"Until the spell is broken, you've got to avoid the other vampires," Bob said to Diego. "And in a few days, I'll reinforce the anti-infective spell I cast upon you."

"I will. Now, please excuse me while I go up front and mesmerize your customers, so they forget what happened and ignore any puncture wounds on their necks."

We were safe for now. But I had the nagging feeling that this emergency was far from over.

# CHAPTER 27

# FENDER BENDER

"**D**o you *really* feel safer with me as your bodyguard?" Cory asked after we got in the car, and I started down Cadiz Street on the way to the home improvement store on the outskirts of town.

"Don't take this the wrong way," I said, "but who else is going to protect me? We can't afford to hire security."

"The police, I would think."

"I'm not an official witness. Most of what I know in the case against Jack, I found out through paranormal means. In the eyes of the law, it's not real."

"Are you sure he knows you took his glasses from the table?"

See, this is what happens when you lie. It forces you to lie to support your lie. It was time to stop.

"Yeah, he noticed. Especially since I actually swiped them off his face."

"You what?"

"He was leaning into my car window trying to intimidate me."

"Darla, what is wrong with you? Why are you so reckless?"

"Adventurous. I like that word better."

"Sheesh. Okay, let's try to look on the bright side. He won't know that you can get information from his glasses."

"That's what I'm hoping. But remember, he's a faerie, even if a hybrid one. He could probably sense the paranormal in me. So, he's got to be wondering if I'm going to use the glasses against him."

"I don't know."

"I've also stormed in on his client and partner, the owner of the recovery company. I saw the guy buying drugs, for Pete's sake. If Jack mentioned me to him, they'll both know I'm a threat."

We drove in silence for a while until Cory broke it.

"If I'm your bodyguard, I should mention that I'm still a lousy shot."

"Have you been training?"

"Yeah. I'm taking a class at the shooting range. And I've been practicing, too."

He didn't sound thrilled about it.

"Let's hope you won't need to use the gun. It's just that Jack Guarini is a stone-cold killer, so we have to be prepared."

I turned onto San Marcos Avenue and headed out of town, crossing the salt marsh and creek.

"I'm a photographer and a handyman. Not an effective body-guard against a stone-cold killer."

"You're all I've got, sweetie."

We traveled down the busy street lined with shopping centers and box stores. Pulling into the parking lot of the home improvement store, I found a spot away from the crowds.

So why did this idiot park right next to me when there are plenty of other spaces?

"Why is that guy so close?" Cory asked. "Can you still open your door?"

My heart lurched. I recognized the car, a Lexus, from Damon's memory just before he was shot.

The car's passenger seat window slid down. I knew how this story went.

I hadn't turned off the engine yet, so I threw the car in reverse. It lurched from our spot and hit a shopping cart.

"Hey!" the shopper shouted.

Tires screeching, I sped toward the exit, the Lexus right behind me.

"What the heck are you doing?" Cory shouted.

"The guy in that car was about to shoot me. That's the same technique he used to shoot Damon."

"I'm calling nine-one-one. I can do that, right? This isn't a supernatural monster attack, right?"

"Call them."

Cory breathlessly told the operator what was going on, along with a description of both cars.

"Did we see a gun?" Cory said into the phone. He turned to me. "Did we?"

"Yes."

"Yeah, we did. And she recognized the guy as a suspect in recent murders. His name is Jack Guarini. Yes. No, I don't know how to spell it."

I spelled it for him. I needed to focus on my driving, not spelling lessons.

I reached the intersection where the shopping center exit met the main road. The traffic light was red. Cars blocked both the left- and right-turn lanes. We were trapped.

"He won't shoot us here, right?" Cory asked. "It's too public."

He was correct. The shooter's car waited patiently behind us.

I studied it in my rearview mirror. Though the windshield was lightly tinted, I saw the big, violent guy behind the wheel and Jack in the passenger seat. He had found a new pair of shades to wear.

The light finally turned green, and I turned right as soon as the car in front of me did. The Lexus followed us closely. I figured they were waiting for an opportunity to drive us off the road and shoot us.

"Where are we going?" Cory asked.

"To the Police Department."

"Good decision."

The problem was, Guarini probably expected us to do exactly that.

As we crossed the bridge over the saltwater creek, the Lexus pulled into the lane to our left and came up beside us. Then, the car moved to the right, making contact with ours, pushing us toward the bridge railing.

"They're trying to knock us off the bridge!" Cory said, reaching for the pistol in the glove compartment.

I slammed on the brakes. Cory's head hit the dashboard.

The Lexus turned sharply right, crunching into us, now blocking us at an angle. I reversed in a panic until the car behind us slammed into us. Cory's head hit the dash again.

Thankfully, the airbags didn't activate.

"Call nine-one-one again with our location," I said. "At least we have a witness now in the car that rear-ended us."

Now, it was Jack who couldn't open his door, as it was crumpled around the left front of my car. Instead, the big thug exited the driver's seat and walked around their car toward my door.

He can't shoot me right here in front of everyone. Can he?

The thug leaned down right outside my window and motioned for me to roll it down. I shook my head no.

"Sorry for the fender-bender," he said through the glass. "Do you want to get out so we can exchange information?"

"No."

"What are we going to do?" Cory asked. "I can't just shoot him like this."

I looked in the rearview mirror. The woman driving the car behind us remained behind the wheel. The traffic behind us was trying to get around the one and a half lanes we blocked. No one else was stopping. No flashing lights approached that I could see.

The man looked around, too. He put on a pair of leather work gloves.

And smashed my window with his fist, repeatedly. The shattered safety glass ballooned inward.

"What the heck?" Cory shouted as he tried to open his door. It was so close to the bridge railing it only opened a short distance. He tried to squeeze through the opening.

The thug was making good progress in smashing the window. All the glass fell away, and he reached right into the car and across me to unfasten my seatbelt. Then he grabbed me and simply lifted me from the car.

My fists beating his face and chest had no effect at all.

He threw me over his shoulder, walked calmly to his car, and tossed me into the backseat. With a scraping of metal, his car disengaged from ours, and he sped across the bridge into town.

A police car with flashing lights passed us in the opposite direction, taking my hope of survival with it.

"Where are we going?" the beefy driver asked.

"Zane's," Guarini replied.

"Really?"

"Yeah. I want to chat with her first. And even though you mangled the side of my car, I don't want to replace the interior, too."

Replace the interior? Oh, he means after it's soaked with my blood. Of course.

We veered off onto a rutted industrial road that followed the shore of the salt creek. Up ahead was a boat ramp, a dock, and a half dozen boat storage houses. The place was deserted.

*I'll make her tell me everything she knows, then pop her. We'll toss her in the creek wrapped in an anchor chain.*

Sometimes my telepathy was helpful. This time, it only scared me to death.

The child door locks prevented me from jumping out of the car. We rolled to a stop on the crunchy dirt lot too soon, anyway.

You should know by now that I don't have powers like a superhero. I'm not a witch with magic to fight back with. I can't shift into a fearsome animal who can tear these guys apart. I basically only read minds and memories left upon objects. Not a good defense against a nine-millimeter pistol.

Maybe once I've grown into the powers given to me by the Goddess, I'll be able to turn the killers into donkeys or something. At the moment, my main ability seemed to be healing. That's not going to help here.

But I do have one very handy ability now that I have the Goddess in me. I can summon gateways as easily as taxis. And a lot faster. The mysterious portal-creatures seem to have more and more of an affinity with me.

I can get one now to whisk me away before I'm tortured and shot. Or maybe I should whisk the bad guys away and send them to the In Between. That would be much more convenient for me. And with them safely out of my hair, I could always send

Samson to retrieve them if the police were serious about charging them.

Or maybe I should just bail on my own.

"Park closer to the building," Guarini said.

As the thug drove forward, I realized the gateway had already shown up. The shimmering air was right in front of us. My stomach was queasy from our proximity to it.

And the meathead drove us right into it.

I ONCE WONDERED IF AN INTERNAL COMBUSTION ENGINE would work in the In Between. I had my answer now.

No.

Guarani's Lexus sat lifeless on the vast expanse of a beach. I'd been on this beach before. The distance from the sand dunes to the water's edge was like two football fields. It was flat, hard-packed sand that would have been perfect to drive upon, if only cars worked in the In Between.

"What the heck?" Guarini said.

"Where are we?" asked his goon.

"We're in the In Between, an alternate plane of existence apart from the earth," I helpfully explained. "Souls of the dead come here when it hasn't been determined yet if they will end up in Heaven or Hell. Mythological creatures, like dragons, hide out here from humans. And persecuted humans hide out here from other humans. Plus, there are tons of deadly monsters that can eat you. It's not a good place to be if you don't have magic."

"I have Fae magic," Guarini said.

"But do you know how to use it here?"

"You're really annoying, Chesswick. I should have shot you before this."

"Well, you need me now if you want to get back to earth. There's no food or water here. Unless you know how to create it with magic."

The angry expression on his face told me he didn't.

"So, how do we get out of here?"

"We walk until we come upon another gateway. That's what the portals are called."

I wasn't going to tell him I could summon a gateway. I had other plans.

"Let's just kill her and find our own gateway," the goon said.

"The gateways know me. They'll only come for me." It wasn't completely true, but there was no guarantee a gateway would appear anywhere near these guys, especially if they're jerks.

"Follow me, boys." I started walking up the beach with the water's edge to my right, almost touching my feet. There were no waves or tides, so I didn't worry about getting my feet wet.

My plan was to bump into a certain creature I had run away from once before. I put myself into a semi-meditative state, focusing on my inner energies and trying to tap into the Goddess.

*I summon you, king of the depths*, I broadcasted with my telepathy. *I need your assistance.*

We walked for a while, and I continued my call. Finally, I felt the connection.

"How far do we have to walk?" Guarini whined behind me.

"Not much farther."

The sea was a lifeless composition of flat, still water and a cloudless sky. No birds flew, and no fish jumped. You would be forgiven to think the scene was all an illusion.

Until the tentacle rose from the surface of the water.

Then another. They were dozens of feet long, thicker farther from their tips, and covered in suction cups.

The kraken had arrived.

*Take them*, I commanded.

The tentacles shot toward the beach like torpedoes, making V-wakes in the still water. Guarini and his goon were too busy arguing whether they should shoot me to notice them. Until the tentacles tapped them on the shoulders.

The two men's screams were surprisingly high-pitched, like those of little girls.

The goon was seized instantly around the waist and dragged into the water. Guarini dodged the tentacle coming for him and pulled out his pistol. He discharged a full clip, but the kraken didn't seem to mind.

The goon, wrapped tightly by the tentacle, was held ten feet above the water. He drew his own pistol and fired wildly as the kraken swung him back and forth.

"Ow! You shot me, you idiot!" Guarini clutched his thigh and dropped to the sand, emptying a second clip at the tentacle that reached for him.

It appeared he had run out of ammo.

The kraken didn't realize this, of course, and decided that one human would be good enough for dinner. It cruised back out to sea, eventually pulling the goon beneath the surface.

Guarini dropped his pistol on the sand and lay down next to it, crying. He was losing a lot of blood.

"You need a tourniquet, dude," I said, kicking his pistol away, even though I assumed it was empty. "Give me your necktie."

He hesitated. "It was expensive."

"You're going to bleed to death. And who wears a necktie in Florida to kill someone, anyway? You're such a tool."

I unknotted his tie and yanked it from his collar. I wrapped it around his thigh above the bullet wound and jerked hard to tighten it.

He yelped in pain.

I jerked harder. "Got to stop the flow. You might have a nicked artery. Since you wanted to talk with me before you killed me, I'll share that I know you killed Damon Borgia."

He didn't acknowledge or deny it.

"Did you also kill Buddy Grimes?"

"The partner? No, not yet."

"I don't believe you."

"Why would I lie to you now?"

Good point. He was close to bleeding out on an otherworldly plane of existence. If not, a monster ghost crab would probably get him. They're attracted to the smell of blood.

It was time to return home, though.

*May I have a gateway, please?* I asked telepathically.

In seconds, an area of shimmering about ten feet by ten feet appeared nearby.

*Can you come over here and pick us up? This guy's too heavy for me to move.*

The gateway came and swept us up. And suddenly, we were back on the bridge, right in front of our disabled car that still blocked the right lane. A police car with blinking lights sat in front of us, and Cory spoke with the officer a few feet from where we landed.

The officer gaped at me like he was about to have a seizure.

"This guy is a murderer who attempted to kill me," I told the cop. "Please put him in handcuffs and call Detective Siwicki."

"I gather a gateway brought you back here?" Cory asked.

"Yeah. I meant to use it to escape from the killers, but it took all three of us, including their car, to the In Between."

"Did you shoot Guarini?"

"No, his goon did it by mistake. They were attacked by a kraken I summoned. I'd encountered it before, and I figured the

Goddess would inspire it to obey me. He took the goon, and I feel guilty about it. I'm supposed to be all about life and fecundity. Not about killing."

"You were feeding the poor, hungry kraken like a true earth-mother would."

"Now that you put it that way, I feel a bit better."

# CHAPTER 28

## LIES

My phone rang with an unfamiliar number.

"Darla, this is Francis. We haven't spoken in a while."

"I know. How are you?"

"I think you'll want to come by the gallery right away."

"Now?" I asked. I was in the middle of breakfast service, and it wasn't a good time for me to leave.

"Yes. There's something you should see. Something very special. And I don't know who else to call."

"Can you give me a hint of what it is?"

"There are people in the sinkhole under my store."

Sophie had just wandered into the kitchen, rubbing her sleepy face. She was pouring herself coffee, ready to relax and eat some breakfast before it was time for her to clean up. I handed her the serving spoon in my hand, the one from the scrambled eggs.

"You need to take over breakfast for me. Another batch of

muffins will be done in fifteen minutes. And we're running low on biscuits and gravy."

I went to the alley, got in my car, and raced to the gallery.

When I arrived, the art installation covering the hole in the floor had been shifted aside. Francis and her assistant reached into the hole, helping people climb up the ladder and onto the gallery floor.

They were men and women, from their twenties to their sixties. Emaciated, pale, and dirty, they still had enough strength to make it up the ladder, with a little help, into the civilized world. They looked around apprehensively, their pupils dilated from their time spent in the darkness. Their clothes were torn and ragged. Their hands were calloused and caked with dirt.

They looked like slaves because that's what they were.

"My God, where have you been?" I asked a woman with a gaunt face who kneeled upon the floor next to the hole, catching her breath.

"We have been digging tunnels," she said, "and harvesting fungus. The little monsters whip us if we don't work fast enough."

"Were you a substance-abuse-disorder patient?"

She nodded and broke into tears. Francis pulled her to her feet.

"We need to get them food and water," I said to Francis. "And see if any need medical attention. But I have to make sure their stories are safe to tell the authorities."

I quickly sent a group text to the members of the Memory Guild with the good news. I also asked for advice on how to keep the freed prisoners from spreading wild stories about the Fae.

"How did you all escape?" I asked a woman who emerged from the hole.

"With our help," said a man who was standing behind me, leaning against an alcove wall.

He was slight and short, though taller than me, of course. He had black hair and olive skin, with dark brown Mayan eyes.

"Are you an Alux?" I asked.

He nodded and smiled with the whitest teeth I have ever seen.

"I am Alfonso. I helped rescue you from the camazotz. You don't recognize me in my human form."

Just like the conventional Fae, an Alux in human form did not lead the observer to think he had faerie blood at first glance.

"You've come to the rescue again," I said, patting him on the shoulder.

"We're outnumbered by these Old-World Fae," he said. "But we've been busy fighting them. We've been digging tunnels to cut off theirs, and today we connected with one. We sent in a raiding party and were shocked to find a subterranean limestone shelf where all these humans were toiling away."

"They made us their slaves," the woman said.

"We led them up through the tunnels of the Fae, large tunnels meant to accommodate humans. The tunnels were unguarded and abandoned, except for one sentry we took out. We sensed it was the most direct route to the surface, and it brought us to the cavern down there. Funny thing, but it smelled like cow poop."

"No, it's not funny. Believe me, it was bull poop."

The next person to climb up the ladder, an African American man, was muscular and wore tactical gear. He looked awfully familiar.

"Hey, you're from the platoon of shifters," I said. "I thought you were all killed."

"We had heavy losses. Our leader, Jeff, eventually died from his wounds. But we escaped the minotaur and wandered lost in the tunnels for two days until the Fae captured us. They put us to work with their other slaves."

"I'm so relieved to see you made it."

"I need to speak to the Executive Council with information that can help us."

I texted the shifter's request to the group.

"Please tell me what you learned," I asked.

"The Fae have a strange issue with running water. I don't understand it. They drink water and bathe in it, but they stay away from underground water pipes and subterranean streams. If groundwater leaks into one of their tunnels, they don't repair the leak—they abandon the tunnel."

I remembered when Cory hid the key in our fountain, he said something similar about the Fae and running water.

"I'd say we flood all the tunnels to drive the Fae away," the shifter said. "But we can't, since there are still human slaves and captives down there."

"We can flood certain tunnels to divide their forces and make the cut-off units surrender. If we could get the city's public works department to help us without revealing the supernatural secrets."

"That's what I was thinking," he said. "And it just so happens two members of the Shifter Guild work there."

I glanced at the prisoners, who were still making their way from the hole to a seating area at the back of the gallery. One woman seemed familiar. Then, the realization hit me. She was the woman in Damon's memories.

Rita.

She was emaciated, with sad eyes. Eyes that still held kindness in them.

"Excuse me, are you Rita?" I asked in a soft voice.

She nodded but seemed unconcerned about why I had approached her. I had second thoughts about what I was going to say, but she needed to hear it.

"I want you to know that Damon truly loved you. He tried very hard to find you after you were taken away from Shady Palms. Sadly, Damon was killed. I believe by the same people who abducted you."

She stared at me blankly for a moment before a tear inched down her cheek.

"Damon was a good man," Rita said in a scratchy voice. "We were never meant to be. I could never be the partner he wanted, not with all I've been through. Was it my fault he was killed?"

"Not at all! Damon was a good, brave man who wanted to stop evil people."

"I don't know. But that's what I'll believe."

Evil must be fought, and you don't have to be a flawless person to fight it.

Which was convenient for me, since I had a lot more fighting to do.

I WAS DREAMING GODDESS DREAMS ABOUT TRYING TO HEAL the world. The realization came to me that humans were sick, and the disease was not an infection from a foreign agent but was from ourselves. The primitive lizard brains in us, that make us fear the unknown and distrust those who are different, need to be suppressed for society to flourish.

Instead, we have let our lizard brains control us. The tiniest sparks of lies and paranoia have been fanned by the bad actors among us, and now a conflagration rages throughout society of hatred, suspicion, and conspiracy theories.

How could I, daughter of the Goddess, stamp out this fire?

The Goddess herself came to me in my dream, and she had the answers I sought. But then I was rudely awakened.

The mattress beside me sagged as Cory sat upon its edge. I opened my eyes. He was barely visible in the light from the clock beside the bed.

"I can't live this lie any longer," he said in a flat, robotic voice.

Was I still dreaming?

"What do you mean?" My words were sluggish with sleep.

"I'd thought I wanted to return to you, but ever since I've been back, it hasn't felt right. Being the little househusband while you run around like you're a superhero, putting your life and all of ours at risk."

My heart froze. Cory couldn't really be saying this.

"All this supernatural nonsense is too much to take," he continued. "Everyone I know leads a normal life, except me. I have to deal with witches and vampires and killer faeries. These things do not exist."

"Of course, they do."

"No. You've woven a world of lies, and I'm trapped inside it. You actually think you're a goddess? That is ridiculous. You need mental health counseling."

"Cory, how can you say this?"

"You know you're not a goddess."

"Technically, *daughter* of the Goddess," I said.

"It doesn't matter. You're lost in a delusion. They call it megalomania. And you need help. Tell me the Goddess is not real, or I will leave you."

"That is unfair."

"Tell me the Goddess is not real. She never was real. Gods and goddesses do not exist. Neither does magic. The world is cruel and hard, but at least it's real. Denounce the Goddess or I will leave you again, this time for good."

I was in pain and disbelief. Cory had never acted like this before. In fact, his usual smells of sawdust and soap weren't there. Instead, he had a funky, humid scent.

"You took a vow when you married me," I said.

"I didn't vow to live in a make-believe world of your insanity. Denounce the Goddess."

"I can't," I whispered.

He stood up. His face was too dark to read.

"Denounce the Goddess."

"Don't ask that of me, please."

"Then, I must leave you to your life of lies."

He stood over me, as if he was going to hurt me.

Suddenly, the toilet flushed, the bathroom door opened, and Cory came out wearing only boxer shorts.

A different Cory. The actual Cory.

The one standing over the bed snarled.

And became a lizard-creature. It had a human face and the body similar to a velociraptor, towering over Cory.

"What the—" Cory uttered, before a loud crack and flash of light threw him backwards into the bathroom. His head hit the floor with a thud.

The lizard turned back to me. "Denounce your lies," he said. "Denounce the Goddess."

"You're The Father of Lies."

He smiled and transformed into the familiar caricature of the Devil: a skinny guy all in red with pointy ears and a forked tail.

My shorts from yesterday were folded on my nightstand. I reached for the Druid Disc in the righthand pocket. It burned painfully in my hand.

"What you say is all lies," I shouted.

The Father of Lies transformed again, this time into a naked woman with long, flowing hair, adorned with flowers, that covered her breasts.

"You are not my daughter," she said to me. "Don't you dare to pretend to be. You are a joke. You're pitiful. Take your own life and spare us your pathetic lies."

Not knowing what to do, I reached out and touched her with the Druid Disc.

With a crackle of electricity, she disappeared.

Sitting in a chair against the wall opposite the bed was an elderly man with a beard wearing a white suit. I couldn't see him well in the near darkness of the room, but his eyes glowed red.

"We need to come to an agreement, you and I," he said.

I shook my head.

"You don't have the power to hurt me, but I admit you're formidable, compared to the typical, feeble-minded human and faerie. If you leave this city, you'll be spared and allowed to live a comfortable life within your normal lifespan. If you stay here, I will enchant you just like the vampires. Just like many of the Fae. And you will serve me."

Not knowing what to say, I shook my head again.

"You were correct when you dreamed about the lizard brains of humans. It's the same with other creatures, such as the Fae. An evolutionary trait meant to help ignorant creatures survive has somehow become ascendant in your species and the others who are supposed to be intelligent. You know what that means?"

I didn't answer.

"It means I'm winning. There will be mass slaughter across the earth, and the survivors will be my worshippers and slaves. I offer you mercy. Go away and leave me alone. You'll enjoy the remainder of your days before all I have foretold comes to pass."

Why did he want me to leave him alone? He must fear the Goddess. But why?

How could a mother-earth goddess defeat him? The truth-telling quality of the Druid Disc appeared to be a helpful tool, but it didn't kill him. I needed to find a weapon to defeat him.

However, what I possessed were healing powers, not weapons for inflicting harm. I enhanced fertility and spurred new growth. I inspired the will to live and flourish. Hope and new beginnings were my stock in trade.

He was about death and negation. Doubt and distrust. Lies and illusions.

Without thinking, I groped for the tote bag beside the bed where I kept the giant pearl, now that I tried to have it with me at all times. Just in case.

Cases like right now. I reached into the bag and held it in my left hand, the Druid Disc in my right. The twin forces of healing and truth. Both began glowing, dispelling the shadows in the room.

I rose from the bed and faced the Father of Lies.

"Come now," he said calmly, "do you really expect those gewgaws to frighten me?"

In the white light from the pearl, and the blueish light from the Druid Disc, the man's face looked concerned, however.

I moved closer to him, and he shrank into the chair.

"You seem to be under the misunderstanding that if you chase me out of your bedroom, you're achieving something," he said. "You're forgetting that I'm in the hearts and minds of billions of humans, faeries, and other creatures."

I had to hand it to him there. He was correct. Driving him from the room wouldn't drive him from those he's infected. I needed to destroy him, if that was possible.

A loud *crack* and flash of light preceded a force that threw me backwards, tripping over the nightstand, and landing on the bed. My hands still gripped the pearl and stone.

Who was I kidding trying to destroy the Father of Lies? He was Satan, or his equivalent. Perhaps the only lasting way to rid the world of him would be to convince everyone to reject him. But that was an impossibly monumental task, especially in this day and age of people listening only to what they wanted to hear.

I needed to weaken him somehow.

The pearl still glowed in my left hand. What was I going to do, heal him? Open his heart to love? Nope. Impossible.

The Druid Disc burned in my right hand. Could I expose the Father of Lies to the truth?

Setting down the pearl, I wrapped both hands around the stone disc and felt its prickly electricity run through me. It was time to bring the power of the Goddess to bear and join it to the power of the disc.

My scalp tingled; my ears popped. And the man sitting in the chair revealed what he truly was: a sack of deflated skin, old, withered, and rotting. Flies flew above the foul, empty hide.

I yanked a small mirror from the wall. Using my power of creation, I projected my vision of truth into the mirror, holding it in front of The Father of Lies, so he could see what he truly was.

He was nothing except putrescence.

"Bear witness to what you are!" I commanded. "You are nothing but rot and deceit. Your power is an illusion. Even the weakest of humans is stronger than you."

The mirror shattered, glass shards spraying everywhere. The wood frame splintered apart.

The chair where I had aimed the mirror was empty now. An anguished howl echoed in the recesses of my head.

The Father of Lies was gone for now, but he wasn't defeated.

A brief glimpse of the truth wouldn't destroy an entity whose entire existence was based on denying and twisting the truth.

Still, my ability to see the truth and project it into someone else's mind gives me a glimmer of hope. I had landed a punch on him. And if I could find a way to make the next punch harder, and the one after that ten times harder, maybe we could lessen his influence on earth. Bringing truth back from the brink of extermination.

After all, that was the mission of the Memory Guild.

A moan came from the bathroom, a very human moan.

I turned on the light and rushed in there to check on Cory—the real Cory, not the apparition the Father of Lies had used to weaken me. He lay on his back on the tile floor with his hands cradling the back of his head.

"Was I knocked out? I came out of the bathroom, and it was like I was struck by lightning. That's all I remember."

I knelt beside him and examined his head, checking his eyes and face for any signs of a concussion.

"Let's get your clothes on and take you to the ER so they can check you out. Just in case."

"Were you having a bad dream? I remember hearing you talking in your sleep while I was in here."

"You would never ask me to denounce the Goddess, would you?"

"Of course not. Are you crazy?"

"I sure am. But you knew that when you married me."

# CHAPTER 29

# FLORIDA MAN GOES SOUTH

With all that's been going on, you probably assumed I'd written Buddy off. Well, I hadn't.

You might have also assumed Buddy was dead. That is a logical assumption, I'll grant you. I learned there were people who wanted him dead, and they had no hesitation about killing.

However, I'd been getting messages he might be alive. Not direct contact from him. No, that would be too responsible and considerate for Buddy. The signs I got were what you'd call circumstantial evidence.

They were in the form of news articles found in our own local newspaper and after I conducted extensive internet searches of other news sites. Perhaps you've seen similar stories in this unique genre of crime story.

"Florida Man shoplifts from grocery store four boxes of cupcakes and six sausages stuffed in his pants."

That one was from the county south of here. Then, in the county south of that came more news:

"Florida Man robs liquor store using juvenile alligator as weapon."

And:

"Florida Man eludes police after driving car through Catholic Church during Communion."

I realized I was onto something, so I continued searching for Florida Man stories. They popped up every day in every part of Florida and neighboring states. But certain stories formed a pattern.

In the next county to the south, Florida Man was similarly busy, according to the headlines.

"Naked Florida man steals police car, leads authorities on high-speed chase, then pilfers prom dress from residence to hide his nudity. Police warn public to be on the lookout for man in pink chiffon dress several sizes too small. High school student devastated by her ruined prom plans."

Why would I assume these are about Buddy, you ask? Out of all the daily Florida Man stories, why do these point to Buddy? I culled these particular ones because they set off alarm bells.

Call it a gut feeling. I was married to the guy, remember? He is the quintessential Florida Man. This is his legacy of his mess of a life.

The stories continued, appearing from places farther and farther southward in the state, as the Florida Man, who was probably Buddy, made his way toward an unknown destination.

Here was another: a tiny article in a chain of newspapers. I easily could have missed it tucked in the page among ads for urinary incontinence treatments and hair pieces.

"Florida Man on Jet Ski, wearing prom dress, exposes himself to cruise ship passengers in Port Everglades. Evades authorities."

He remained busy.

"Florida Man discovered sleeping in nuclear power plant. Workers report he fled while emitting 'eerie glow.'"

The next day there was another:

"Florida Man spotted crossing cemetery on stolen airboat. Crashes into crypt and escapes on foot."

And another:

"Florida Man causes brawl in Little Havana demanding tacos at Cuban restaurant."

Yeah, it sure as heck sounded like Buddy. So, he was heading to the very bottom of Florida. It was only fitting, since Buddy was always headed straight to the bottom of everything in his life.

Then, the trail went cold with the final Florida Man story in the pattern. I prayed that this one was not, in fact, about Buddy.

"Florida Man found inside stomach of giant Burmese Python in the Everglades. Body too digested to be identified."

Was this the end of the story of Buddy? I feared it was.

Fortunately, bail bondsmen do not like to lose money. If a client skips town, they do whatever it takes to retrieve him and make sure he shows up in court.

Enter Ralph Thungus, bounty hunter, and his magnificent handlebar mustache.

He created quite a sensation when he marched into the inn during breakfast, dragging with him Buddy Grimes in handcuffs. Fortunately, Buddy was wearing a T-shirt, shorts, and flip-flops, not a prom dress. Even so, my guests, who have seen ghosts and homicide investigations here, appeared to be more fascinated by Thungus parading my ex-husband like a captured tiger.

"I thought you were eaten by a python," I said.

"No. Why would you think that? I was chilling out in South Beach when this jerk shows up and drags me out of a bar. I was chatting with a table of beautiful college girls on spring break when I was totally embarrassed by Mr. Fungus."

"Thungus," said the bounty hunter, jerking the chain attached to Buddy's handcuffs.

"Ow! Stop that."

"The perp wanted to see you before his rescheduled court appearance today," Thungus said.

"Why hasn't Jack Guarini returned any of my calls?" Buddy asked me.

"Because he's the one who killed Damon. Now tell me, why did you run away? You were afraid of going to prison?"

"I was afraid Damon's killer, whoever he was, would come after me. So, I left my SUV parked at Shady Palms to confuse him and skipped town in a rental car. Which I lost in a poker game the next day."

"Well, it turns out you were right. They were going to go after you." I gave him an abbreviated version of what I had discovered about Guarini, Williams, and Hopeful Recoveries. I mentioned the human trafficking but avoided any reference to the Fae.

"Wow," was all he said in reply.

"If you hadn't left town, you could have helped the investigation, and we could have wrapped it up sooner."

"Or I would've been shot by Guarini."

He might be right.

"You could have told me you were going into hiding," I said. "I was really worried about you."

"Sorry. I had to travel incognito."

"That's no excuse. And you weren't exactly incognito. I found several news stories about your brushes with the law on the way to Miami Beach."

"Really? I was in the news?"

"Not by name. And, really, you robbed a liquor store with an alligator?"

He chuckled. "Pretty clever, huh? But I didn't take any of their money. The gator was getting irritable, so I ran right back out the door."

"And you stole a prom dress after stealing a police car while naked?"

"That's totally untrue," he said, indignant. "It wasn't a prom dress. It was more of a cocktail dress."

Thungus yanked his chain. "Come on. We can't be late for court. You've already missed one appearance."

"But everyone knows I'm innocent now."

"You have to show up, so your bail bondsman gets his money back," I said. "I'm sure today, or in the near future, they'll drop the charges against you. Please, be responsible for once. No drinking and no airboat rides."

I called Siwicki to inform him of the triumphant return of Buddy.

"Will the state drop its charges against him now?" I asked.

"Oh, I would say they will. I shouldn't divulge this, but we've been working Grady Williams really hard. Between your affidavit that you saw him buying drugs, our arrest of the dealer, and testimony from patients, we've got him nailed for drug trafficking. We also have plenty of patients willing to talk about the human trafficking. Let's just say Williams is ready, willing, and able to plea bargain and testify that Guarini murdered Damon Borgia."

"I hope Williams doesn't get off easy."

"No way," Siwicki said. "I bet Guarini will flip on him. He's the attorney. He has a paper trail of dirt a mile long."

"When will Buddy be in the clear?"

"Don't be in such a hurry." Siwicki chuckled cruelly. "He also has a little matter of health insurance fraud to wriggle his way out of."

I had almost forgotten about that. Leave it to Buddy's all-you-can-eat buffet of stupid.

Dr. Noordlun, Arch Mage Bob, and I stood in the closed art gallery on a bright morning. Imelda was with us, too. Francis was in her back office working. We didn't tell her what might happen in her gallery if our plan worked.

Outside in the street, the city water department was flushing out a mysterious tunnel that had appeared near the main pipelines. The city had no idea how the tunnel had been dug. Dr. Noordlun had the right connections to arrange for this work to take place today.

Running water was the key.

Meanwhile, Alfonso and his partner, Izel, led a team of Aluxes deep underground. They had been creating a map of the extensive Fae tunnel network beneath the city and discovered an exceptionally deep main passage that ran beneath the Sangre River. The river, and the bay it widened into, separated mainland San Marcos from the beachside barrier island. The Fae's tunnel ran beneath the river, connecting their principal network of passages with a smaller one near the beach.

Alfonso and I had come up with this plan. The Fae's aversion to running water intrigued me to no end. There had to be a way to capitalize upon this. Our solution was quite simple.

Imelda closed her eyes and moved her lips, communicating telepathically.

"Alfonso says they have finished their digging and cast the

demolition spells," she reported. "His team is evacuating now. The time is soon."

We waited, tense. Bob spoke in a low voice into his phone, warning his team of mages and wizards to prepare for action. I had nothing to do but watch, yet I was nervous, nevertheless.

Time ticked by with painful slowness. Outside, the sound of rushing water came from the open utility hole in the street.

Imelda nodded. "The spells have been triggered."

The ground vibrated beneath my feet from the explosions, only a few blocks away, but deep underground.

You see, the Aluxes had located the Fae's main tunnel beneath the river. They dug a smaller one that crossed just above the Fae's tunnel, between it and the bottom of the river.

And they placed mines. Like I had worried the Fae would do.

The underground explosions broke through the roof and floor of the Aluxes' tunnel, allowing the river to gush into it and the Fae's tunnel below it.

The river water would be flooding directly into the Fae's main tunnel now, flowing both east toward the beach and west beneath the town. It would spread into the smaller tunnels that fed off the main ones.

The Fae would be in absolute panic.

"The wizards stationed at the beach have made the first contact with evacuating faeries," Bob said, phone to his ear. "They're casting their warding spells big-time."

The faeries, fleeing from their tunnels in fear of the flooding waters, would be weakened and disoriented by the sunlight. The warding spells should be highly effective upon them.

"The faeries are flying away from the beach in a big swarm," Bob said excitedly. "They're headed inland and to the south."

"Will humans be able to see them?" I asked.

Bob shook his head. "They escaped from the ground in a

state park that isn't open yet this early. No humans were around. The faeries are so high in altitude now that people would just think they're birds."

The main forces of the Fae were directly below San Marcos and the surrounding areas. There was no way we could flush them all out, but we hoped to make a big impact.

Cool air rose from the hole in the gallery floor from the sinkhole below. It smelled earthy and damp. I thought I heard the faint sound of running water in tunnels below the sinkhole.

The water flooding in from the river would cause faeries to flee in this direction. The Water Department's flushing of the tunnel beneath the street would prevent the Fae from using it to escape further inland.

High-pitched squeals and scratching sounds came from below, as if a horde of rats were down there. Those of us in the room exchanged wary glances.

I jumped from the loud clang of steel on the street outside. I turned toward the window and saw a utility hole cover had popped off and lay wobbling on the cobblestones.

Faeries, in their natural forms, flew from the utility hole one by one like wasps from the eaves of a house.

Movement in the shadow of the building across the street caught my eye. A mage stood there, furiously sending a warding spell at the emerging faeries like insect repellant.

The faeries changed course away from him and continued to climb into the sky.

That was when the earth below us erupted with a teeming mass of faeries. They scurried up the ladder from the sinkhole, knocking each other off in their desperate attempts to escape. Others simply rose on their wings into the gallery.

The room filled with faeries, and we humans had to flee behind the counter. This was where two of Bob's mages stood, a man and a woman. They looked like any random humans and didn't wear robes or anything. But up close to them like this, I felt the pulse of power flowing from their fingers as they cast the warding spells. The air smelled like a recent lightning storm.

The faeries couldn't remain milling in the gallery. And they couldn't return to the underground tunnels where water flowed. Even if they were in no danger of drowning in the higher tunnels, the simple proximity of running water was repugnant to them.

So, with a massive shattering of glass, they burst through the windows of the gallery and fled into the bright sunlight, shrieking like panicked birds.

Francis ran out of the rear office, horror in her face. Okay, I admit we didn't fully brief her on how extensive the evacuation of the Fae could be. And it must have been pretty upsetting to see all the windows of her gallery blown out. I wasn't surprised to see how upset she was.

I *was* surprised to see her shrink to faerie size and take off into the air, especially since she had pretended to be ignorant about the Fae when I first met her.

No, actually, once I thought about it, I wasn't so surprised.

"Do you have insurance?" I called out after her as she flew from the nearest broken window. My bad for forgetting that insurance doesn't cover supernatural damages.

"Pretty cool, huh, dude?" Bob asked, beaming.

"Yeah." I didn't want to be a downer, but I had to add, "It's not over, I hope you realize. There are still hostile Fae in San Marcos, and the ones we drove away could return. This was a big victory for us, but we haven't won the war."

"You are such a buzz-kill, dude."

I felt bad about that. But when sunset arrived, my troubles only multiplied.

# CHAPTER 30

## ROOMMATES

I returned to the inn to find the smaller, secondary refrigerator moved from its usual spot hiding the door to Roderick's crawlspace. When my resident vampire went out, he was always careful to replace the fridge. What was up?

"You look as distressed as I am," Archibald said, perched on the subway tile above the sink.

"It's not like Roderick to be so careless. And he knows better than to come out so early when guests might be around."

"Exactly. I saw him when he left the inn. He most definitely was not himself. He had a hunger beyond which I'd never seen in him."

This was not good. Had Roderick been affected by the spell that had sickened Pedro's guild members? I explained my worries to Archibald, who was only too aware of how the magic affected vampires.

"Blimey, that is concerning," he said. "Does this mean he'll be enthralled to the Fae?"

"That's the case with the other vampires, but the Fae gave

them explicit orders to attack us at Bob's surf shop. I don't believe Roderick has had any contact with the Fae."

"In any case, it appears to have stimulated his appetite. You should have seen the bestial look in his face. He could very well get in trouble since he lacks the ability to mesmerize his prey.

In today's modern world, vampires must be exceedingly careful when feeding on humans. They rarely kill us, which would be counterproductive. Why kill the hen that lays your eggs? And why attract law enforcement's attention?

Mesmerism, a type of hypnotism, is the key to feeding upon humans and making them completely forget the experience. It is erased entirely from their memories. That, plus avoiding any witnesses, is how vampires feed and get away with it.

Roderick, though, didn't have that ability sufficiently, only just enough to charm his prey into his clutches. Afterwards, they call the police, thinking they'd been sexually assaulted. Roderick needed a way to adapt and survive for more than a century since he'd been turned.

His solution was effective, though hardly elegant.

Animals: dogs, cats, possums, raccoons. Cows and horses were ideal if he was willing to travel outside the city to find them. His minimal trace of the ability to mesmerize was just enough to immobilize a possum or poodle.

Roderick once lamented to me that human blood was so much tastier than that of animals, yet he, alas, could rarely sup it.

In the state he was in tonight, I was afraid he would attempt to do so.

"Do you think he'll go after humans?" I asked Archibald.

"I would not be the least bit surprised."

Outside, a dog yelped. Archibald and I exchanged glances.

The dog barked frantically, the volume decreasing slowly as it moved further away.

I grabbed a flashlight and ran outside onto Cadiz Street. I swept a beam of light across the street. It was empty aside from parallel-parked cars.

Wait—there was a white dog on the opposite sidewalk. It faced in my direction, retreating slowly down the street.

The shadowy figure of a man came from behind a car and sprinted across the street toward the dog. The dog took off and disappeared.

"Roderick!" I shouted. "Is that you?"

The man stopped and turned toward me. Glowing red eyes pierced the darkness. It was Roderick.

I jogged toward him but stopped before I got close. The feeling of danger was too strong.

"Are you okay, Roderick?"

"Something has come over me. I've never felt this famished before."

"Evil magic has escaped in San Marcos that is affecting vampires. I thought you'd be safe from it, since you weren't near where it was released, but I'm afraid it's affecting you, anyway."

"I have the strongest urge to feed on humans," he said, ashamed. "A most brutal urge. To feed on someone until he's been emptied. It's not simply hunger, it's. . . it's hatred. Why would I feel such hatred?"

"It's how the magic works. It corrupts your mind with lies, paranoia, mistrust, anger, resentment, hatred."

"Oh, like social media?"

"Exactly."

"I'm trying to resist the urge to attack humans," he said, moving slightly closer to me.

"Good," I said, moving slightly away from him.

"The dog should have been easy prey. I must be off my game."

"Why don't you go to the dairy farm on Highway Nineteen? That will be the safest meal for you and your prey."

"Good suggestion."

"Come home immediately afterward. I want to try something to see if it helps fight the effects of the magic."

He nodded and sprinted away, so quickly he was a mere blur of motion.

I hoped he didn't bump into any humans along the way.

SOPHIE AND CORY WERE HOSTING WINE HOUR. NOW THAT I've become so wrapped up in supernatural affairs, I was relying more and more on them to handle the mundane human details of inn-keeping. Would Sophie still be willing to do this when she became more advanced as a witch? Seeing as there weren't many full-time jobs out there for witches, I assumed she would continue working at the inn.

I went to say hello to the guests mingling in the foyer, sipping wine, and nibbling on cheese. One of the attendees stood out like a sore thumb, an elderly man who looked like a monk in a brown floor-length woolen robe, sampling a chardonnay.

"Hi, Wilference."

"Good evening, Daughter of Danu."

I still haven't gotten used to being called that.

"What can I do for you?"

"Perhaps we can speak somewhere in private?"

"Yes, of course. Please follow me."

I led him into the kitchen, and we sat at the small table near the fireplace. After he glanced around and seemed assured no one else was within earshot, he looked me earnestly in the eyes and spoke.

"I come to you, throwing myself upon your mercy, with two requests."

The last time a faerie came to me with a request, it didn't work out so well. Nevertheless, I nodded for him to continue.

"You must understand how grateful the Faerie Queene is for your healing of her. Despite how underhanded Jaekeree behaved afterwards."

"She is feeling well?"

"Yes, despite being held under house arrest by the coup plotters."

"So, with her being healthy, does this mean all the Fae are healthy?"

"No." He frowned. "Not at all. The morale of our people is higher now that we needn't fear for her survival. And the overall vitality of our magic has improved slightly."

A benefit for them, I thought, but not for us humans.

"As you saw for yourself, our people need to have direct contact with the Queene, and they have been denied it because of the coup."

"What about your, um, fertility problem?"

"That is still of grave concern," he said. "Many factors other than the illness have caused it."

I knew the Aluxes might have a fix for that, but they were currently on the opposite side in the war with the Fae. There would have to be peace before the Aluxes could heal the Fae.

"So, Wilference, you haven't mentioned your requests yet."

"Ah, yes. I was getting to that. The Queene ordered me to ask you to assist in rescuing her."

I was floored. "Say what?"

"Free her from the coup plotters and restore her to her throne."

"How the heck would I be able to do that? Our people are still at war. And I'm just a psychometrist."

"You are the Daughter of Danu."

"I heal stuff. And inadvertently cause seedlings to sprout everywhere in my inn. I can't blast my way underground and rescue her."

"She is confident you will eventually find a way."

I wondered if the Queene was healed after all. Her mind seemed to be off its rocker.

"I doubt I will find a way."

"In time, the Goddess will reveal it."

"I have to be honest with you and the Queene," I said. "Please go back and tell her that as much as I would want to help free her, I simply can't."

"I can't go back."

"What do you mean?"

"The coup plotters believe I'm too loyal to the Queene. I've been banished under threat of death. I'm officially in exile now."

"Where will you go?"

He smiled and glanced around the kitchen. "You have such a lovely inn."

"Wait a minute, you're not implying that you—"

"Wish to be your guest here. I'll pay. In the currency humans use, of course."

"Wouldn't you prefer a tunnel or burrow or something?"

He laughed. "We faeries are just as comfortable living in human form in well-appointed residences. You saw Dorn's home and the Queene's Winter Palace."

I did indeed. Dorn lived in a huge house outside of town.

And the Queene's palace rivaled the grandest mansions in Palm Beach.

"Isn't it unsafe for you to stay here? Jaekeree knows I live here."

"No matter where I go, their magic will tell them where I am. When you speak of safety, it will be safer for you with me here. I will be able to sense if they intend to attack your inn."

I figured he was right. Could I deal with having a faerie live here? Well, if I can deal with multiple ghosts, a gargoyle, and a vampire, I guess I can handle a faerie.

Speaking of my vampire, the back door opened, and Roderick stepped in. He was brimming with energy after his recent meal.

"Oh, a faerie?" he asked when he saw Wilference.

"A vampire?" Wilference asked.

"Yeah. You guys are going to have to put up with each other. Oh, you have some blood on your chin, Roderick."

While he wiped himself with a handkerchief, I introduced them to each other. They shook hands warily.

"Pardon me for mentioning it, but you appear to be infected by evil magic," Wilference said.

"I caught a touch of it."

"He's not as infected as the bulk of the vampires in the Clan of the Eternal Night," I said. "And I'm planning to try to heal him."

"How interesting," Wilference said.

"Gentlemen, please follow me to a more private location."

I led them to the utility room in the back of the ground floor, where the laundry and workshop were located. Asking them to wait for me, I hurried to the cottage to pick up my tools.

When I returned, the two were in the middle of a laugh.

"You think *you're* old? I remember when crackers came in a tin!" Roderick roared and slapped his knee.

"I remember when they came in wooden boxes," Wilference said, one-upping him.

"I'm glad you two are hitting it off," I said. "Wilference will be joining our freaky family here at the inn."

"Splendid," Roderick said. "We'll get on just fine. So, how many humans does it take to change a lightbulb?"

"Knock it off, Roddy. Time to get this evil magic out of your system."

Like when I was battling the Father of Lies in my bedroom, I had the pearl and Druid Disc with me, one in each hand. I wasn't going to burn Roderick with the truth. Nor did I want to cleanse his heart temporarily, like my goddess song had done to Pedro's vampires.

I wanted to wash the lies and hatred out of Roderick for good. For that, I needed the healing power of the pearl and the truth revelation of the Druid Disc.

And I supposed some singing couldn't hurt either, as I felt the song swell inside me flow from my lungs.

It was the same song I'd sung at the surf shop, just not as loud.

The pearl glowed in my left hand. The disc burned in my right. An energy like electricity arced between the two objects right in front of my face.

Wilference instantly dropped to his knees and bowed his head in reverence.

Roderick stared at me as if I'd gone mad.

But in mere moments, he staggered backward as if he'd been pushed. His head tilted toward me, his eyes bulged, and his mouth dropped open.

*Cleanse your heart of the hatred for humans*, my song said with words I wouldn't normally have understood. *Clear your mind of the lies. Open your soul to the truth.*

Wait—do vampires have souls?

Yes, of course they do.

Soon, Roderick closed his eyes and smiled, humming along with the song.

"The magic is gone," Wilference said. "I'm certain of it."

Roderick settled down and came out of his daze.

"How do you feel, Roddy?"

"More like myself. I don't have the urge to prey upon and kill humans anymore. It could be because I'm still full from dinner. But, no, I don't have that irresistible need to kill you anymore."

"I'm glad to hear that."

"I still feel superior to you, of course. That's only natural. But I have none of the contempt and loathing I had for you and your species earlier, after I'd been infected."

"I didn't realize you felt that strongly."

"Yes, I hid it quite well, didn't I?"

"What is going on here?" asked Archibald, who had suddenly appeared on the concrete wall above the washing machines. "Another faerie visiting our inn?"

"Archibald, this is Wilference. He's a priest of the Fae. He's on our side now."

"Don't be too quick to believe that," Archibald said.

"He's also your new housemate."

Archibald sputtered with indignation, unable to get a single angry word out.

"Don't worry," I said. "I'm sure you two will get along fine."

So, it had come down to this. I was serving as resident dorm advisor to a menagerie of supernatural and mythological creatures. I was somehow burdened with the task of healing the city's magic-infected vampires—a task that would be much more difficult than what I'd just accomplished with the lightly infected Roderick. And I was still embroiled in the war with the Fae—a conflict with the freedom of humanity at stake. Oh, and there was the matter of the veil being torn asunder, letting forgotten monsters back into the world. That could pose endless problems.

Sophie walked into the room, startled to see the party going on.

"Mom, several seedlings popped up in the foyer during Wine Hour. And the woman in the Honeymoon Suite just complained about a ghost haunting the TV remote. I think it may be a new ghost we haven't encountered yet."

Yes, on top of all the burdens I just complained about, I had the daily responsibility of running this historic inn with all its problems and idiosyncrasies. The place was called The Esperanza Inn, named after the Spanish word for hope. And hope, it seemed, was all I had to offer.

Welcome to my world. Stay as long as you'd like.

# WHAT'S NEXT

## ENJOYED THIS BOOK? PLEASE LEAVE A REVIEW

In the Amazon universe, the number of reviews readers leave can make or break a book. I would be very grateful if you could spend just a few minutes and write a fair and honest review. It can be as short or long as you wish. Thank you so much!

## NEXT IN THE MEMORY GUILD:
### Book 8: The Goddess's Touch

**News flash: I'm a psychic, not a superhero.**

The small city of San Marcos, Florida, rarely experiences murder. But when a human is killed, reportedly by the legendary Questing Beast, it threatens to shatter the secrecy cloaking the supernaturals living among humans. That could be a catastrophe for all of us who aren't normals.

Why is that *my* problem? Well, as a member of a supernatural guild, I share responsibility for keeping the secret. And, more personally, the victim was my dentist, and I had an appointment for a root canal. With the help of my psychometry, I embark on a frantic quest to find out if the Questing Beast really did it, and if so, how to explain it to the police.

Plus, why is it, and other mythological monsters, here in San Marcos?

Meanwhile, I have a Fae priest living in my inn (and creating an absolute mess). He won't shut up about the Faerie Queene being held prisoner by a rogue faction of her court. Like, *I'm* supposed to rescue her? Why me?

So, what exactly *can* I do, aside from use my newly discovered healing powers? I'd better find out, and fast.

**Get enchanted by an alluring world of magic, murder, mystery, and mischief. Order *A Faerie's Touch* on Amazon or at wardparker.com**

**GET A FREE E-BOOK**

Sign up for my newsletter and get *A Ghostly Touch*, a Magic Guild novella, for free, offered exclusively to my newsletter subscribers. Darla reads the memories of a young woman, murdered in the 1890s, whose ghost begins haunting Darla, looking for justice. As a subscriber, you'll be the first to know about my new releases and lots of free book promotions. The newsletter is delivered only a couple of times a month. No spam at all, and you can unsubscribe at any time. Download your free book for all e-readers at wardparker.com

# ACKNOWLEDGMENTS

I wish to thank my loyal readers, who give me a reason to write more every day. I'm especially grateful to Sharee Steinberg and Amanda Peters for all your editing and proofreading brilliance. And to my wife, Martha, thank you for your moral support, Beta reading, and awesome graphic design!

# ABOUT THE AUTHOR

Ward is the author of the Memory Guild midlife paranormal mystery thrillers. The Goddess's Daughter urban fantasy series continues the adventures.

He also writes the Monsters of Jellyfish Beach paranormal mysteries, set in the same world as his Freaky Florida series.

Ward lives in Florida with his wife, several cats, and a demon who wishes to remain anonymous.

Connect with him on Facebook (wardparkerauthor), Book-Bub, Goodreads, Bluesky (wardparker.bsky.social), or Threads (wardparker2223). Check out his books and sign up for his newsletter at wardparker.com.

## PARANORMAL BOOKS BY WARD PARKER

### Freaky Florida Humorous Paranormal Novels
*Snowbirds of Prey*
*Invasive Species*
*Fate Is a Witch*
*Gnome Coming*
*Going Batty*
*Dirty Old Manatee*
*Gazillions of Reptilians*
*Hangry as Hell* (novella)

## The Memory Guild Midlife Paranormal Mystery Thrillers

*A Magic Touch* (also available in audio)
*The Psychic Touch* (also available in audio)
*A Wicked Touch* (also available in audio)
*A Haunting Touch*
*The Wizard's Touch*
*A Witchy Touch*
*A Faerie's Touch*
*The Goddess's Touch*
*The Vampire's Touch*
*An Angel's Touch*
*A Ghostly Touch* (novella)
Books 1-3 Box Set (also available in audio)

## The Goddess's Daughter Urban Fantasies

(Sequel to the Memory Guild Series.)
*Of Envy and Empaths*
*Of Fear and Fae*
*Of Vampires and Valor*

## Monsters of Jellyfish Beach Paranormal Mystery Adventures

*The Golden Ghouls*
*Fiends With Benefits*
*Get Ogre Yourself*
*My Funny Frankenstein*
*Werewolf Art Thou?*
*In Sprite of Herself*
*Worms of Endearment*